PLOUGHING ON

Liam Cox is twiddling his thumbs, willing the priest to take a shortcut to that part where he says, 'Go forth, the Mass is ended', the answer to which is quivering on Liam's lips, ready to come out: 'Thanks be to God!'

But the priest is taking his time, sending out fumes of frankincense and pronouncing the glory of the Almighty left, right, and centre. Mother must have paid a fortune for this memorial service and she expects good returns on her investment. It will be a while yet. Liam has to grin and bear it. He remembers those long church hours of Sunday Mass stretching into infinity, a purgatory for a small boy with his mind on climbing trees. Today, nearly forty years later, his mind is still on earthly matters, such as his stumbling business. Mother could help, if she wanted to co-operate, but before they get to that he must sit through this spectacle, biding his time. This will please her. 'Your father will be proud of you,' she will say, as if Father would have given a toss even when he was alive. Now that he is dead, and has been so for two years exactly, he cares even less. But it matters to Mother. She still believes in all this mumbo-jumbo of praying for the dear-departed in the hope that it will make their afterlife easier.

Oh well, you can take a nun out of a nunnery, but you

can't take the nunnery out of a nun.

'God, give me strength!' It is rather hypocritical of Liam to pray for divine intervention under the circumstances of his uncharitable thoughts, but he hopes the loving God will overlook them.

He fidgets, and Mother shushes him, just like she used to when he was a youngster. She puts her forefinger to her lips and frowns at him, whispering, 'Sit still!'

Liam turns to sit on the other cheek, because the bench is hard as hell and his backside is aching. He catches a glimpse of people on the back benches. Not many people. Maybe ten in all. They are old faces he remembers vaguely from his childhood, faces of no significance now. Right at the back sits a man. He also has a face that is vaguely familiar, but Liam can't put a name to it. He isn't that old either: late forties, thick blond hair and beard, Liam's build. What is he doing attending a mid-week memorial Mass? Who is he? Liam has a strong feeling he should know who that man is.

The priest bellows, 'Go forth, the Mass is ended!'

'Thanks be to God!'

When it rains, the freshly turned soil glistens with its own oily sweat. It gives out the scent of musk. It is carnal. Unwashed. Intimate. Mildred loves the smell of ploughed fields in the rain. It makes her feel alive and, at the age of seventy-six, it is a feeling to be cherished. She inhales deeply and holds it in, getting intoxicated on fresh air. Her thoughts ebb and flow inside her skull, the rows of turned earth an extension of her brain waves. She pauses for the hundredth time, and scans the fields. They permeate her.

2

It isn't so much that she owns them as it is that they own her.

Raindrops crack open against the sou'wester she is wearing over her scarf. It is an old scarf – they don't make scarves like that anymore. It's the kind the Queen favours, with a bold floral pattern and a rich, aged-gold border like a picture frame. Her green waterproof anorak keeps her bones warm and dry inside. She could stand here and look at the fields for hours. And inhale them. Mildred sucks in the air greedily. Young people don't appreciate the simple pleasure of drawing breath, she thinks. They take in air and spit it out without relishing it, like fast food.

'Mum, we've got to be moving. I've got millions of things to do back at the office,' Liam points out with an exasperated scowl. He is a big bull of a man; fleshy, flushed with the effort of walking, already short of breath. And patience. Just like his father, Mildred observes. Reginald too was always annoyed, always had something better to do, something urgent waiting round the corner. He was chasing it relentlessly, like a dog chasing its own tail. He had had no time or patience for Mildred – he simply tolerated her. Nor had he had the time or patience for the land. He had cultivated it without love, without a pause for thought.

'Mother!' Liam is talking to a brick wall.

'Give her a break. She's catching her breath,' Colleen tells him.

Mildred smiles at her daughter. In her doe-brown walking boots and a knee-length pleated skirt of demure black under the frills of her exuberantly purple poncho, standing under a green-and-red check umbrella, Colleen is

3

a mismatch of colour and style. Her ripe-plum coloured hair, pinned on top of her head, has fallen out of the bun in thin wisps and is clinging to her neck and cheeks as if the purple hair dye has run. She is puffed and frumpy. She has never cared about her appearance. No wonder she has never married. It used to worry Mildred, but it no longer does.

It is four p.m. Mildred was hoping she could offer them a snack before they left, considering the effort they have made to be here. They didn't have to come to the service. She half-expected to hear the usual excuses: a dentist appointment, a meeting with a client, the car has gone for service...They surprised her. Seeing them arrive gave her that tiny flutter of motherly pride deep inside her stomach. Liam had even herded in Stella. She stepped out of the car wrapped in a slinky black fur coat, wearing six-inch heels, looking like a penguin on stilts. She used to be a beautiful girl – peachy complexion, slender body. No wonder Liam put up such a fight over her and used every trick in the book to seduce her away from his brother, David. Would he do the same nowadays? He probably would. He is his father's son. He owns things and he owns people. He won't let go of what's his without a fight.

They are standing together. Stella is desperate to squeeze under his umbrella and save both her fur and her hair from ruin. Her narrow heels have sunk deep into the ground and she is leaning forward to maintain balance. An expression of angelic patience graces her face. 'She's going to catch her death in this rain,' she says, unwisely presuming that Mildred can't hear her. Mildred can, but she is selective about responding. She won't waste her breath on flippant remarks. She won't get herself wound up. Sometimes it is easier to pretend she is deaf as a post. That way she can keep track of what is said behind her back.

'Mother, please, let's get a move on!' Liam is such an ankle-biter.

Mildred stirs. 'Will you stay for a snack and a cup of tea?' she asks. 'It won't take Grace a minute to whip up sandwiches. I have scones and fresh clotted cream. Strawberry jam, homemade…'

'I'm in, Mum. I'd kill for hot tea. And your strawberry jam…' Colleen takes her gently by the arm and leads her down the path.

'Thank God for that!' Mildred hears Liam mumble under his breath. She is not sure what he is so grateful to the Lord about: the strawberry jam or her being on the move again. His shoes squelch on the muddy ground. Stella's heels dig into the clay like chisels. When did she become such a madam? She used to live two houses down the lane, on Dove Farm. She used to run about barefoot.

It was his mother's idea to walk to church. There was the civilised option of taking the car, but she would have none of it. 'There's a perfectly good shortcut,' she'd said. 'I'd be the laughing stock of Sexton's Canning being driven five hundred yards in a car! It's only ten minutes on foot.' So they went treading through mud and cowpats to please her.

At the gate, Esme is talking to that farmhand – an Irishman whose name Liam never remembers. He became a permanent feature on the farm after Father's death, or

5

perhaps it was only then that Liam started noticing his sulky presence. All sorts of scum crawl out of the woodwork when a man dies. They feed on hapless senile widows, like ticks on blood.

They are standing by the stables where Esme keeps her horse. Rohan, she calls him. It costs a fortune in insurance. Liam wishes his daughter would spend his money in a more constructive way. But she won't. She has always been *contrary*, like her grandmother. Chose to study biology. He asked her why she couldn't go one step further, become a vet. Push herself a bit. It would give her something concrete in hand, but no! – biology is what she wanted. What do you do with biology? Put your diploma in the bottom drawer and volunteer to do odd jobs for the National Trust; let your father pay the bills.

The farmhand sees them approach, hangs his head low, and disappears inside the stables, taking the horse with him. There's something shifty about that man! Liam is a good judge of character, and he doesn't trust him as far as he can spit. He will have to get rid of him. He will have to make lots of changes around here.

Esme is waving, a big smile on her face. She is pretty - strawberries and cream, like her mother used to be at that age. What is she doing talking to that man? What can they possibly be talking about?

'Sorry, Nan! Couldn't make it to the service,' Esme has to bend practically in half to kiss her gnarled grandmother. She is looking guilty. Judging by the fact that she's wearing her riding boots and jacket, she clearly had no intention of making it to the church.

'No matter! You're here now.' Mother pretends not to

be bothered, but she is. It means the world to her – the church, the service, all that hocus-pocus.

'Was the service good?'

'It's a new priest, you see. He didn't really know Reginald, but still -'

'He must've known him. He's been here for five years, if not longer. He probably doesn't stay in touch with his parishioners.' Stella points out in a tone that implies gross irregularity.

Mother ignores her, or simply can't hear her. 'Still, he knew Reginald's name and got the dates right, and read out the prayer I gave him. He even added a few bits from himself ... Good voice – I heard every word he said. Unlike Father O'Leary.'

'Father O'Leary! His speech was incomprehensible. I couldn't get past his thick accent and on top of that, he mumbled and grunted... and whistled through his nose. Remember how silly it sounded?' Colleen chortles.

'Even when he was young,' Mildred adds.

'Was he ever young? I can't imagine him as a young man.'

'Now you don't have to. He died last winter -'

'Let's go inside and have that tea,' Liam butts in, bristling with impatience. "I really ought to be going soon, but there are matters to discuss. Since we're all here...'

The kitchen is large and airy, as a farmhouse kitchen should be. The pots are hanging high up on hooks under the ceiling where Reginald installed them fifty years ago – now too high for Mildred to reach. Thank heavens for

Grace! She is tall and robust. Nothing is ever too high or too heavy for her.

Except that Grace is not here yet. She was going to cycle home after the service, check on the dogs, and come over straight after that. Something must have got in the way. Mildred is disconcerted. She doesn't know where Grace has put the butter – it isn't in the fridge. It may be in the larder, but you need a torch to search in there. The torch should be in the top drawer, but isn't. If she starts opening all the drawers, she will look confused. She most certainly cannot afford to look confused in her own house.

'I'll put the kettle on. I say, everyone could do with a cup of tea,' she says, assertive and competent. Stella stares at her, alarmed by the old woman stating the obvious. She has taken off her fur, folded it inside-out and placed it on the bench next to her. Her hand rests protectively over it, pressing down hard as if the thing was about to come to life and run away.

'Let me help you,' Colleen offers and reaches for the bread. She lifts it to her nose and inhales. 'God, I love the smell of a fresh loaf!' The sharp knife slides through the crust.

Mildred is picking out the mugs. So many of them are chipped or cracked, or stained inside. Some commemorate Charles and Diana's wedding. Two of them go back as far as the Silver Jubilee. Eventually she carries five carefully selected mugs to the table, one by one. It is then that she sees the rosebud tea set she washed and dried earlier, ready for tea this afternoon. Flustered, she takes the mugs back to the cupboard. Stella is still staring. Liam has just put down his mobile phone, and is now tapping his fingers

8

on the table, watching her.

Where *is* Grace?

Mildred succeeds at prising open the tin of tea leaves. With a shaky hand she takes a few scoops, then fills the tea pot with boiling water. Some of it spills out and leaves a wet ring on the bench top, but she carries the pot triumphantly to the table. The milk is definitely in the fridge – she put it there this morning. Mildred pours it into a small jug. The tea is ready. She sits down at the table and feels like bursting into 'Glory in the Highest'.

'Mum, where do you keep the butter?' Colleen's question makes her heart sink. She doesn't know where the butter is. And even more to the point, she does not know where Grace is. Where on earth is Grace?

'Why don't we wait for Grace?' she says. 'She's in charge of the butter.'

'Forget the sandwiches, Colleen. We can have the scones instead,' Stella proposes.

'I sliced the bread for sandwiches… and the ham looks delicious,' Colleen looks disappointed.

'We can have them without butter,' Esme shrugs.

'Grace would know,' Mildred says faintly.

'I'll just have the scones. Did Mildred mention clotted cream?' Stella inquires through the medium of her husband.

Mildred gets up to fetch the jam and cream. The jam is in the cupboard – the bottom shelf - but the clotted cream… It is in the same place as the butter, only Mildred doesn't know – doesn't remember – where. She surrenders.

'I wish Grace was here. She knows where everything

9

is.'

'Let's just drink the tea.' Esme is a good girl.

'Only I've already sliced the bread,' Colleen insists like a stubborn old mule.

Liam stops tapping the table and points at his mother. 'This is precisely why you can't go on like this!' he bursts out, sweeping his arm around the kitchen as if it was a freak show.

'Like what?' Mildred blinks nervously.

'You aren't coping. You can't cope on your own.'

'Grace is usually here. Something must have -'

'Grace can't be here all the time, Mother,' his tone is placid and patronising, as if he was addressing a five-year-old. 'If anything - God forbid - was to happen to you, Grace couldn't cope. Like I said, half the time she isn't even here.'

'Not to mention she isn't a qualified carer,' Stella adds. 'Mildred needs professional support.'

Liam glares at her. He dreads what Mother will do. She has this uncanny propensity to dig in her heels just to spite Stella.

She does exactly that.

'I don't need a carer – qualified or not. I'm perfectly capable of looking after myself.'

'She doesn't even know where anything is in this house,' Stella goes on, oblivious to the effect she is having.

'Grace does the housekeeping. I don't have to know where everything is as long as she does.'

'Stella, honey, leave it to me,' Liam fixes his wife with an icy glare.

She snorts, suitably admonished. 'I don't feel like the scones anymore.'

'Why don't you go outside then? Get some air. Clear that pretty little head of yours.'

'It's raining and it's cold. Why would I want to go outside and stand in the cold?'

'I really don't care what you do,' he grits his teeth, 'so long as you shut up and stay out of it.'

There is a moment, a glimmer of realisation, when Stella's lower lip quivers and she swallows the insult loudly and pointedly. She is blinking rapidly, holding back tears.

Suddenly Mildred brightens up. 'The butter! Grace said she would take it out for us. It's on top of the fridge,' she points it out to Colleen. She is a master-evader, avoiding the subject. She may come across as scatty, but she knows what she's doing.

'Oh, so it is! Smashing!' Colleen is overjoyed. Little things make her happy. 'How many sandwiches? I'll have two myself.' No one answers.

'I feel like such a pig,' Colleen chuckles. 'I really ought to lose some weight. I think that'd be my New Year's resolution.'

'Mother, I've had a good look around residential homes.' Liam thrusts three spoons of sugar into his tea and stirs frantically. 'There's a lovely place in Werton. Grace could visit you every day. We could, too – it's a ten-minute drive from my office. Mind you, it costs an arm and a leg, but we can afford it if we sell the farm. It's better to pay a bit more and have peace of mind…'

He reaches for her hand. 'I'm worried about you,

Mother… Here on your own. What if something happens? You see where I'm coming from? At Autumn House they have all the facilities you could ask for: medical nurses, beautiful grounds… You'll love the gardens!'

'But I love it here. My farm… I've got everything I need. You shouldn't have troubled yourself, son.' She squeezes his hand.

Stella snorts again and raises one eyebrow at Liam, as if saying *I told you it'd be a waste of breath*. He rubs his shiny, well-exfoliated chin, exhales and composes himself again.

'That's just the point, Mother: the farm. It's a business - it has to be run like a business. It'll go to waste. You can't run the farm by yourself! I've given you two years – just to humour you. To give you time to get over Dad passing, and all that… But without him and at your age, let's face it, you can't manage a working farm on your own.'

'Who said I want to?'

A glimmer of hope lights his eyes. 'I'm glad you see it this way. We must sell up before it's run into the ground.'

'It won't come to that.'

'But it will if it isn't properly managed. It has to go into capable hands, I'll take care of that. I've given it some thought. We have to market it as a going concern, together with the outbuildings and the farmhouse – all as one. So you see, you'll be so much better off -'

'I'm not selling.'

'But I thought we agreed the farm can't go to waste. We owe it to Father…'

'The farm is doing well. It *is* properly managed.'

Liam gawps at her, incredulous. 'By who? You? You don't know the first thing -'

'Sean does. He runs the farm, keeps accounts for me, the payroll – the lot. Grace takes care of the house and the chores. I'm in good hands. Everything is taken care of.'

'Who the hell is Sean?'

'Sean! You must've seen him around. He's here from dawn till dusk. In fact, he lives in the cottage. He's refurbished it – a fresh coat of paint, all the plumbing, patched up the roof. To think that only -'

'You mean the *farmhand*? For God's sake, Mother, we're talking business management here, we're talking big money!'

'We're talking farming, Dad. He's good at that, knows his stuff. His family had a farm in Armagh,' Esme interjects without an invitation.

Liam gapes at his daughter with disbelief as if he is making a great effort to remember who she is. The veins on his neck are swelling. His face is flushed livid red. 'Didn't I ask you to shut the hell up!' he thunders.

'You asked Mum, not me,' Esme says evenly.

Mildred gets up from the table. 'That settles it, then.' She smiles, though her blood is pounding frantically at her temples. If she took her cardigan off, she is sure, her throbbing arteries would show through her skin and the thin fabric of her blouse. Has she taken her blood pressure tablets this morning? She panics. And *where is Grace*?

Colleen bites off a big chunk of her sandwich and chews hurriedly. Then she wipes her hands, looks at Liam with a crooked smile, and again assuming that Mildred can't hear a thing, says, 'I told you she wouldn't listen.

What made you think she'd change the habit of a lifetime?'

They are leaving. Mother looks away. Stella cocoons herself inside her fur coat and trots to the bathroom. Liam resumes his table-tapping while waiting for her. He hasn't even taken his coat off. It was meant to be a flying visit, a mere formality, but nothing is ever straightforward these days, and hasn't been since Mother took it upon herself to run the farm. Liam is losing his patience.

'Coming with us, Esme?'

'I was going to go for a ride when you came. I should still like to do that.' Like her grandmother, Esme is looking away.

'Suit yourself.'

Colleen is helping Mother to take the dirty dishes to the sink and insists on doing the dishes while Mother hovers around. She will soon drive off to her big city flat; she will make herself indispensable to the snotty brats at her school – Liam will stay behind, holding everything together, putting up with their mother's eccentricities and everyday disasters. Ever since he can remember he has always been the one to stay behind, to do the donkey work and pick up the pieces while Colleen romped around the world, abandoning one pointless degree for another and squandering her supposed talents. And still, after all those years of her counterproductive existence, she looks beatifically pleased with herself. It is time somebody enlightened her about how deluded she is.

But it won't be Liam. She is his sister, like it or not, and perhaps the only person on this planet he could trust –

if he cared to take her seriously enough.

Liam goes to the sink to kiss his mother and sister goodbye. 'I'll wait outside. Tell Stella.'

'Give me a minute and I'll come and see you off,' Mother says. 'We're nearly finished here.'

'No! No, don't bother. It's cold.' It would take Mother half a day to get ready to see him off to the gate. Just remembering where she has put her scarf may be a challenge. Then there is the extracting of her feet from plimsolls and the pulling on of wellies. Once found, the scarf might take a while too. And what if she decides to have another cup of tea before tackling the coat? The concept of time is foreign to her. Time is money, and Mother has never been any good with either. 'No, it's all right. I'll come over next week. We'll talk some more in peace.'

'I think we've talked already. Aren't we done talking?' Mother – when she wants to – can be sharp as a knife.

'By no means!' He kisses her on the cheek. It feels lukewarm. Her hands are white and bony in the soapy water, like chicken claws.

The rain is taking a break. The air is still heavy and threatens more downpours, but for now it seems the sky is holding its breath, seeing how long it can last before it spits it all out again. Liam crosses the yard to the back of the stables. The ground is covered with filth, and the smell of shit and sulphurous fertilisers assaults his senses. Scowling, he heads for the cottage. It is an overstatement to call it a *cottage* – it is an old wooden hut with rotting floors and smashed window panels. Tiles are missing from the roof. As children Liam, David and Colleen weren't allowed to play there. The broken glass and rusting blades made the place into a tetanus hazard. Their father had cut his hand on a dirty nail there and had to go to hospital for painful injections. After that the cottage was off limits. Liam is curious to see how somebody could make a home out of it.

He steps gingerly over an ancient plough overgrown with nettles and negotiates his way down the makeshift pathway built from tyres pressed into the soggy ground. From outside, the cottage appears untouched since his childhood, but for the roof which has been covered with roofing felt. He tries the door. It is locked. The windowsills are green with grime, unwashed for years, but the broken glass has been replaced. A power cable runs from the main house to the cottage. The Irishman has wired the place. It looks amateurish. It is probably a disaster waiting to happen.

Liam peers through one of the windows. It is almost empty inside: only a single bed, an oil heater, three built-in shelves running along the whole width of the wall, filled with books. There is a chest of drawers, which Liam recognises. It used to stand in his parents' bedroom. How did *he* get hold of it? Preying on Mother's kind heart! Cardboard boxes are piled up against the wall with God knows what hiding inside them. But yes, the walls have been given a coat of white paint, the floorboards are new, and a small lamp topped with a Spiderman lampshade stands on one of the cardboard boxes next to the bed. The lamp must have been stolen from some unsuspecting little boy in the village or, at best, bought at a car boot sale.

Liam circles the cottage and reaches the kitchen

16

window. He steps closer and rips his trouser leg on the barbed wire that lies concealed in the knee-high weeds. He curses under his breath, his trousers are ruined, but since he's already here he may as well take a look. He is surprised to see a fridge. He doesn't know why he finds this sight of domesticity disturbing.

'What are you looking for?'

The question comes from behind him and it makes Liam jump. Firstly, he sees a dog – a great big, nasty thing, a German Shepherd baring its teeth and padding towards him, head down, eyes still and watchful. The beast is closely followed by the Irishman. He is almost as tall as Liam, but much leaner: narrower around the waist, squarer around the shoulders. He is stooped a bit and seems younger than Liam – early forties? Despite the weather-beaten complexion and his sullen expression, his eyes are round and clear-blue and he has a full mane of dark hair without a single streak of grey. Mother must have fallen for his Irish charm and taken him in. Some sort of solidarity with her compatriot – madness of old age.

'I see you've made yourself comfortable in the cottage,' Liam observes coolly.

'Mildred offered. I took her up on her offer.'

'As you would.'

'Is that all?'

'You pay rent, I take it?'

'Free board is part of my pay.'

'What's the rest of your pay?'

The man fixes Liam with a steely stare. Those innocent blue eyes can be very deceptive.

'That's between me and Mildred. I've got to go back to work. Duty calls. Come on, Corky!' He turns and is walking away, the dog by his leg. There is something insolent – offensive – about him. It infuriates Liam that he thinks he can just walk away like that.

'I'm afraid we'll have to let you go. A month's notice, I think, is more than generous.' Liam is following him. They are heading for the stables. Without stopping, without acknowledging Liam's words, the Irishman picks up a pitchfork and starts shovelling manure from the stables out onto a hefty pile in the yard. Once stirred, the shit stinks heavens high.

'We're selling the farm. Mother is moving to a retirement home.'

'Mildred never said anything to that effect,' the man responds calmly from the recess of the stable and chucks another forkful of straw and horseshit onto the pile outside.

The kitchen window overlooks the backyard, with its discarded old junk, cracked concrete conquered by weeds, and the cottage where Sean now lives. Mildred remembers how it used to be. A swing, made from a plank suspended on two lengths of rope, was attached to the lowest bough of a sturdy chestnut with a thick trunk and foliage like a giant cauliflower. The children used to play there and Mildred could keep an eye on them from the kitchen window. But then Reginald got that rusty bit of metal under his nail while retrieving a ball, and sent the kids away, out of harm's way. Truth be told, the cottage and its surroundings were an accident waiting to happen.

And now Sean has resurrected the poor little place. It is nice to see it occupied and to see a feeble red light glowing in the cottage every night before she goes to bed. She finds that comforting and reassuring. Without that light she would have to accept she was alone and vulnerable, and she would have to leave the farm. Go to a home. Concede defeat and get ready for dying.

The last saucer nearly slips from her rheumatic fingers. She dries it thoroughly and puts it with the others in the top cupboard. Did the cupboards mysteriously move up or has Mildred sunk another few inches into the floor?

Liam is snooping around the cottage, peeping through the windows. He tears a perfectly good pair of Sunday trousers on some barbed wire. What on earth is he doing? Behind her, Mildred can hear Stella asking where Liam has gone to. She ignores it, but Colleen, always obliging, says, 'He's waiting for you outside, I think.'

Mildred follows Stella into the yard. The daughter and the daughter-in-law part with cool indifference. They have never taken to each other.

'I'll be off then. It was a lovely service.' Stella declares in a big voice normally reserved for the deaf, but Mildred sees no need to respond.

Sean is talking to Liam. This must be their first face-to-face encounter. Mildred cannot see their faces, but the body language seems friendly enough and even Corky is at ease. The two men maintain physical distance, but the conversation goes on as they walk together towards the stables, followed by the dog. Clearly, they have found something to talk about. She hopes they get on. Liam must see that Sean is taking good care of the farm. And of

Mildred. He is her right-hand man.

The rain is gone and there is a promise of a dry afternoon.
Patches of clear blue sky drift from the south, pushing out
the low-lying clouds and hanging them high up to dry,
where they look rather threadbare. After the rain, the air is
thinner and lighter. Mildred waves goodbye to the
stoplights on the rear of Liam's four-wheel drive as it
splutters mud before vanishing around the sharp curve of
the driveway. The day is still young.

Esme and Sean emerge from the stables, Esme leading
Rohan who tries to pull away from her grasp, excited at
the prospect of a ride. Sean pats the horse on the neck to
calm it down. Corky trots ahead of them.

'Rohan needs some exercise,' Esme calls over to her
grandmother. 'Just look at him!'

'Sean exercises him when you're not around.'

'I know.' Esme gazes at Sean. If Mildred didn't know
any better she would've sworn there was a subtle
undertone to that gaze, like those two are in on a secret.
'Rohan loves Sean more than me. Something needs to be
done about that.' Esme laughs.

'Nah, Rohan knows what's good for him,' Sean
returns the gaze, but his seems a bit self-conscious - a bit
tortured. He holds the horse's bridle while Esme mounts.
Rohan is a large beast and Esme looks tiny sitting atop
him. She may be tiny but she is strong and firmly in
charge. Esme is an impetuous young lady. She knows
what she wants and she goes for it – more like her dad
than her mother.

She takes off at a full gallop, her bottom high up, her

thighs pressed tight to the horse's sides. Corky runs after her, but soon gives up and returns to his master. He never leaves Sean's side for longer than the blink of an eye.

'You're from County Armagh, Esme tells me,' Mildred says. Bizarrely, it never occurred to her to ask him before. Three years ago, perhaps more than that, he wandered into the farm out of nowhere and asked for a job. Any odd job, he said, he was good with his hands, he knew about farming. He had no references and Mildred didn't ask for any. Reginald had just had his first stroke and was lying in bed, partially paralysed, mentally fragile. Little chance he would get up and get going. Mildred was at her wits' end; she needed someone to lean on. The newcomer brought with him distant memories of Ireland and of her youth. He reminded her of her father. It was in the way he carried himself, held his head on her level so as to look her straight in the eye. She would trust him without references and she didn't see it fit to ask any questions. If he wanted to speak, he would say who he was and where he was from, but it was up to him to decide.

'Aye, from Armagh. Just outside. My family had a farm – a smallholding – west of Armagh, towards Killylea,' he tells her now.

'I know the area. I was with the Sisters of Mercy at Newry for a couple of years before I came here. And my parents had a smallholding too, near Banbridge, and nine mouths to feed. Not easy. I joined the Sisters when I was scarcely seventeen.'

'My mother took on odd jobs in town – the dry laundry, the greengrocer's, all sorts. She was forever

saving for my schooling. It was me and my four sisters –
she believed I stood a better chance of making it.'

'And here you are helping on the farm,' Mildred
scrutinises his face. Has something gone wrong for him?
How did he end up here? Is he here to stay?

'And here I am,' he nods, a bright smile in those deep-
blue eyes. 'Happy as can be.'

'Glad you are. I need you here.'

'Your son tells me you want to sell the farm?'

'He does, I don't.' Mildred speaks resolutely, but she
finds herself breaking out in a cold sweat.

Grace is approaching from the road, waving her arms
as if she was under attack from a swarm of wasps. 'Sorry
I'm late. Blinking rain! Got a leak in the roof, just above
me bedroom. All the bedsheets wet, blimey! We had to do
some patching up, me and Henry. I was holding the
ladder, Henry stuffing rags into the hole, between the
tiles. Must be the birds what done it! It's only for now,
mind. We'll have to pay someone to do a decent job of it.
It never ends!' Grace shakes her head.

'I'll have a look for you tomorrow morning,' Sean
offers. He's a good lad, and Mildred knows he won't take
any money for his trouble.

'Oh, bless you, Sean!' Grace is delighted. 'That's a
relief, believe me! Right, I'd better start on the dinner.
How many staying?'

'Liam and Stella have gone, so it'll only be Colleen,
Esme and us here,' Mildred says. 'I was thinking of that
silverside in the fridge, with gravy and mash? Everyone
would like that.' They start walking away towards the
house, leaving Sean and the dog behind to receive Esme.

She is coming back, at a trot, unhurried and full of beans.

Dinner is on the table. As much as she could, without getting under Grace's feet, Colleen has helped with the vegetables, and she has committed herself to washing up, feeling guilty that Grace should be Mum's mainstay while she comes only during school holidays – tokenistic visits. It was different when Dad was alive, they were there for each other and didn't need anyone else. But since his passing, Mum has grown frail and confused. She puts a brave face on it, but she can't carry on as it is. It has crossed Colleen's mind to move back - find a teaching post in Sexton's Canning or in the village itself, and offer Mum a helping hand - but she hasn't got a clue about farming. Her head has always been in the clouds or inside a book, and she simply wouldn't know where to begin. Perhaps Liam is right – perhaps Mum should pack it all up and move into a nice and cosy retirement home.

'The dinner's getting cold,' Grace complains. 'Didn't I tell Sean to be here by six? I did, but was he listening? And where has Esme gone off to? Still with the horses, I bet!'

Colleen shakes herself awake from her musings. 'I'll go and find them. They're probably on their way anyway.' She wraps her poncho around her shoulders. When the sun goes down here, it gets cold rapidly. The house isn't too warm either. Mum doesn't believe in central heating outside the winter months, and even then the heat is thriftily rationed. She crosses the yard to the outbuildings but finds nobody there. She will have to try Sean's cottage. She hasn't visited there – was never invited. In fact, she feels a bit nervous and awkward around Sean. He is handsome and surprisingly well-spoken for a simple farmhand, and he looks at her suggestively, as if he knows that she – perhaps – fancies him, a little. Comparisons with *Lady Chatterley's Lover* crowd her head as she proceeds along the overgrown pavers to the back of the house where the cottage stands.

'Corky, here you are!' Colleen finds the dog asleep on the porch. He lifts his head and lazily wags his tail before putting his head back between his paws and peering at her watchfully, just in case she may do something he doesn't approve of. Colleen is wary of dogs ever since she was nipped by that nasty mongrel next door. Gingerly she steps over Corky and is about to knock on the door when she hears suspicious noises – an alarming tangle of grunting and panting performed to a vigorous beat; both male and female, deep and soft, mingling with each other and growing in intensity.

Colleen doesn't knock on the door. Something tells her not to. She retreats to the path and creeps through the knee-high weeds under the kitchen window. Her eyes rounded with anticipation, she looks in. Her gaze is drawn to a small lamp with a bright lampshade. It lights streaks of blue and red on the bare walls - and on two figures standing in the doorway. The woman's arms are stretched out and she is gripping the doorframe. The man stands close behind her, his face buried in her hair and his hands guiding her hips towards him, pulling them in then pushing them away, and as her buttocks slam against his thighs, he and she groan in perfect harmony. A pair of riding boots stands to attention at the foot of the bed, which is odd considering the urgency and chaos of what is going on in the doorway.

When it is all over the man kisses the woman on the back of her neck. They both laugh as she twirls to face him.

Sean and Esme.

Colleen grasps her chest – her heart is about to jump out of her ribcage. She turns on her heel and forces her way across the weeds and the junk, and away from the barking dog, back to the main house. Something catches at her poncho – she yanks it, and runs.

She is trembling like a leaf when she finally shuts the door behind her and collapses into a chair. Mum and Grace stare at her.

'So,' Grace says, 'where's Sean? You found him?'

Colleen shakes her head, catching her breath and recovering her heartbeat.

'Didn't you see Esme anywhere?' Mum asks. 'I have a feeling she went home without even saying goodbye.'

'No! I mean, no, she didn't.' Colleen manages a semi-coherent response.

'I wouldn't have done that!' Esme is speaking from the hallway. 'Would I now?' She enters the kitchen, beaming and carefree, as if she had nothing to be ashamed of. Of course, she doesn't. She is an adult. She can do what she likes. Sean is one step behind her. He's also full of smiles. He is carrying something colourful, something very much like Colleen's poncho. He passes it to her.

'That'd be yours, I imagine. Corky found it. Sorry about the state of it.'

Full house! Mildred enjoys having a full house. It would have been nice if Liam and Stella could have stayed, but Liam is forever in a hurry, so much so Mildred often fears that if she ever accidentally strayed into his trajectory she would be run over and slammed into a roadside ditch like an unsuspecting badger on a motorway. Liam is probably much happier in town, dining in fancy restaurants, and to be perfectly honest Mildred is much happier not being told what to do by a son who wants nothing more than to put her in a little cell in an old people's home and throw away the key. Mildred has had her share of living in little cells, firstly in Newry, then here in England. Clearly it wasn't her true vocation to be a nun, hard as she tried. The little cell had something to do with it. She won't be forced back into it now that for the first time in her life, she is in charge.

With Grace restored by her side, Mildred is back in the saddle – cool and lucid like morning dew. With Sean on the other side, she is invincible. Without sounding blasphemous, Mildred often feels that she and those two, three as one, are like the Holy Trinity. Only perhaps not that holy.

She needs them. She will have to tell Liam not to take it upon himself to hire or fire her employees. Because they are more than employees – they are her extended family. 'The meat is lovely and tender,' she praises Grace, and she means it. 'Grace, you are a miracle worker!'

'Coming from you, Mildred, I'm minded to believe it – in miracles, that is! But it was a decent piece of beef – lean it was, without a hint of fat on it.' Grace looks very pleased with herself, and so she should.

'Very good, Grace,' Sean agrees.

'Another helping, pet?' She is keen to please him. That leaking roof in her house won't mend itself.

'Don't mind if I do.'

Grace gets up and whizzes to the stove to fetch the pot. When she returns, she heaps up a second helping onto everyone's plate, like it or not. Colleen squeals, 'Not for me, please. I can't, I won't...' It isn't like her. She likes eating. She hasn't been herself in the last half an hour or so – since she came back with a wild look in her eye. What happened? Did the dog snap at her? Not like Corky, but then with all those colours and frills flying in his face even he could get a bit wound up. Colleen needs to think about her dress code. Those clashing colours, honestly, could raise the dead.

As if on cue, Corky breaks into a volley of barks. His habit is to lie on the step outside the door, waiting for his master to come out. Sean gets up. 'Someone at the door,' he says and goes to restrain the dog.

He returns with a man. Mildred's eyes aren't what they used to be, and perhaps she shouldn't be trusting them right now because, sure as anything, they have to be deceiving her. Or else the dead have indeed been raised. Mildred crosses herself, her face pale, her jaw slack. Her eyes tell her she is looking at Reginald. Not as he was towards the end, but in his prime: wide-shouldered, thick blond hair never quite brushed and screaming to see a barber, even the unkempt beard... Is this a hallucination? Has she finally lost it? Perhaps she should pretend that he is a stranger. Perhaps she should ask him if he is lost and needs directions.

'Ma... Colleen...' the man says, and it is only then that she knows, as does Colleen, who he is. They say it at the same time.

'David!'

Colleen runs to him and throws herself into his arms. She is crying, loud and unashamed. That poor girl can conjure up tears at the drop of a hat! Is that why she has been acting strangely? Did she know he was coming? Why didn't she say?

Mildred takes time to get up – her legs and her senses have temporarily abandoned her. She has no strength to hold herself upright so she leans on the table, heavy and ungainly. She won't be able to walk to him, but that's just the same as he frees himself from Colleen and comes to her. She tells herself not to cry, but she does nevertheless, the same as Colleen who is good at making a spectacle of herself. Mildred finds it embarrassing. When she finally speaks, she tries to sound casual, 'My God, David, where have you been all these years?'

'Canada,' he replies, just as casually.

The others are blinking, staring at David and throwing curious glances at each other. Grace is the first one to recover her wits. 'I know you – you're the David what left, mmm, years ago – going on twenty years...'

'Twenty-seven to be exact.'

'That long!'

'That long.'

'Ha, I'll be damned!' Grace is the only one to maintain a thread of conversation. 'Well, sit down, make yourself at home. You hungry? I got some silverside left, mash and gravy.'

'No, thank you, I've eaten.'

'You can still sit down, can't you?'

'I suppose I can.' He takes a chair and pulls it away from the table, away from everyone else. David has always been a loner, the odd one out.

'You haven't changed one bit,' Colleen exults, her hands animated and restless. She throws them up in the air, then clasps them to her cheeks, finally binds them together and rests them in her lap. Not for long.

Mildred has to disagree with her. 'He has. He's broader, bigger somehow, I say.'

'That's because you're smaller, Mildred!' Grace chuckles. She gets up from the table and starts collecting the plates. Colleen is too flustered to help her even though she has promised to do the dishes. Mildred can't blame her – she is flustered too. It has been such a long time. She thought she had lost the boy for good.

'I'll make tea,' Grace informs everyone. 'And no one's touched the scones!'

'We couldn't find the butter and when we did…' Mildred isn't sure what she wanted to say. She is captivated by David, by his sudden return, by how much he looks like his father. Guilt weighs heavily in her ribcage.

'So tell us about Canada,' Colleen's hand reaches towards him, as if she wants to touch him to check if it is really him. She withdraws it quickly.

'What's there to say? It's a big country. Cold most of the time.'

'What have you been up to down there?'

'The usual: lived, worked, had a wife…'

'Wife?' Colleen cries out with excitement. 'Did you bring her? Is she here?'

'She's dead. Cancer.'

'I'm sorry!'

'It's been six years.'

Silence creeps into the conversation. Grace brings the rosebud tea set to the table. She knows when the occasion calls for it. And it does – it does big time! David is back.

'Are you staying?' Mildred asks.

'I think so,' he says, and qualifies it quickly, 'I might.'

'How long have you been back?'

'Five days.'

'Five days! Just five days back in old Blighty!' Colleen is beside herself.

'Five days and it's only now that you come home?' Mildred is less disposed to euphoria.

'I stopped calling this home twenty-seven years ago.' He looks hard at her. He hasn't forgotten, hasn't forgiven – despite the lapse in time. Time doesn't always heal old wounds, not for everyone.

'So why now?'

'The solicitors found me. They're holding some money in trust for me, from Father.'

'He left equal shares to all the children,' Mildred says. What she is trying to say is *He loved all his children in equal shares, including you,* but she can't say that for fear of offending him.

'And he left the farm to Mum,' Colleen tells him.

'Just for now, until I die.'

'I hope it isn't *just for now*! You must stop talking about dying, Mother. I can't bear it! Tell her, David!

She'll listen to you.'

David smiles awkwardly. 'You look good, Ma.'

She is glad he came back. She wishes he sat a bit closer so that she could take a better look at him and touch him. Despite what he may think in that stubborn head of his, she loves him dearly, like her own – has done so since the day he was born.

He gets up. 'I'd better be going. Thought I'd say hello... The service was really good.'

'You were there?'

'Just in passing.'

He can't admit to having feelings, or memories. He used to wear his heart on his sleeve – no longer, it seems.

'Must you be already going? I won't have it! You haven't told us anything. You must tell us all about Canada and what you've been up to. You can't just come and go,' Colleen is a tenacious character. And she is innocent of any wrongdoing. She has the right to speak. 'You've done a runner once, and once is enough.'

This time his smile is genuine. 'You haven't changed, Colleen. Still the mulish little girl, stomping her feet and having it her way.'

Colleen snorts. 'Whenever was that me? It sounds more like Liam! Wait till he hears you're back!'

The mood stiffens. Mildred sighs. David is no longer amused. 'I must be going nonetheless.'

'Stay,' Mildred says. 'Stay here, on the farm, please. I could do with your help. God knows, we could do with an extra pair of hands. Couldn't we, Sean?' She can't look David in the eye in case he says no and walks out of that door, and disappears for good.

31

'Definitely,' Sean agrees. 'I was going to look for someone permanent. Things don't work as well with casual labour, but then Liam said you were selling the farm – I thought I'd hold my horses.'

'Are you?' David looks interested. 'Selling the farm?'

'No, not me. Liam wants me to. He says I can't cope, time to move to a home. He's used to getting it his way.' She doesn't care if she appears weak and vulnerable. This is her worst nightmare – losing the farm, getting locked up in a home. Sometimes putting on a brave face is too much for Mildred. Perhaps she is too worn out to carry on with the posturing. David's return has stirred something in her – her deepest anxieties.

'I'm booked into the Holiday Inn. My things are there. I was going to look for a place as soon as I collected the money.'

'Why pay for a hotel? Plenty of room here,' Grace takes it upon herself to point out the obvious since no one in this family seems to be talking any sense.

'At least until you find your own place,' Mildred adds.

'Yes, OK. Until then.'

It is only when everyone has gone that Esme asks the question, 'Who is that man?'

Mildred has just been drifting into her mid-evening nap. She is emotionally exhausted and that translates into sleep incontinence. She only needs to close her eyes…

'He called you *Ma*. If he's my uncle, why haven't I heard of him? If he's no relation of ours why did he call you Ma?'

'I have been a mother to him.' Mildred must stay awake for this conversation. A trip down memory lane is something she normally takes on her own, and usually it is an inward journey which requires no words and no explanations. Not so this time. It's time Esme was introduced to David. 'Your grandfather was married when we first met. At the time I was in a convent, Sisters of Mercy... What was it you used to call it? *My previous life.*'

'I know that. I can almost picture Grandad seducing you away from God, and into the kitchen,' Esme chortles. 'I always had you as the pure and innocent one. Are you telling me there was someone before Grandad? Naughty, naughty...'

'No, God forbid!' Mildred chuckles. 'David is your grandad's child. His first wife had a hard time with her pregnancies. In those days it wasn't uncommon, people buried their stillborn babies and kept trying. She'd had three stillbirths before David and she feared it would happen again – it was raw fear, so real you could smell it... It was tearing her apart. She was convinced she would lose this baby, too. The worry got her into hospital with complications. To me it was her mind that was her greatest enemy – she was beside herself and was losing hope. I was there, only a young lass, a nun for goodness' sake – what did I know about having babies? But it was my job to offer her support and hope, and keep her going. We grew close. She relied on me being there every hour of the day, and I was. Reginald would come and go – he had a farm to run, singlehandedly.

'On the day of David's birth, she knew she was going to die... I was there right through the birth while Reginald sat outside, waiting. She grabbed my arm, I can still feel the pressure of her fingers digging into my skin. She made me promise that if the baby lived I'd look after it as if it were my own. I made a solemn promise. David was born. Patricia died giving birth to him. I took the baby, still covered in blood and birth waters, wrapped him in a blanket, and carried him to his father. The child was mine, I thought, God's will… Reginald took time before he dared hold his son in his arms for the first time. He grieved for his wife, of course he did, but without knowing her will, he begged me to stay with him and David. He asked me to marry him – off the cuff, not much fanfare there, just a simple question, and I said yes. What else was I supposed to say? I'd made a promise and besides, I already loved that boy like my own. Jesus didn't want me for his bride – God wanted me to be a mother to David and a wife to Reginald.'

Mildred smiles at her memories. It isn't often that Esme has nothing to say – no smart comments to make. She is listening, taking in Mildred's every word.

'Within a year your dad was born, then Colleen four years later. We brought the three of them together, loved them all the same. Yes,' Mildred feels truly spent. 'That's about it, about your uncle David.'

'I suppose I need to get to know him,' Esme says. 'Do you mind if I stay the night, meet him tomorrow morning when he comes – really meet him?'

'Be my guest. You know where the bedsheets are. Get the bed in the south room ready.'

Esme looks pensive. 'I still don't get it - why has no one ever told me anything about David's existence? And why did he disappear all those years ago, without a

34

forwarding address? Did you have a fall out?'

'It's a long story, and it is way past my bedtime.'

'What happened? Come on, Gran, tell me!'

It's a painful memory, one that has been buried for years. Now that David is back there is little point in digging it out. It is best to leave it in the past. 'It's not for me to tell you. Let's not go there.'

'Who, then?' Esme is a persistent little pest, has always been. 'Who can tell me?'

'Ask Stella. Ask your father.'

Mildred regrets it the moment she says it.

REAP WHAT YOU SOW

Liam forces his way into the lazy stream of cars heading for Sexton's Canning. An idiot in a Corsa - miles behind him – punches his horn, and holds his fist down on it for a few annoying seconds. Liam glances at his rear view mirror. The trigger-happy idiot is foaming at the mouth. With a deliberate and relished slowness Liam sticks out his middle finger at him and waves it from side to side like a pendulum. That makes him feel a fraction better.

'God, you're so crude!' Stella peers at him over her shoulder, her eyes full of contempt. She picks the sides of her fur coat and wraps them tightly across her chest, distancing herself from Liam, the crude peasant. It's convenient for her to forget that the same crude peasant paid for that bloody coat! Liam thinks it, but he doesn't say it. He holds his tongue. It's important that she plays the hostess tonight to the best of her ability. Last thing he needs is Stella being a prima donna. Not tonight. Her mood swings will have to wait until tomorrow. He won't care then if she slips into her habitual silent treatment. He has too much on his mind to care for Stella's airs and graces.

She continues to try his patience. 'I really didn't

appreciate you talking to me that way in front of your mother. In front of everyone! Who do you take me for?'

Despite his best efforts not to rise to the provocation, he snaps, 'You don't realise it, do you? How you always – *always* – rub her the wrong way. You *always* say something -'

'Stupid! Is that what you want to say? *Stupid?* Because – let's face it - I am stupid!'

'No.' He tightens his grip on the steering wheel and puts his foot down. 'I never said that. You just provoke her. She's just sitting there and waiting for you to say something -'

'*Stupid.*'

'No! To say *anything* – clever or stupid, if you must know! Whatever you say, Mother will use it against me. I can't afford this. Not at this time, when I'm trying to get her to see the light!'

'She won't go into a home. And I'm sick and tired of you blaming it on me!'

'Just stay out of it, all right? Leave it to me. She'll go.'

'Why? Why is it so important that she does? She's happy where she is. You'll only antagonise her if you push her too hard.'

Liam doesn't mean to lose his nerve, but Stella has a knack for pushing his buttons the wrong way. He doesn't know when it started but it has by now come to a point that he can't control it. 'Told you to fucking stay out of it, didn't I? So do it – shut the fuck up! Or we'll all end up in the gutter!'

It is easy to talk to Dimitri when he has a full stomach.

Despite her earlier antics, Stella has outdone herself: the lamb was succulent and dripping with flavour, and the selection of cheeses would please a true connoisseur. Dimitri is purring with pleasure. He is sitting in Liam's armchair, knees far apart, the sagging sack of his stomach unfolding into his lap. He is huffing with exhaustion. His digestive system is in overload, but he likes it this way. Food is his religion – second only to money.

The stink of his cigar makes Liam retch, but he endures it with grace. Once upon a time this fat Greek saved Liam from financial ruin – the least Liam can do is to let him smoke his foul cigars in the lounge.

'People aren't buying real estate in Greece anymore – even fools know not to. No one wants to take the risk in this bloody climate. Too volatile. It's a pit. I'm washing my hands of it. Moving on.' Dimitri has never lost his guttural South African accent. His fat forefinger is curled over his cigar as he takes a drag and exhales a series of perfectly formed rings.

'We've had a good run while it lasted.'

'Can't complain.' He attempts to cross his legs, but his stomach won't allow that. 'I'm thinking rural France – a bit of property recycling: buy an old farmhouse, make it into a chateau, and throw in a coat of arms. I'll need to free most of my capital here, I'm afraid.'

Liam has been expecting this for some time now. 'Everything is tied up in Cox Properties -'

'I don't want to know, Liam.' Dimitri speaks softly, but there is unmistakable menace in his tone. His *associates*, two beefy heavies without a word of English, shift behind him. Liam leans towards the possibility that as much as they choose not to speak, they damn well understand every word that is being said. 'What's the story with your mother's farm? That's worth a few bob, no?'

'I was getting there. That's what I wanted to talk to you about.'

'Oh? Go on then – I'm all ears. Keeping my options open.'

'I'm getting my mother into a home -'

'Yeah, yeah, you've been telling me this for some time. Business won't stand still.'

'I know. She's going – like it or not. It's prime land, the farm, right on the outskirts of Sexton's Canning, almost within the town boundary. Shouldn't be a problem to have it re-zoned from agricultural to residential.'

'You want to build there?'

'Yes. Before someone else snaps it from under our feet.'

'Development – I don't know, mate. It didn't work for you in Ireland, remember? If it wasn't for yours truly,' Dimitri chuckles, swallows a ring of cigar smoke and starts coughing. Liam wishes he would choke on it. He doesn't like being reminded of his failed ventures. Ireland is a distant memory, well buried – six feet under.

He waits for Dimitri to recover his breath and says, 'It wasn't just me, it was everyone. You know that. We all had to take a fall – the bubble burst.'

'Speak for yourself.'

'I know, and I am grateful, Dimitri – I truly am!' Without the Greek's injection of cash Liam would've been bankrupted within days. The sword of Damocles was hanging over his head, about to fall, when Dimitri stepped in. But once Dimitri had invested his blood-stained cash, he had his hands wrapped around Liam's throat and he wouldn't loosen his grip. He had him. He controlled him. Liam had to live with it – and tread carefully – until the loan was repaid. With interest.

'I don't want your gratitude, mate. Get down to detail. What do you propose?'

'I provide the land and organise building permits and re-zoning, I get the team going- I know people, old contacts. I will need a small cash injection to get us going -'

'And that's coming from me?' Dimitri dons his trademark Godfather's smirk.

'Well, we can't wind up Cox Properties – we need a corporate structure, a front – you said that yourself. My money is tied up in the company…'

'As you keep telling me. But it is *my* money – strictly speaking.'

'When the project is complete, and I imagine two or three hundred houses, fifty per cent of net profits is yours. That should cover the loan.'

'Net profits?' Dimitri stubs out his cigar. 'You're not saying you want to deduct the cost of the land from my share? I am not an idiot, Liam. Fifty-fifty on gross profits, provisionally. The land will be your gesture of goodwill, and if you don't have any, I'll consider accepting it in lieu of interest repayments. We'll see about the final figures later, see how the sales pan out. Do we have a deal?'

Liam cringes. Mother's farm is the main asset in this enterprise – it is his inheritance. He knows he won't be paid a penny for all his work, but what choices are there? He needs Dimitri's money. Without it, he will sink. 'OK, then. Deal.'

He has brought the paperwork with him. This has been a business meeting from the moment Dimitri soaked his first olive in the virgin oil dip Stella prepared for starters. Liam knows it because Dimitri has come alone – without his wife, Persa. That's when Dimitri means business. 'Right, these are the budget projections, see what you think.' Liam passes his folder to the Greek.

'I'll take it home.' He hands the folder to one of his associates, the shorter one with a slightly more intelligent face. 'We wouldn't want to spoil the party.' A big grin on his face tells Liam he is buying into it. All the knots in Liam's arteries begin to loosen up. Until Dimitri delivers a final blow just below the belt.

'One thing to remember – I don't care how you get your hands on that farmland, but I'm not holding my breath till the old lady kicks the bucket. No disrespect there, mate, I know she's your mother, but we're working to deadlines.'

Another baby is on its way. It isn't any old baby – it's a boy. After three girls and a few adjustments to their mating rituals, Mr and Mrs Webber are expecting a boy. The news was broken to them this morning when they attended their second scan. DS Mark Webber is positively glowing – you'd be excused for thinking that it is he who carries the foetus inside him. He caught up with Gillian in the car park and for one uncomfortable second she thought he was going to hug and kiss her. Never before did she see him so animated. He was flapping his arms around him like a runaway windmill. Gillian picks up her pace to avoid being judged unfit for duty by association.

'So, Kate asks – I was thinking it too, but had more sense than to say it out loud – so she asks: "Could it be a finger, or something other than a little penis?" and the bloke looks at her, straight face, and says: "No. In my experience, no." So there – it's a boy, officially!'

'Subject to him not having six fingers on one of his hands,' Gillian qualifies. 'Stranger things have happened, you know.'

For a brief moment, Webber takes her flippant comment seriously. 'You're joking, aren't you?'

'Would I ever?'

As they enter the station they find PC Miller besieged by a loud-mouthed man laying down the law about who is fit to hear his complaint. 'I'm not talking about a run-over hedgehog! This is serious. I want to speak to a detective. This is fraud, you understand? An old lady is being defrauded of her money, and she happens to be my mother. You can't expect me to sit back and do nothing about it!'

'If I may take down all the details, I can assure you the matter will be referred to an appropriate officer.' PC Miller is his usual stoic self. He has heard about thousands of serious crimes, much more serious than any other in the history of criminality, and he has learned to take them all in his stride. With the recent cuts in the departmental budget, even if Jack the Ripper walked in the door to give himself up, he would have to stand in line and wait his turn.

Gillian and Webber sneak behind the loud-mouthed man's back and take the fire stairs instead of waiting for the lift, thus avoiding attracting unnecessary attention to their plain clothes detective statuses. PC Miller is perfectly capable of deflecting him all by himself.

'Right! I can't win this one, can I?' the man huffs. 'You'll have to send someone in charge to Nortonview farm, just off the road leading to Little Norton – you know the place?'

'We'll find it, sir.'

'I bloody well hope so – before it's too late, before he gets away with it! So the man's name – or so he tells my mother, who'll believe anything he says – so his name is Sean. He works there, he lives there actually!'

'Sean who?'

'Don't know, do I? That's the problem. He could be anyone!'

'And your name sir?'

'Liam Cox.'

This is where Gillian makes a U-turn and turns back down the stairs. 'I'll take it from here, PC Miller.' She introduces herself to Mr Cox. He is suitably impressed with her rank and the speed with which she has responded.

In Interview Room 3 Liam Cox leans over, elbows on the table, relaying his suspicions about a farmhand called Sean, Irish by the sounds of him, a nobody who, since Mr Cox's father's death, has climbed up the ranks from casual manure shifter to become manager, accountant and all-round major-domo. He has established himself on the

43

farm, taking up lodgings in a cottage for which he pays no rent. He has coerced Mr Cox's mother into business arrangements the poor old dear can neither understand nor control. She is elderly, senile and of weak constitution. The man is bleeding her of all her wealth, which is substantial, and this has to stop now.

It is a sob story, one of many similar tales made up by prodigal sons intent on covering up their own neglect of their parents. Webber fidgets next to Gillian, looking rather bewildered, no doubt trying to work out why this pathetic man has not been left whining downstairs at the duty desk, bending Miller's ear. How has his domestic angst become a police priority? Aside from the backlog of real police work, Webber has just learned that he is having a son, and that alone couldn't possibly be overshadowed by this nasty character and his tantrums. Webber ventures a remark, 'You may wish to consider referring this matter to Social Services -'

'No!' Liam Cox, understandably, and Gillian, inexplicably, shout in unison.

'We'll investigate your complaint, Mr Cox,' Gillian adds, 'and stay in touch to keep you informed about our progress.'

My arse, she can read Webber's expression. *Fact is you'll never hear from us again.* How wrong he is!

After raising their glasses (twice) to Webber's successfully conceived son, Gillian feels obliged to explain to him her earlier enthusiasm about the obnoxious Mr Cox. Unlike every other day, they aren't lunching at the staff canteen, where the cleaner, Mrs Clunes, doubles as a sharp-tongued chef - her only resemblance to Gordon Ramsay, and given the poor food - they have relocated to the nearest pub. It would be their first choice of dining venue every time were it not for its prices - way too high for your average copper's pocket, especially one who is misguided enough to insist on paying the bill despite having a fourth bun in the oven, so to speak. But Webber is an old-fashioned gentleman and Gillian stopped trying to convert him to living in the twenty-first century a long time ago. She simply orders the cheapest meal on the menu.

Webber dabs his beer-froth moustache. 'Now, can you explain to me what the story with that Cox character is all about? I assume there is a story?'

Gillian wipes her tomato soup moustache. 'He is under investigation – Serious Fraud Office, nonetheless.'

'Blimey – a big fish then!' Webber is appreciative.

'Perhaps not so much him as his supposed business partner, Dimitri Papariakas – a Greek national, as the name implies, but he's cast his net wide: South Africa, Europe, now Britain. And Mr Cox appears to be his British link. We don't know how deep he's in it so we're treading carefully. When he waltzed in this morning, raving about that farmhand, I thought – perfect! A way of getting close to his operation without raising any suspicions!'

'Another one?' Webber raises his empty pint glass and points to Gillian's. 'You can tell me all about it over a pint.'

'I can tell you all about it, DS Webber, by all means, but I must remind you we're on duty.' Gillian needs to rein him in. Since the news about his imminent paternity, he has lowered his professional standards. It's Gillian's job to keep the man in line. What is it with men and their sons?

Webber smiles sheepishly and gawps into his glass, probably expecting a miraculous spring of cold beer to burst out of the bottom and towards his thirsty lips. One miracle in a day will do.

'Yeah, you're right. Getting ahead of myself, the news and all,' he concedes the point. 'So when did you find out about the SFO's investigation? How come I know nothing about it?'

'I referred a case – a number of cases, in fact. It started with a woman making a complaint that her parents had been duped by – her words – a con artist, and by that she meant Liam Cox. Karen Watson was the concerned daughter. She came to us about three weeks ago – tears, drama. She'd had to transport her father back from some Greek island for medical treatment. Poor devil had suffered a stroke and was in a pretty bad way, stranded in Greece, with no access to proper care. The wife was in a state, called their daughter, and the ball started rolling from then on. Turns out the parents, enticed by Mr Cox, had made one of those part-exchange deals: traded their perfectly good family home in Sexton's for a,' Gillian forms virtual speech marks with her fingers in the air, '*luxury villa* in a Greek retirement village on some God-forsaken island in the Aegean. It all looked good on paper – glossy brochures, Ms Watson showed me: secluded white sand beaches, socialising with like-minded expats, but in reality -'

'Let me guess,' Webber barges in, 'a run-down caravan park on the wrong side of town, scores of refugees on your doorstep, no medical insurance and serious language barriers.'

'Pretty much. The poor parents, and many more others in the same boat, were too ashamed to write home about their plight. The guilt stopped them from complaining. After all, they had only themselves to blame – losing their children's inheritance on the cheap con they had fallen for. Not something you'd want to brag about. They kept quiet until the stroke. Then it all came out. Ms Watson consulted a solicitor who perused the watertight contract and told her he could do nothing to rescind it and get her parents' money back. He recommended reporting the matter to the police, but not to hold her breath. It would be hard to prove a crime had been committed. Perhaps the Greek property did not live up to their expectations, but there weren't any blatant misrepresentations in the contract to support those expectations. It was a construct of their minds inspired, perhaps, by verbal exaggerations. In other words, the old dears got more than they bargained for.'

'Tragic!'

'Yes, tragic, but not exactly criminal. I knew Scarface wouldn't approve an investigation into the sanctity of the contract under English law. He'd hide behind the tight budget, and he would be right. So I thought about referring the case to the SFO to see what they made of it.'

'That's how you found out about that Dimitri chap?'

'Dimitri Papariakas, yes. He's behind this scheme and a few more just like it. Each time the same modus operandi: charming unsuspecting pensioners into a tight deal they can't get themselves out of. Taking their hard-earned savings, homes, you name it, in exchange for a fantasy, but with just enough substance to it to make the exchange unassailable. He has a team of brilliant lawyers behind him. And he's unscrupulous – already known to the South African police, and to the Greeks. Under investigation by Europol – apparently going nowhere. Now, our Mr Cox here provides a new angle. He may be eyes-deep in it, or he may be just a hapless scapegoat. For Papariakas this is just another money laundering operation, but he's a clever old fox. SFO are cautious. They have to be very, very cautious.'

'So Cox coming to us of his own free will with this half-baked complaint -'

'Is one in a million.'

Liam is not a good listener. He has come to meet Warburton – and is paying his extortionate fees – not out of love, but to get some action. Fast. He doesn't need to hear about the procedures and prospects of success. He knows the usual disclaimers by heart – they don't need to be repeated ad nauseam over endless cups of coffee in this windowless lawyers' conference room. Liam is feeling claustrophobic.

'All I need is power of attorney,' Liam interrupts the flow of legalese.

'If she's prepared to sign it -'

'That's the problem – she isn't! Would I be here otherwise?'

'Then you won't get power of attorney.' Warburton

48

peers at him from behind his rimless glasses that sit right on the very tip of his Roman nose. He claps his hands together and is holding them to his lips as if saying: *my lips are sealed*.

'Well... Can we get it *without* my mother signing it? She's obviously not thinking straight. That's why I need to think for her.. That's the whole idea of getting the damned power of attorney, isn't it?'

'If Mrs Cox can't think straight, as you put it, then you can't get a valid power of attorney for her. Power of attorney, you see, can only be given by a person with full mental capacity.'

'So, what?' Liam's patience is wearing thin. Maybe he doesn't need a lawyer. Maybe he needs a priest – a priest would get Mother to sign her soul away, not just the damned farm. 'What do I do? Do I just leave her to her own devices? She's alone on a farm – not counting the bloody cows. She thinks she runs it – how delusional is that? Obviously she's senile. Obviously she needs to be in a home, properly looked after. And I need to take care of the land – develop it most likely, to cover the cost of her care. Dairy farming isn't viable. It's losing her money. I must step in before -'

'Hold your horses, Liam!' That patronising smirk again. 'One issue at a time. We can go the Mental Capacity Act route – have your mother declared incapable of handling her own affairs.'

'That's what I'm asking for!'

'You asked about a power of attorney. That is a different matter altogether.'

Liam wishes he could wipe that smirk from

Warburton's face with something like a thump right between his eyes. He is a busy man – he needs straight answers. 'Just tell me what needs to be done and how long it'll take.'

'Firstly, there will have to be a capacity assessment. We can start the ball rolling procedurally, but it's a minefield, trust me.'

Where would I be if I did, Liam ponders.

'We'll need to get a medical practitioner – your mother's GP, I imagine, would be best placed – to comment on her mental capacity, and health in general. But the test is quite stringent – it has to be clear that her dementia severely impairs her ability to understand, to weigh the pros and cons of her situation, and to make decisions, even to communicate them clearly to others.' Warburton is enjoying the sound of his own voice. It hovers in mid-air like a buzz of an invisible fly, coming closer and fading away only to return with renewed force – a flaming nuisance.

'OK, I'll get a quack to produce a certificate – is that what's needed?'

'It isn't as simple as a medical assessment. We need that, of course, we do, but your mother will also have to be provided with an independent advocate to make sure that any decisions you make will be made in her best interest.'

'That shouldn't be too difficult – an old senile lady needs to be in a home. If that's not in her best interest then what is? Then we need to deal with the farmland. It can't lie barren. I'll develop it, probably. Most likely, I will. Of course, that will pay for her care and all that. It's not for me! I'm her son, for God's sake – I have her best damned interests at heart.'

'I don't doubt that, Liam, but we can't jump the gun. Every decision will be judged on its own merit. But first things first: the capacity assessment.'

'How long will that take?'

'You must arm yourself with patience.'

Easier said than done with Dimitri breathing down my neck. He has to act. There is hope that with that bloody Sean out of the equation, Mother may just cave in. Without him, and without that damned Grace of hers, Mother will see for herself how helpless she is. Liam is onto it. He'll pay Grace off, get her to undermine Mother's resolve. He'll get the cops to sort out the Irishman, a nasty piece of work, that! He'll find a doctor who will sign the certificate – whatever paper needs signing. Liam is a fighter. He won't roll over. And most importantly, like Warburton says, it is all being done with Mother's best interest at heart.

'This can't wait, no matter what the cost. Get the ball rolling,' Liam tells his lawyer. 'I'll take care of the rest.'

A frumpy woman in her forties is trying to push a case on wheels onto the passenger seat of a tiny car. She hasn't folded down the retractable handle which is now stuck in the door – the fact of which the woman is clearly unaware. She is pushing. A frayed – or torn – shawl has slid from one of her shoulders and is trailing in the mud under her feet.

'Do you need some help with that?' Gillian offers and takes charge of the suitcase.

'Oh, no need, really! I almost had it... I...' the woman stammers.

With the flat of her hand Gillian slams on the retractable handle and forces it all the way down.

'Oh, that! I always forget...'

The suitcase is safely on the passenger seat alongside bags of crisps, a cardboard box full of exercise books and what looks like a dead fly suspended in a web in the corner of the window.

'Oh, thank you! Sorry for the trouble.'

'No problem.' Gillian presents her ID card. 'DI Marsh.'

'Oh, dear!' It is irritating that she has to start every sentence with an emphatic *oh*. It's like talking to someone in a state of permanent shock.

'I'm looking for Mrs Cox.'

'Oh, Mrs Cox...' she seems puzzled. 'That's my mother. She's at home. I was just on my way there... Oh, dear! I was just on my way home – I don't live here, just visiting. I'm her daughter, you see -' Gillian raises a single eyebrow in response to this blindingly obvious revelation that this woman is her mother's daughter, 'but I live in Wensbury. I work there... I teach. Yes...' She looks troubled. Her train of thought must have left without her.

'It's nothing serious. I only need to speak to your mother, Mrs...'

'Oh, me? Cox – Miss Cox.'

'Miss Cox, could you show me to your mother?'

Miss Cox sends a hopeless glance towards her wheelie case, now sitting comfortably on the back seat of her car.

'Oh, I ought to take the suitcase…' The indecision is killing her. 'Is it going to be long? Only I don't know if I should bring the suitcase with me. I could lock it in the car, I suppose…'

Gillian contemplates the possibility of a mutilated body hiding in the wretched suitcase. 'Don't worry!' she says. 'I'll see myself into the house. I take it Mrs Cox can be found there.'

'Oh, but I suppose I should take you. Mum doesn't like surprises. Imagine a visit from the police! I'd better take you… I'll just lock the car, simple! There!' She shuts the back door and clicks her remote key. The car responds with a cheerful wink. 'So yes, this way, um… officer. Can I ask what this is all about?'

'I'll explain to Mrs Cox, if you don't mind.'

'Oh! Not at all! Not at all…'

'Does your mother have someone called Sean working for her here on the farm?'

'Oh, Sean!' Miss Cox's face flushes bright pink. She lowers her eyes and hastens her pace, the frayed and muddy end of her shawl dragging behind her, leaving a snail-like trail in the mud. 'Yes, yes, she does. Sean. Has *he* done something against the law?' She glances at Gillian furtively from under her lashes. 'What kind of *offence*? If you don't mind me asking… Only I'd be worried for Mum. Gosh!'

'Nothing that I'm aware of. I'm just making inquiries. It may be nothing at all. I just need to chat to your mother first.'

Miss Cox utters a strange hiccup in response to that, but as soon as they enter the house she blurts out, 'Mum, the police are here to arrest Sean!'

It takes a moment to calm everyone down and clarify the nature of Gillian's intrusion. Mrs Cox has sunk into a chair and looks bewildered. She is a small person, pale and frail; her thumb is trembling, her gaping lips have lost all colour. As Gillian explains the cause of her inquiry Miss Cox erupts into sporadic *Ohs!* and most sincere apologies. Another Miss Cox – apparently Liam Cox's daughter – growls, 'That's vintage Dad! Wouldn't expect any less of him! I really wouldn't take him seriously if I were you – he's just wasting your time for his own wicked ends.'

'Oh, you can't say that, Esme! We can't be sure. What do we know about Sean? What do we really know? Let the police do their job.'

'Aunt Colleen, you don't know Dad as I do. You don't know what he's capable of when he wants something. He controls people out of habit. I'm twenty-six and he still sneaks behind my back to look at my mobile. I know he does that, and he knows I've got a fool-proof password, but he keeps trying. Each time he tries, he has three attempts. I've lost count of the times I grabbed my phone only to discover it was locked. My papa, I'm afraid, is unashamedly controlling, and what he can't control, he will go out of his way to destroy.'

'Oh, you're so unkind – truly – towards your own dad…'

'I know him!'

'Oh, do you? And you know Sean, I imagine, rather well…' The older Miss Cox purses her lips and narrows her eyes.

'What exactly do you mean?'

Gillian, Mrs Cox and the younger Miss Cox fix Auntie Colleen with an inquiring look, under the weight of which she loses her steam and falters in her resolve. Her cheeks are trouble-pink all over again and her eyes desperately search for a hole to jump into. 'Nothing… nothing. I… I don't know what I'm saying. Do what you think is right. I should be going… I must be going. My suitcase is in the car.'

She scampers, her frayed shawl discarded on the floor.

'That was odd even by Aunt Colleen's standards,' Esme Cox declares. 'Oh well, we'll never know what she meant. She probably doesn't know either.' She turns to her grandmother. 'Gran, are you all right?' Getting no reply, she walks to her and plants her tight and perky bum on the arm of the chair occupied by her mute grandmother. She puts her hand on her shoulder, kisses the old woman's forehead. 'Good thing I stayed here overnight. You mustn't worry about these silly things Dad comes up with. You know how he is.'

The old lady manages a feeble smile and pats the young woman's hand. 'He means well.'

'I seriously doubt that! Believe me,' Esme Cox informs Gillian, 'there's nothing to Dad's accusation against Sean. Sean is the one who keeps this place going. He looks after Gran, doesn't he, Gran?'

'Sean does, yes,' Mrs Cox nods. She seems to have recovered some of her wits. 'I don't know what I'd do without him.'

'You see?' Esme addresses Gillian. 'Waste of your

time.'

'Probably,' Gillian has to agree, 'but it is only an informal inquiry – a follow-up, if you like. I'm not accusing Mr... What is his name?'

Esme looks at her grandmother for answers. She in her turn scowls and puts on a pair of spectacles, which have so far been dangling on a thin silver chain on her chest. Obviously, the spectacles have some magical powers. But not on this occasion - she mumbles under her breath, confusion reigning supreme. 'Sean... Sean... I knew it, damn it!' The exclamation, coming from a delicate old lady, sounds comical. 'I know his name, of course I do. It escaped me... Hang on!' She looks inspired, but the light quickly goes off. Remembering names clearly isn't her strength, and that seems to frighten her. She looks troubled. 'I can't remember, I'm sorry. But Sean is a good man. I don't know what I'd do without him.'

Gillian doesn't want to unsettle the old lady any more than she already is. She tries to sound conciliatory. 'No problem. I can always ask him myself.'

'Yes! Why don't you?' Esme says. 'Why don't I fetch him and you can ask away?'

'Oh, I don't know,' Mrs Cox mutters. 'I wouldn't want him to think we don't trust him. It'd put him off.'

'He can take it, he's a big boy!' Esme laughs.

'Oh dear, dear...'

'Gran, if we don't let her speak to Sean, it'll look like we've got something to hide. And we don't. Neither does Sean.'

'If you say so... I don't know... I wouldn't want him to feel...'

'He won't!' And that convinces the old lady better than any logical argument Gillian could advance.

Sean Corrigan is his full name, he informs Gillian. He looks her straight in the eye, without hesitation and without a trace of guilt. His manner is relaxed and self-assured. If Gillian were to judge him on his demeanour alone, she would proclaim him an innocent man. He tells Mrs Cox – Mildred – not to fret and not to worry. He's got it all in hand – it's merely a misunderstanding.

'Told you, Gran,' Esme is speaking to her grandmother but gazing at Corrigan, 'Sean won't mind answering any questions. He's got nothing to hide.' Mrs Cox nods. She's also looking at him, but her spectacles are off her nose, hanging redundant on her chest. Clearly, now that she has Mr Corrigan about her, she doesn't need any more magic. He seems to have a soothing, or rather mesmerising effect on both women. That doesn't come as a surprise – he is, indeed, very easy on the eye. Lean, angular, in his prime – a man who can be trusted. He has the innocent round eyes of a boy. His attire is that of a farmhand - dirty and smelly overalls, muddy boots that have never seen shoe polish - but his manner doesn't go with his clothes, for he comes across as very polished and well-educated.

'I do keep books,' he admits smoothly, 'as well as payroll and everything else – from capital expenditures on the farm equipment to Mildred's household expenses. Grocery shopping is Grace's domain, but she brings all receipts to me and I balance the petty cash.' He speaks with an unmistakable Irish accent. His voice has a clear ring to it.

'Mr Cox expressed his concerns for his mother's financial security, which in the circumstances -'

'Dad's just fishing around! Wasting police time! I'm fed up with his antics, I really am!'

'What can I do to assuage those concerns?'

'If you could give us an insight into the books – with Mrs Cox's permission, of course. I don't have a warrant, this isn't an official investigation so you're entitled to say -'

'I don't see why not,' he interrupts her. 'Let me show you to my office.'

It isn't an office at all – it's a table in a poky lounge in a poky ramshackle cottage where Corrigan apparently lives. They are accompanied by an enormous dog, a German Shepherd going by the name of Corky. It is only slightly less shabby and slightly more malodorous than his master – not the kind of beast Fritz would care to fraternise with, Gillian thinks. It plonks itself on a matted rug on the floor and from that vantage point keeps a close eye on Gillian. Corrigan has offered coffee and biscuits, a highly civilised gesture which scores him bonus points with Gillian. She likes him – she likes him very much.

When he returns with steaming mugs and a selection of shortbreads and jammie dodgers, he puts them on the table and joins Gillian on a settee – the only piece of furniture fit for the purpose of seating guests (not counting the matted rug on the floor which is already taken by the watchful dog). A whiff of masculine scent teases Gillian's senses. What she originally took for *smelly* is on second thoughts rather tantalising. The smell of a real man: sweat, hay and horses, something musky and earthy. She likes it. It is bizarrely arousing. She almost wishes – against common sense and propriety – that he would put his arm around her and pull her closer into him so she would be wrapped in his warmth and his manly scent. When was the last time that she sat this close to a man, feeling his presence through osmosis? This brief moment of closeness awakens a yearning in her she has not felt in years – has been too busy to permit herself to feel. She reaches for her coffee, stirs in two sugars and pours in some milk, thus keeping her hands occupied with something practical and her hormones out of mischief. The milk – poured too rapidly – splatters onto the table.

'Sorry about that,' she mumbles.

Corrigan has shoved a whole jammie dodger into his mouth. He shakes his head as if to say what his full mouth can't verbalise: 'Don't worry.' Thankfully, he gets up and heads for a stack of cardboard archive boxes. He wipes biscuit crumbs on his thighs and retrieves an arch file. 'How far do you want to go?'

Gillian nearly chokes on her dodger. 'Uh?'

'How far back in time? The ledgers?'

'Oh, I don't know,' she sounds just like poor Colleen. 'The last financial year, would that be OK?'

'Anything's OK with me. I honestly don't mind. I took over book-keeping in the last few months of Reginald's illness – Reginald being Mildred's late husband.'

'When did he die?'

'Two years ago – almost to a day. We had the memorial service yesterday – second anniversary.' He is ploughing through the content of the archive boxes, pulling out files and envelopes. Gillian watches him as if she wants to eat him; the dog watches Gillian with a similar intent. 'We can go through the business ledgers first – it shouldn't take long, I'm bloody well organised, I fancy, a bit on the OCD side.'

'Do you mind if I borrow the ledgers, for a day at the most?'

'I'd need a receipt before I let them go, but I don't mind – why should I?' He brings the folders to the table, and with that he brings that manly scent of his. He puts his hand on one of the folders. 'Here you'll find bank statements so you can cross-reference them with the ledgers. Sorry, it's all in paper format. I abandoned technology a long time ago. I don't even possess a computer and my phone, you'll find, can only make and receive basic phone calls.' He is smiling, a mock apology in his blue Irish eyes.

'Lucky you,' Gillian returns the smile. Are they flirting? She wouldn't know – it was such a long time ago when she last tried it. With disastrous consequences – the bloke was married and didn't really mean anything by it, Gillian got her knickers in a twist. A distant and best-forgotten memory. She swallows the last of her coffee and gets up. 'I'd better be going. Thank you for your cooperation, Mr Corrigan.'

'Nothing to hide, like I said,' he shrugs.

'I don't expect to find anything untoward. Just following up on a complaint,' she repeats herself.

'I know, and that's OK. I don't want there to be any doubt, any shadow over my handling of Mildred's affairs.

She trusts me unconditionally, and I'll do nothing to betray that trust.'

'Very commendable.'

'Nothing commendable about that. She's like a mother to me. She took me in, no questions asked – I was a bit of a stray. I owe her.'

'You weren't always a farm worker?' Gillian probes. The man is too articulate, too polished to be just a *farmhand*, as Liam Cox put it.

'No, not always.' He picks the folders from the table. 'I'll carry them to your car. They're rather heavy. You accumulate tons of paper and before you know it...' he points to the stack of archive boxes. Clearly, he's avoiding the conversation about his past. Does he have something to hide after all?

That is exactly where Gillian's sniffer dog instinct kicks in. 'What did you do before you started here on the farm?'

'This and that. It was a different life, different era...'

'In Ireland?'

'Yes, in Ireland, as you can tell by my accent. Shall we go?' He is holding the folders, piled up to his chin, keen to get rid of her. Corky has got up and is eyeing Gillian with hostility. Clearly, she has overstayed her welcome.

He throws the ledgers and bank statement onto the back seat of Gillian's car, and shuts the door. A net curtain twitches in the kitchen window of the main house. They are being watched.

Gillian doesn't want to go. She is drawn to this Irishman, a confusing man: friendly and easy-going on the surface, secretive and impenetrable below it. It could be that earthy scent of his. It could be his innocent blue eyes. It could be his chosen lifestyle. He has chosen it – no doubt about that – because he is someone else, not a farm boy, despite what he tells her, or rather fails to tell her.

She lingers by the car, scans the paddocks beyond the gate, where a herd of cows grazes idly. The sky is swollen with clouds – they are white and innocuous, the sort of clouds that keep the world warm rather than threatening rain. The cows seem to return Gillian's interest – a few of them have raised their heads and begin to watch her, their jaws still moving, grinding the grass.

'There were twice as many,' Corrigan tells her, 'but we cut down on the numbers to make it more manageable, less manpower, less trouble. We leased out fields to the north to Mildred's neighbour.' He sweeps the horizon with his hand. 'You wouldn't believe it but financially it makes no difference. The rent money is almost the same as the profit we would make from those extra numbers. Dairy farming isn't profitable, not any more. You aren't in it for money.'

'What are you in it for then?'

He smiles under his breath, his eyes fixed on the horizon. 'For the love of it. Look at that! It's beautiful.'

Gillian's gaze travels from the fields to the man. He is beautiful, she thinks. 'Yes,' she nods. 'Very beautiful. But it isn't your scene– am I right?'

'Wrong! I'm a country boy, raised on a farm in Ireland. Smallholding, really, not much of a farm. My parents were tenants. This is my scene, believe it or not.'

Somehow Gillian finds it hard to believe that this is all

there is to him. She extends her hand. 'Thank you again for your help.'

He takes her hand and holds it in his for a little too long. He says, 'I love it here. Mildred loves it here. I'll do what I can to help her hang on to this.' His hand is soft and warm – not the hand of a farm worker. And now Gillian doesn't want that hand to release hers, but she must go. She nods. 'I'll return the files tomorrow, once we've had a chance to look at them.'

'See you tomorrow then.' He lets her hand go and opens the door for her. It comes naturally to him to be gallant. No, he is not a simple farm boy.

Mildred backs away from the window the moment the policewoman looks up. It may be too late though – she may have seen Mildred spying and being altogether a nosy busy-body. Mildred wonders if her silhouette is visible from behind the lace of the net curtain. She dares not move in case it is, so she stands still and cold, pretending to be a shadow. They are talking. It's a shame Mildred can't see their faces. Are they smiling or frowning? Her eyes, even with her glasses on, aren't what they used to be. Most of it is a blur and it seems that the policewoman and Sean are standing behind a screen of thick gauze – two fuzzy outlines. Are they shaking hands? It goes on. You don't shake hands for this long…

The police woman gets in her car, and drives off. Such a small pixie of a woman and yet she has caused Mildred so much anxiety! It's good to see the back of her.

Sean remains immobile on the driveway, with Corky by his leg, both watching the car disappear behind the bulge of the hedge. Then he looks up – towards the window, towards Mildred. He must be able to see her for he is waving. She waves back. Things can't be that bad: he's waving and she could swear he's smiling too, though it is more of a guess than an observation. His face is blurred. He heads for the outbuildings. He hasn't been arrested.

'Is she gone?' It is Esme's voice.

'Yes, gone, thank God!' Mildred abandons her vantage point by the window and sits with Esme at the kitchen table. 'Shall we have tea?'

Esme laughs, reaches out to her and squeezes her hand. 'If I have another cup of tea, I'll burst!'

'I could do with one.' Mildred needs to have her hands occupied, even if it means making tea which no one will drink. Just refilling the kettle with water and putting it on the hob validates her existence. It's a reassuring ritual – it puts her mind at ease and stops her hands from shaking. You have something to focus on so that you don't spill it.

'What do you think happened to Uncle David? He said he'd come today. I was looking forward to meeting him, properly.'

In all this commotion with the policewoman and silly Colleen with that frightening talk about Sean being arrested, Mildred forgot all about David. He did say he would come to stay. He did say it would be today. 'Maybe he's got some things to do first.'

'Maybe, but I can't wait for him. Must be going.'

'You're always in a hurry. Stay, we could have a cup of tea.'

'Not for me, Gran. Come, sit with me, I've got

something to tell you.'

Mildred is reluctant to take herself back to the table and hear about that *something*. It doesn't sound good. She doesn't like surprises and it will probably be a surprise. She has to brace herself. Maybe, she thinks, she can avoid the subject of that *something*. She says, 'What time is it? Grace should be here any minute, to start on the dinner. If you don't want tea, we'll wait for dinner. Grace's cooking is -'

'I can't. I really can't. I need to tell you something.'

There is no escape. Mildred is cornered into listening to that *something* she is probably better off not knowing anything about.

'I'll be going away for a while – a year, maybe two, maybe a bit longer. It depends.'

'A year!' Mildred is horrified. 'Will I live for another year?'

'Course you will!' Esme has a beautiful laugh. It's so carefree and resonant that it makes Mildred think of a xylophone. 'You've been around for eighty years – what's another year for you?'

'Not eighty! Seventy-six, to be exact. That's a long way from eighty.' Mildred lives one year at a time. It has become an effort to get through every day without dropping something or forgetting where she has put it. A year – that's three hundred and sixty-five days; sometimes sixty-six.

'You'll have to manage, OK? I need you to look after Rohan while I'm gone. I've asked Sean, but -'

'So where are you going? Is it that far that you can't come and visit, and ride Rohan from time to time. The

poor animal will go to waste – he ought to be exercised.'
Mildred will use any form of blackmail to keep her family
close to hand.

'Zimbabwe.'

'Zimbabwe!' That may as well be the other side of the
moon as far as Mildred is concerned. She has a vague
recollection of where Zimbabwe is – somewhere in
Africa, somewhere where people don't usually travel.
'Why, in God's name, Zimbabwe?'

'I managed to secure a post, working in a national park
in Zimbabwe. They're crying out for people out there with
all the poaching and shortages going on.'

'Surely you could find something closer by? Longleat?
Half as dangerous, I bet!'

'It's a once in a lifetime opportunity for a biologist,
Gran. I wouldn't be true to myself if I didn't take it.'

Mildred thinks Esme may be dead if she does take it.
Mildred isn't as out of touch with today's world as
everyone thinks. She knows what goes on in Zimbabwe.
There's that dictator – what's his name? 'Must you
really?'

Esme kisses her forehead – she likes doing that, and
Mildred likes it too, but not now, because now her mind is
on keeping Esme close to home. And Esme isn't listening.
No amount of kissing can change that. 'Does your dad
know?'

'I'll tell him tomorrow, and I'm leaving the day after
tomorrow. So,' another kiss on the forehead, 'be good,
Gran. Don't get up to any mischief while I'm gone!'

As if Mildred would. She knows it's a joke, to make it
light, but she isn't in a mood for jokes. She doesn't want

Esme to go. But Esme won't listen to her. No one listens to Mildred anymore. You'd think it was them who are all deaf, not Mildred.

Esme has left and Grace hasn't arrived yet. No pot-banging, no village gossip, no weather forecast for the next week or two – only silence. Mildred has nothing to do, nothing to occupy her poor hands with. She can't keep making cups of tea for herself and then pouring them in the sink. She could consider having one of those leftover scones with cream and jam, but that would spoil her appetite before dinner. Grace wouldn't like that.

It is difficult to sit and do nothing. Normally, Mildred would have a nap, but not now. Her mind is full of anxieties: the police woman wanting to arrest Sean, Esme going to some dangerous place to fight poachers, and Grace not yet here to start on the dinner. Not to mention this dreadful silence. Mildred can't do all these things that need to be done. She can't see, can't hear, doesn't have her finger on the pulse. Emptiness takes so much effort to fill out when you're on your own.

In the past, in her nun days, Mildred was used to solitude: sitting in her cell, praying, or working in the garden or the laundry, in perfect silence. But then she was young. Her head was full of ideas. When did all those ideas turn into anxieties?

Mildred takes her rosary from the drawer in the kitchen table. Prayers will dispel those anxieties. Only prayers can do that: the repetitive, comforting hum of Hail Marys, hands occupied with the glass beads rolling between her fingers – peace.

Gillian was right – her pitbull terrier instinct wasn't deceiving her. Sean Corrigan isn't a simple farmhand, or at least he hasn't always been one. Once upon a time, he was somebody else, and not exactly who she thought he would be. He doesn't have a record – not even a caution. The man is clean as a whistle. This comes as a relief. Gillian has taken to him like a little girl to a shiny charm the minute she lay her eyes on him, but she had to hold herself back. What if he were a fraudster, just like Liam Cox alleged? What if he were worse than that? A drug addict. An escapee from prison. A wanted man on the run, say an IRA bomber… He could well be that – he's Irish, he's secretive and he lives under the radar of respectable society. He is single, though bloody good-looking. Why? He won't speak about his past. He could well be a terrorist.

But he isn't.

Gillian has been through every bit of information she could find about Sean Corrigan in Records. Born in the middle-of-nowhere County Armagh, Northern Ireland, Sean Corrigan swiftly rose from his humble beginnings to study chemistry and forensic science at Queen's University Belfast, and upon graduation joined Northern Ireland's Forensic Science Services where he remained until seven years ago. It was seven years ago when suddenly and without an explanation or a forwarding address, he simply gave in his notice and vanished without a trace. Midlife crisis? Going back to his roots? Change of air? Gillian is dying to know.

Sailing past Erin's desk, Gillian is confronted with the

content of Corrigan's ledgers strewn across every available surface. Erin is down on the floor, hard at work. There obviously must be some method to her madness for she is slowly fitting together all pieces of the accounting puzzle, and those that fit she puts in a neat pile on her desk. The pile is growing and the floor under her desk is beginning to see the light of day, or at least the artificial light of the energy-saving LED spotlights.

Erin is Gillian's treasured find. There was a false-start in their working relationship when Gillian mentored Erin some nine months ago, at the time when she was on the Poulston head-on case. That turned to custard for Gillian as she was briefly suspended (through no fault of her own, she knew, though Scarface may beg to differ) and Erin was promptly dispatched to complete her induction elsewhere. Apparently something to do with Gillian setting a *bad* example. However, two months ago Erin – now a fully fledged DC – went through a swift but acrimonious divorce and immediately thereafter put in for a transfer to Sexton's Canning CID – a new beginning. Here she is now, doing Webber's job. Webber left the office at the civilised hour of five p.m. sharp to be with the mother of his son-to-be. Erin is wading through the Nortonview farm's accounts all by herself. She is kneeling on the floor, her shoes discarded under her desk. Gillian finds it endearing to discover that Erin's tights harbour a hole with the tail of a segmented ladder running from her big toe towards her heel, and that she's wearing a black bra under her white blouse – a state of dishevelment Gillian is particularly at home with. They'll get on, she is certain of that.

'Found anything yet?'

'No, everything seems to be in perfect order. I'll tell you for sure tomorrow morning – I'm going through it with a fine tooth comb. It takes time and it's doing my back in.' She gets up to her feet and arches her spine, hands on her hips, her head rolling from shoulder to shoulder. She looks pasty.

'I'm going home and I think you should, too.'

'Nothing to go home to. Not that I'm complaining. I like my peace and quiet. Nah, I'll finish it.'

'Suit yourself. And don't let Mrs Clunes near the papers. Everything she finds on the floor after hours is fair game for her. You won't see it again.'

'No worries. I'll guard this shit with my life.'

Gillian injects a spring into her stride to appear purposeful on her home-bound journey, but in all honesty she, just like Erin, has nothing to go home to (if you exclude Fritz).

Unlike all other estate agents around town, Cox Properties does not scream at random passers-by with images of houses for sale against the background of invariably blue skies in window displays. In fact, Cox Properties does not have a shop window in the conventional sense of the word – instead it features a plain sign with its name and telephone number, and behind it hangs a venetian blind – at half-mast. It strikes Gillian as a very low-profile enterprise, clandestine, which is the exact opposite of what she has come to expect from estate agencies. It seems as if Cox Properties do not wish to be found, which makes sense considering that most people looking for them want a refund.

Gillian enters and finds Liam Cox in the company of a fat man with a distinctly Mediterranean complexion and a cigar between his chubby fingers. There are two other men in the shop – beefy but otherwise nondescript, wearing expressions of total boredom or perhaps incomprehension. They are standing while Mr Cox and his cigar-wielding customer are seated in fine-looking leather chairs, their heads nodding over what appears to be an architectural drawing.

'Mr Cox,' Gillian grins, 'I thought I'd pop over to keep you abreast with my findings.'

'Findings?' Cox looks shifty. He steals a sheepish glance at his customer, who raises his eyebrow in an expression of mute inquiry.

'The complaint you made at the station yesterday,' Gillian reminds him innocently, 'about the handling of your mother's finances… Is this a convenient time to talk?' She looks at the fat man pointedly.

'Um, not really. Can I call you?'

'You may not be able to catch me – busy schedule. Rarely can I be reached on the phone, to be honest.' She smiles half at Cox – half at his *customer*. She takes out her ID badge, 'DI Marsh, Sexton's Canning CID.'

The fat man shifts uncomfortably in his leather seat, the leather screeches and the chair groans. He puts out the cigar, attempts to smile back at Gillian, but it comes across as weak and slightly constipated. He says, 'Don't mind me. I'll come back another day. My business can wait.' He sounds foreign – South African. Gillian knows South African when she hears it – she lived there long enough to recognise that guttural Afrikaner tone from the first syllable.

'No, it's nothing serious. Please don't leave on my account, Mr?'

The fat man stares blankly at her and doesn't give out his name. He must be Dimitri Papariakas. Any other South African in Liam Cox's shop would be too much of a coincidence, and Gillian doesn't believe in coincidences. 'Oh well, since I'm here… I mean I only stopped by because I was in the neighbourhood,' she continues smoothly. 'And there is nothing to worry about. I thought you may want to know that to put your mind at rest. We went through the farm's accounts thoroughly – everything's spick and span.'

'It is?' He looks distinctly disappointed and altogether rather uncomfortable. Beads of sweat have formed on his forehead. Then maybe it is the temperature in the shop. It's hot. Dimitri Papariakas, at least that's who Gillian believes the fat man to be, is also sweating. His silver-grey silk shirt has dark undertones around his armpits. Maybe it's her presence that has unsettled them. 'Well, that's done then,' she chirps on her way out. 'At least you don't have to worry anymore. I'll be closing the case but if there's anything else, don't hesitate to contact the police station – they'll pass the message on to me.' She throws her card on the spread of architectural drawings, and leaves.

In the street, heading for the comfort food of Greggs, Gillian is humming under her breath. As soon as she has her Belgian bun – her belated breakfast caused by an empty fridge this morning – she will ring the chaps at the

Serious Fraud Office. They need to know that Dimitri Papariakas is definitely in the picture, definitely with his fat finger in Liam Cox's pie. Gillian is very pleased with herself as she sinks her teeth into the white icing.

'You cannot be serious, man!' Dimitri pulls the perfect McEnroe at Liam the moment the woman leaves the shop. 'You bring in the cops – why? What the fuck were you thinking?'

'She's got nothing to do with our dealings, calm down,' Liam tries to sound conciliatory and calm, even though deep down he also finds himself in the grip of deep angst. 'It's another matter – my mother, she fancies she's running the farm... this bloody Paddy... I need to get rid of the bastard before I can move on with the land. Don't worry, it's my business.'

'*Your* business?' Dimitri's chin is wobbling with fury. 'Your business is *my* business, yah? *Mine!* You don't bring the cops into the equation, you understand? Not when I'm around. I don't do cops, yah? You do your business, you do what you must, *without* bringing the cops into it, yah?'

'Yeah, all right! I get the point!'

'No, I don't think you do.' Dimitri heaves his bulk off the chair. He is taller than Liam, larger and louder. He towers over him, his finger in his face. 'I don't want cops snooping around my affairs, but you've done it – you done it already! You got cops involved, yah... So now you'd better move fast. I'm not waiting. The deadline has just been brought forward. You deal with it – your mother, the land, the fucking lot – quick and clean. You get my drift?'

'That's what I'm doing, Dimitri…'

The big fat bastard isn't listening. 'And get rid of all paperwork. Get it out of here, today! You have one month to get your arse into gear.'

Before she reaches the farm, Gillian finds herself held up by a herd of cows, ambling across the road to a new grazing paddock. The cows take their time, as cows do. A group of them have halted on the green and juicy bank of a roadside ditch, and are straining their necks and sticking out their tongues to get to the freshest grass and a drink of water. As they eat they simultaneously release steamy cowpats which land on the road amidst the litter of straw and mud. A dog runs in circles around the herd; Gillian recognises Corky. The cows are forced forward; they aren't particularly obliging but they must know all resistance is futile. Still some of them make a point of lingering on the road and gawping at Gillian – the only other road user, a rarity here, which naturally arouses their curiosity. Soon a man emerges, closes the gate and waves the most malcontent cows into an orderly road crossing. He waves to Gillian, and smiles. He is Sean Corrigan.

Her heart skips a beat. It is such a silly expression but it is pretty accurate. Gillian winds down the window. 'Hi there! I'm returning your ledgers!'

The dog barks. Corrigan calls out its name and pats the side of his leg to calm it down. 'Good,' he says. 'I'll meet you down on the farm. Give me five minutes.'

Gillian watches his back as he ushers the remaining rebels from the herd into the paddock and shuts the gate behind them. He has a tight and narrow behind which Gillian observes with a tinge of pleasure. He waves her through as if she were royalty – with an exaggerated bow. She laughs and puts her foot down, cow dung splattering from under the wheels of her car at Corrigan, who side-steps it nimbly, and wags his finger at her.

He catches up with her a few minutes later in the forecourt. 'Good news, I hope?'

'Yes, all in order. It was only a formality.'

'You'll have to tell Mildred. She worries too much. Must have been beside herself with worry since yesterday.'

'I'll tell her.'

'Did you tell her son?' His eyes narrowed. It must be the sun. It has temporarily popped out from behind a feeble cloud.

'Yes, he knows. I don't think he'll trouble Mrs Cox or yourself again.'

'Good. That puts the whole matter to rest, I hope.'

'It does.' Gillian steps out of the car and opens the boot. 'All ledgers present and accounted for. Where do you want them?'

'I'll take them to my office, where else?' He grins.

'I'll help you.' She doesn't want to part ways with him just yet. There won't be another excuse to come and see him. She really likes Sean Corrigan. Perhaps she even fancies him. Nothing wrong with that – the brief inquiry into his account handling is over, and let's face it, it was never a serious investigation in the first place. She can afford to fancy a man. She may be married to her job, but otherwise she is free for the taking.

They are heading for his shabby lodgings, excitement building in Gillian's throat. She is hanging on to a small folder – her reason to spend a few more minutes with him. At last she says, 'I was right – you haven't always been a farmer.'

He chuckles. 'I knew you'd check on me. Couldn't resist, could you?'

'It was part of the inquiry – checking your credentials.'

'Of course it was.' He winks at her.

'An intriguing transition from forensic scientist to a farmhand?'

'Like I said – I'm a country boy at heart.'

'What made you leave your career behind? And your country… I hope you don't mind me asking. It isn't in my professional capacity – just curiosity, really.'

They are standing on the porch, the dog already splayed across the step, blocking the entrance to the house. Corrigan takes the folder Gillian is carrying from her hand. They are facing each other, only the pile of ledgers between them. He says, straight and without any preamble, 'Why don't I satisfy your curiosity over dinner? Tonight?'

'Why don't you,' Gillian grins like a teenage girl, totally incapable of adopting the poise of hard to get.

'Golden Dragon, at seven?'

The rosary has not left Mildred's hands since yesterday. It is wrapped around her wrist and even though she is not saying it this very minute, it provides her with immeasurable comfort. Mildred needs plenty of comfort and reassurance. The policewoman offered some, but it was too little too late. The damage has been done – the anxiety is planted in Mildred's mind and once there, it is so hard to tear it out. It lingers, it spills and soaks into every crack, and it torments her.

She had almost forgotten what caused the anxiety in the first place, but when the policewoman – DI Marsh – came to tell her everything was OK and there would be no further investigation, Mildred went weak at the knees. Had it been that serious? She didn't know, or perhaps she had forgotten. DI Marsh telling her to forget about it has had the exact opposite effect. Mildred is sitting in her rocking chair, but she is still and alert, unable to rock herself into a nap. She is clutching her holy beads, seeking the comfort that is too slow to come. A premonition of some unclear, ill-defined evil spins her anxieties into a frenzy. She can't run away from it. It's no good trying. She is an old woman, she can't run.

Soon after the policewoman leaves, a man stands in the doorway. His bulky frame blocks the light behind him. She knows him, of course she does. She recognises his shape, his height, the way he moves – like Reginald. It must be David. He is so like Reginald, and he promised he would come to stay for a while. Before she manages to greet him, he speaks first, 'Mother, we have a few things to talk over, and you really have to concentrate.'

It isn't David. It is, of course, Liam.

'I'm not ill, I don't need to see a doctor,' Mildred digs her heels in.

'I've made an appointment -'

'I didn't ask you to make any appointments. Nothing's

wrong with me.'

'It's a check-up, to see how you... getting on, health-wise.'

'I'm getting on fine, thank you.'

'Don't be obstinate, Mother! You're going, and that's final. I'll pick you up tomorrow at two. Get yourself ready so we aren't late.'

'You set the police on us,' Mildred remembers her anxieties from only a few minutes ago. Liam is to blame for them. He must know how much grief he has caused.

'*Us?*' Liam's voice breaks upon travelling up an octave. 'Mother, I am trying to protect you against unscrupulous, opportunistic-'

'You makin' false accusations, that's what you doin'.' When Mildred is upset her accent becomes as thick and broad as if she had never left Ireland. She can hear her own mother in her speech. 'I know you – I know what you tryin' to do. I won't go to a home. This is my home. This is where I stay till I die.'

'Two o'clock, tomorrow. Be ready!' It isn't a request – it's an order. He is used to giving orders, and that is Mildred's fault. She brought him up, made him into this bully, this sergeant major. Everyone always gives in to him, sooner or later. Stella, David, Mildred... But not this time. She won't be ready tomorrow at two. She won't be ready at all. She is not going anywhere. 'Over my dead body,' she says.

Liam snorts, like a horse, shifts his feet, hesitant as to whether to reinforce his demands with more shouting or leave her to stew in it. He chooses the latter. Slams the door on his way out. From her rocking chair, through the

78

window, Mildred observes him as he hurries to his big nasty car, pushing past Sean, and driving off in a black cloud of smoke. Mildred's fingers begin to move faster and faster rubbing the beads of her rosary as she chants relentless Hail Marys.

Gillian hasn't had a date in ages. She left work early by her standards, at the same time in fact as Webber, both of them looking radiant though for different reasons. Webber said something about considering nine-to-five job opportunities out there and whether she would be prepared to act as his referee. She nodded keenly – she wasn't really listening to what he was saying.

'I want to be a proper father to my son, spend time with him, like fathers do,' he elaborated, and again Gillian agreed. She had no idea what he meant.

It caught up with her when she was going through the content of her wardrobe, and she made a mental note to speak to him about it tomorrow. Increasingly, to her dismay, she had begun to realise that everything in her wardrobe, other than work suits, dated back to the nineties, at the best: little black numbers, style-less and shapeless blouses and pencil skirts, shoes with silver buckles. On reflection, who was she to lecture Mark Webber about work-life balance?

She arrives at the Golden Dragon fifteen minutes late, already reconciled with the distinct possibility of Corrigan having given up on her and gone home. On some level she would welcome it – the stress of dating while wearing her daughter's mini dress with the low back will probably prove too much for Gillian. Luckily Tara is much taller so the dress is long enough to just about cover Gillian's behind. The low back prevents her from wearing a bra, which is another challenge Gillian grapples with rather awkwardly by clutching close to her chest a large purse in which she carries nothing at all. Gillian never knew the purpose of possessing a handbag, money and cards being sufficiently accommodated by her pockets, house keys living under the flower pot by the front door, and items of a lady's personal grooming remaining as superfluous to her as the idea of pyjama bottoms.

To her disappointment, she spots Corrigan at a window table – not very cosy, not very private and most certainly not suited for wearing a low back dress with no bra underneath. Gillian musters a phantom of a smile and staggers to the fish bowl table (wearing the early nineties shoes with silver buckles).

'I was just about to finish the bottle and go home,' Corrigan gets up to greet her. Unlike her, he is at ease and is wearing a funky, body-hugging shirt and suit trousers – smart but casual, happy in his skin. The scent of hay, mud and cow dung is gone too, replaced by something so sensual that Gillian has to stop herself from biting into his neck to taste it.

'Sorry, I was going through my daughter's wardrobe, looking for something to wear.' Gillian doesn't lie as a matter of principle. It makes life easier. 'Can I have some of that wine, please?'

Over the second bottle, Gillian gets into the swing of sharing all there is to know about her. Corrigan is a better listener than her, which surprises her. It will usually be Gillian asking the right questions and listening to the answers, but he has managed to turn the tables on her, so she goes on.

'I was only nineteen and head-over-heels in love with Deon. Followed him all the way to South Africa and there, fell in love with him even more. It wasn't just him, I guess. It was the world he came from – so different! Wild!' Gillian downs what's left in her glass, and Corrigan instantly refills it. 'It was like the Wild West and Deon, on his vast farm in Natal, was so… so…' Words are beginning to escape Gillian. She knows she might have had a glass too many, but doesn't care. It's such a pleasurable moment to remember the good life, the adventure. 'He was like a *voortrekker*. Have you heard that term?'

Corrigan shakes his head. 'It sounds very romantic.'

'They were the first Dutch settlers, and Deon was like that: broad-shouldered and hard-working, a mule of a man. And there I was, in that unrelenting African heat, hallucinating about being his woman. I guess I like a solid country man.'

'Darn! I shouldn't have taken off my overalls!'

Gillian points her finger at him in mock accusation. 'But you're not really a country squire, are you? Forensic scientist – now, now… You're virtually one of my own kind. So what made you give it all up?'

'I've discovered women prefer farmers.'

'Is that so?'

'You told me yourself.'

'Deon and his cornfields was a mistake.' Gillian sobers up at the memory of their violent arguments – violent on his part, argumentative on hers, both guilty as hell. She has consigned that to the past. 'But we have a daughter, Tara. She's twenty and a pain in the neck, and if nothing else, she was worth the trouble of living on a dusty farm with a shotgun under my pillow.'

'You must tell me about that.'

'No. You must tell me. I asked you first. I asked you yesterday. How did you end up on Nortonview Farm?'

'Do you ever leave your policewoman's hat at home?'

She wags her finger at him. 'Don't try to get out of it. I went to great lengths to be here!' Tara's minidress and the missing bra remind Gillian to cross her chest and cover her unruly nipples from poking their heads through the thin fabric. Oh, the sacrifices! 'Go on, tell me! Before they bring green tea. That's the cue to go home, did you know?'

'I don't do tea on a night out. I'd rather we ordered another bottle of wine? What do you say?'

'I'd say you want to get me drunk, but I need to warn you – I have drunk many a big man under the table in my day.'

'I'm up for a challenge!' He picks up the empty bottle and nods to the ever-watchful Chinese waiter to bring another one.

'And I want to hear it.' Gillian, the pitbull terrier – even a tipsy one - knows how to tighten the grip on her intended victim. 'Why did you give up your career? Something must have happened.'

His blue eyes, clear and round despite the alcohol in his bloodstream, focus on her and he suddenly appears as sober as a nun. 'You obviously heard about the Omagh bombing.'

'Yes – late nineties. Tragic.'

'Ninety-eight. I was on the forensic team investigating that incident, plus many other related ones. We handled things badly, we at the NIFSS, the police… The evidence wasn't bagged properly, labels held with Sellotape had come off and got lost, items not recorded in the Special Property Register; evidence collected at the scenes was flying between us and the police stations and hardly anything was verified against the records. It was mayhem, and we were overwhelmed, but that's no excuse, as you probably know.'

Gillian knows. She nods.

'In ninety-eight we tested all forensic evidence, including fibres – what was left of them after the explosions - and no one reckoned with any potential for DNA testing, but then in 2003 the exhibits were recalled for transmission to Birmingham for LNC DNA examination. You've heard of the LNC method – Low Number Copy DNA?'

'Vaguely. I don't think it's been validated.'

'It has been found unreliable – the quantity of DNA profiles was so tiny that the results could not be conclusively reproduced. But we didn't know that at the time. We were asked to collect all exhibits from various parts of the lab for that LNC profiling. All of it, and there was a lot. It wasn't just Omagh, you see, there were a number of other car bombs and mortar attacks during that period that had been bundled together on five trolleys.'

'Trolleys?'

'Yes, trolleys. You couldn't just carry it. We packed it on trolleys and they were wheeled to a police van and taken to the station. Some bags were leaking – glue had dried up, bags opened – a fertile ground for DNA cross-contamination. And that is the crux of the matter - a young man died as a result of that, and it was my fault.' Sean doesn't flinch under this confession. He is looking at Gillian. 'Do you want to go home now?'

'I want to hear the rest of it. How did he die?'

'Hanged himself – couldn't take the pressure. Everyone presumed he was guilty, and I think he too believed it in the end. It was bizarre... The same day we transmitted the Omagh evidence to the police station, before it was flown to Birmingham, that young man – Dermot McAuley – was being detained at the station for disorderly behaviour. Silly lad stuff. He had been out with friends, celebrating his graduation. He would have been a civil engineer... Somehow, between the leaking exhibit bags and the boy's personal belongings collected at the station, the DNA cross-contamination occurred. Within months Dermot McAuley was arrested and charged with conspiracy to murder, conspiracy to cause an explosion and possession of an explosive substance with intent. The DNA evidence was apparently, to everyone's mind, irrefutable, no matter how hard the young man tried to plead innocence. He was only seventeen at the time of the bombings, for God's sake!' Sean's voice trails off. He bites his upper lip. 'No one listened. Your lot had a suspect. We had rock-solid DNA evidence against him. Not only did he fit the DNA profile, he was Catholic, his deceased father once suspected of IRA sympathies... He was the perfect candidate for a scapegoat. No one believed he would get out of it. Nor did he. So he hanged himself in his cell long before the trial began. He was an only son – his mother a simple, working-class, Catholic woman. Her heart couldn't take it – the stigma of killing all those innocent people now on her son's head… Tough luck, we all thought. We had a DNA profile match. He was guilty as hell. I was sure of that. I was a scientist. Science doesn't lie. But I was wrong. We were all wrong. The truth came out at the Sean Hoey trial years later. He was an electrician implicated in the Omagh bombing on the basis of that wrong evidence. He was of course acquitted, but that was far too late for Dermot and his mother. I had two choices: I could sweep it under the carpet, pretend it was one of those freak misfortunes, or I could pack up science.'

'You did the latter.'

'It turned out science wasn't omniscient and Dermot McAuley died because of our arrogant belief that it was. I couldn't continue doing that job. I chucked it in. It wouldn't bring the boy back, but I owed him at least that – an admission of guilt.'

Gillian understands. She might have done the same thing, she thinks, in the same circumstances. 'I see.'

'You know, the funny thing is, he was just like me – Dermot McAuley. I am that boy from a poor Catholic family with little prospects and all odds stacked against me, but I made it through with hard work, through university, through the ranks at the FSS… And he didn't. Same starting point, but only I struck it lucky. And it was my fault that he didn't and that his mother had lost a son while my mother got to keep hers. The damned Irish luck – more of a curse, really.'

Gillian reaches for his hand. It is cold. She squeezes it. 'Don't be too hard on yourself. Error of judgment – in our line of work we have to take that into account.'

'Nah! I don't do judgments, I do conclusions based on facts. I like it black and white – I'm a scientist! Was...' He pours the rest of the wine from the bottle into their glasses and raises a toast: 'To atonement!'

They drink in silence and as soon as their glasses are empty, the Chinese waiter serves Chinese green tea. Gillian makes a mental note to read up on the Omagh bombing and Dermot McAuley.

Like a love-struck teenager, Sean insists on walking her home.

'I can look after myself,' Gillian giggles – she too is a love-struck teenager. 'I'm used to catching criminals with my bare hands, you know?'

'That might be so, but you have a bottle of wine in your bloodstream.'

'Hear yourself speak! You've had more than me!'

'But I am a man and I don't look half as vulnerable as you. Attracting trouble – you are.' He gazes pointedly at her chest where her nipples, pinched by the cold evening air, stand hard and erect. Gillian crosses her arms and rubs her bare shoulders. She accepts his jacket, which he wraps around her naked back. He leaves his arm on her back, and she accepts that too.

His jacket is longer than Gillian's dress – she becomes painfully conscious of the fact. If she were to be hit by a bus, what would the hospital staff think of her? A drunken, middle-aged slapper... Oh dear! The compulsion to explain herself is stronger than ever. 'I wasn't joking,' she says, 'this isn't my dress. It's my daughter's. I didn't have anything appropriate to wear, for a date...' She blushes, hopelessly. 'I mean, assuming... this may be a date...'

'Funny that – I've made the same assumption,' he chuckles. 'Problem is I don't have a daughter to borrow outfits from, so I had to go and buy the whole thing! You'll find the price is still attached – in case there aren't any more dates after this one. Bloody expensive those suits and designer shirts! Too expensive for a farmhand.'

Disbelieving, Gillian fumbles with the lining of his jacket, and finds the label, still intact attached to the inside pocket. 'Fancy that! You're worse than me!' She laughs and reads the label. 'Blimey! Look at that price! It's daylight robbery!'

'I was keen,' he says. 'Still am.'

The fact that she has not had sex in living memory is no hurdle. Things just happen naturally, one leading to the next as if this were a textbook rehearsal of what nature intends when the male and the female of the species run into each other. She bends over the flower pot to recover the key and immediately feels his eyes drilling into her behind. She wonders, only briefly, what knickers she has put on – they must be on display. She didn't have time to think about the knickers – pity! She turns the key in the keyhole and pushes the door open.

'You'll come in for a cup of coffee, or -' she tries to follow the preambles to the mating rituals she sees on TV, but it is too late for preambles. He pushes her inside and kicks the door shut behind them. From the corner of her eyes, Gillian spots Fritz scuttling from under their feet and dashing up the stairs to the safety of her bedroom. Sean's jacket has just missed the cat as he pulled it from her back and tossed it on the stairs. She leads him to the sofa in the lounge – there is no time to follow Fritz up to the bedroom. There may not be time for the sofa either. His impatient hands slide inside her dress and rip it from her neck to expose her breasts. She will have to mend the blinking dress before Tara discovers the damage. His lips are pressing into hers, his body is pinning her to the wall. She pushes him away to give herself room for manoeuvre. Her torn dress, held up until now by their bodies pressed together, falls from her hips to the floor, leaving her naked but for her black knickers and the shoes with silver buckles. He takes her body in with his eyes, admires it with open greed. She is hungry for him too. She unbuttons his shirt and his trousers. He cups his hands under her buttocks and lifts her – she wraps her legs around his hips and allows him to carry her into the lounge. The sofa might yet get some action.

'It's now or never,' he wheezes.

'Now,' she says.

Fritz yodels from the stairs.

Gillian's mobile lights up and vibrates on the table.

'Shit. Sorry, I have to take this. It may be work.' She scrambles up and grabs the phone, crossing her fingers behind her back that no one managed to get themselves killed while she is in the middle of a surprisingly successful date. It's a text from Tara. Gillian never hears from her daughter, but when she does the timing is usually found wanting.

She skips through the text. Something about Easter. Is it Easter already? She will read more carefully later, and respond to it then. For now, she slides back into Sean's arms...

'Where's Sean? Not like him to be late for dinner. He's usually first at the table, with that dog of his panting on the porch, waiting for scraps.' Grace has put her hands on her hips and is watching Mildred sip her soup.

Mildred puts on a knowing expression, 'He's out on a date.'

'No!' Grace's eyes bulge in disbelief.

'Oh yes, with that policewoman. He even got a new suit – dressed up to the nines he was when I saw him last.'

'A policewoman?'

'The same one that was investigating him for embezzlement.'

'Charmed her with his blue Irish eyes,' Grace marvels at the developments. She sits at the table, next to Mildred and whispers in a confidante tone, 'It may be a good thing, our Sean and the policewoman... I had my suspicions he had his eye on young Esme.'

Mildred nearly chokes on a piece of bread. 'Where did you get that idea from! Sean and Esme? He could be her father. You Grace, you have to watch that tongue of yours, you really do! Sean and Esme!' Mildred makes a hurried sign of the Cross on her chest. The very concept of Sean and Esme feels to her like incest.

'All right, all right... No need to get all up in arms, Mildred. Maybe I was wrong – just saw them two together a lot -'

'That's only because Sean looks after Rohan and Esme is here every other day to ride the beast. You see me with Sean a lot too – does that give you any ideas?'

Grace chuckles with merriment. 'Oh Mildred, you know how to make a point!'

Mildred smirks. She has recovered her wits. The soup tastes strange, though – tasteless though it is her favourite cream of mushroom. She pushes it away.

'What's wrong with the soup?'

'Too much, Grace, too much.' Mildred doesn't want to hurt Grace's feelings. And perhaps it isn't just the soup, perhaps it is the worry nibbling at the back of her mind. She sighs and tells Grace, 'Esme is leaving – going to Africa to fight poachers. Won't listen to reason.'

Grace shrugs, 'The youth today – full of fancy ideas! She'll go, see the grass ain't any greener on the other side of the world, and she'll be back.'

'But when, Grace? When will she come back? It may be too long for me to wait. I'm not getting any younger...'

'On that note, Mildred,' Grace looks uncomfortable. Mildred knows her – she knows Grace is about to say something Mildred won't like. She waits for Grace to bring herself to say it, which she does without meeting Mildred's eye, 'With Esme going, and mind you – Sean might go at any time, you never know with him... And I can't be here for you all the time... Fact is, I ain't getting younger myself – don't know how long I can carry on -'

'What are you saying, Grace?'

'You can't be here by yourself, all alone, like a sore thumb... What if something happened with you? Nobody'd be any the wiser, God forbid!' Grace grabs

Mildred's bowl and pours its content into the sink. She begins to give it a good scrub, as if it needs it. With her back to Mildred, she finally says what's been on her mind. 'Don't you think you should pack it all up and go to a nice home? Where they can take care of you, proper care…'

Mildred feels all her anxieties, none of which have gone away, come up to her throat to choke her. 'Has Liam been talking to you? Has he been telling you things? Has he? I know he has!'

'You mustn't get yourself into a state, Mildred. We all want what's best for you.'

Grace is gone. Sean hasn't come back from his date with the policewoman. David hasn't arrived to stay like he said he would. After all that – he hasn't. It isn't like him. He always kept his word, but that was years ago – he may have changed since then, and who would blame him?

Mildred is alone. Everyone has been warning her of being alone of late. Like they are all conspiring against her. Even Grace. Mildred shudders. It is chilly in the house when she is the only person in. Her body heat isn't enough to fill it with warmth. The blanket is in the sitting room, on the settee where she left it last night – where she always leaves it. She knows it's there and she knows it would offer her warmth, but she can't bring herself to get off the stool and walk all the way there to fetch it. Her legs feel too heavy to lift so she stays slumped on the stool with her arms propped on the table, staring at the now cold cup of tea in front of her. Her rosary lies abandoned next to the cup. She will get back to it in a minute, as soon as she has her tea. But the tea is cold. And the house is cold too.

She shivers. They all want to get her out of here. Where to?

She's too old to build a new home for herself. And she can't go anywhere. Her legs feel too heavy. Something squeezes on top of her stomach. A touch of indigestion. That mushroom soup did taste funny. Something was off, maybe the cream. Mildred hates to admit it but it could have been her anxieties that took away her appetite. Esme leaving, Liam's relentless badgering, and now Grace... He got to her. Somehow he did. He got Grace to take his side. Why do there have to be sides?

The indigestion is getting worse: it is burning inside Mildred's chest. She has to remember to breathe, but it comes out more like panting. Is it because she is so worried. Sean has gone out on a date. His absence tonight is drilling a hole in Mildred's chest. That may be it! Not the indigestion! Esme has gone to Africa. Who will take care of the horse? Mildred can't – her legs feel too heavy and her ribcage is caving in, crushing her chest like a vice. Breathe! David promised he would come to stay with her – give her a chance to make amends. She needs to explain that it was all for the better, that it couldn't have been done any other way. Not in Mildred's world. She is a good Catholic. Where is the rosary? She sees it right in front of her on the table but can't reach for it. It isn't just her legs that feel heavy – her arms do too. Especially her left arm. It aches with all that weight and pressure that has built inside her, all that worry...

Liam started it with his stubborn talk about residential homes and seeing doctors. What for? Nothing is wrong with Mildred, apart from this nasty bout of indigestion. It is sharp! More like a knife. Maybe she should see a doctor after all – Liam will have it his way, fancy that! He always gets it his way. No-one can stand up to him. Not even David – he couldn't either, he preferred to leave and let Liam have it his way. Always. Her breath shortens as if her lungs have been punctured, and the pain is so distinctly like a stab… The light is fading. It's getting late. No, there is someone standing over her, blocking the light. A man. Reginald?

'Ma? Are you all right?'

It has to be Liam. He looks just like Reginald, especially when the light is bad. He is leaning towards Mildred, blocking not just the light but also the air. That makes it harder to breathe, and when she tries the pain stabs.

'Ma, it's me, David? What's wrong?'

He came, after all. His face is blurred and distorted. It grows as if someone's put a magnifying glass to it.

Why is he crushing her chest? It hurts.

AT THE END OF THEIR TETHER

'Don't expect any money from me!'

'I don't.'

'I won't be financing this madness... this... this juvenile behaviour!'

'I was only asking for a lift to the airport,' Esme shrugs and gets up from her backpack. It is huge – bigger than her. How on earth is she going to carry it around? It will break her back! No, it isn't his problem. Liam won't fall for it. She can break her back for all he cares. That may just bring her to her senses. Despite the laws of gravity she manages to heave the backpack over her shoulders, tightens a belt on her waist and clasps a plastic buckle on her chest.

'I'll be going then. I'll take a bus.'

'You are not to do it – I prohibit you,' he says, and even to his own ears his prohibition sounds weak and powerless.

'Father, I'm a twenty-six year old woman. I can do as I please.'

'Not while you still -' He realises that what he is about to say no longer carries any weight: *not while you still live under my roof.* She no longer does. She is leaving. He

94

shouldn't be shouting at her, shouldn't be throwing his weight about – he should be begging her: *Please, don't go. You are my child, my baby daughter. I can't look out for you where you're going. I can't bear the thought of anything happening to you, and me not being there to hold your hand. Please...* But he doesn't know how to beg. He never had to – not once in his whole life. The words just won't come. He only knows how to make demands and how to be in charge. Because he is her damned father. Because he knows what's good for her. Because he knows better. 'You'll bloody regret it! But I won't come running to you to save your neck. You're on your own! Hear me?'

'Bye, Dad,' Esme says from the doorway. 'Try to take it easy.'

And she is gone: his porcelain doll of a girl who could break so easily that it makes his hair stand on end just to think about it, his daughter who almost didn't happen, his jealously guarded treasure, his joy, his reason to soldier on with his gloves off and clenched teeth. Gone. All reason gone with her. He can't let her go. Not like that.

'At least,' he says, 'call me when you need a lift back!'

But she can't hear him. She is already out, walking towards the gate with her huge backpack obscuring her narrow frame.

Sean left at daybreak – something to do with relieving the cows of their burden. As soon as he was out of the door, Fritz crept out from under the bed and plonked himself next to Gillian, reclaiming his rightful place in her life. He is now glaring at her, relieved but unforgiving. His ears wear chandeliers of cobwebs draped over his head, making him twitch. He sneezes.

'Don't tell me you've got cat flu!' Gillian reaches out to the forlorn cat and removes the webs. 'It's only a bit of fluff. Honestly, Fritz, you're such a drama queen!' He is swiping his tail over her face, his bottom up in the air, as she strokes him. 'You'll have to get used to the competition, I'm afraid.' Fritz bares his needle-sharp teeth, and yodels. 'You can sulk all you like but he's coming back.'

Gillian stretches in bed and lets herself daydream for a few precious moments of semi-alertness, remembering the urgent lovemaking of last night, which soon, as the days and nights roll on, will become slow and luxuriant, ageing with time like good wine. A faint whiff of his aftershave is lingering in the bedroom, trapped in the sheets and on Gillian's skin. They made love again, in her bed, with her in charge, on top of the world. She can feel her thighs ache pleasurably.

Gillian takes unusually good care of herself this morning. Instead of her usual mad rush, brushing her teeth with one hand and zipping up her trousers with the other, she runs a long, hot bath where she lazes and soaks at her leisure, closing her eyes and catching the few last snippets of her memories of Sean just like she used to catch melting snowflakes on her tongue when she was a girl. She puts conditioner in her hair and then blow-dries it. She spends a quarter of an hour choosing her outfit. It should be a dress or a skirt – she must look, and feel, and smell like a woman since they are meeting for lunch - and after that she will ask him over for dinner, and after that...

Webber is pulling funny faces. What's that all about? He's making a gesture of having his throat cut and points his finger at Gillian. She raises an eyebrow. 'You feeling all right, Mark?'

'Where have you been?! Scarface has been looking for you all over!'

'Fancy him being here before lunchtime – that one day when I'm running a few minutes late. What does he want?'

'He wants your head on a platter. Really pissed off with you!'

'What about?'

'DI Marsh! In my office – now!' Scarface has materialised before her like the Phantom of the Opera, his face livid-red, the scar over his lip like a shabby white stitching in a piece of scarlet cloth.

Meekly, Gillian shuffles behind him and wisely chooses to stand rather than take a seat. It feeds well into the sense of the dramatic tension Detective Superintendent Scarfe is so fond of. *What is it this time?* she wants to ask, but again, bides her time, offering him her undivided attention.

'I got a phone call from SFO. Would you care to guess what that was about?'

'I've been working with them on a case – money laundering, fraud. A man going by the name of Dimitri Papariakas. It could be something to do-'

'No, you haven't been working *with* them,' Scarfe bangs his desk with his fist, and that brings Gillian's explanation to an abrupt halt. 'You, DI Marsh, have been getting under their feet! Effectively, you have just sabotaged a case they'd been putting together for months! Congratulations!'

'I... How? I...' Gillian is aghast. It was she who contacted the SFO in the first place – she who alerted them to the goings-on between Liam Cox and Dimitri Papariakas and to the whole Greek islands property scheme!

'You went there yesterday, I understand?'

'Yes. A follow up on a complaint by Liam Cox. It gave me an opportunity to cosy up to him.'

'Cosy up! That's so charming!' Scarfe snorts. 'Cosy up! You walked in on them, you alerted Papariakas to our interest in him – you jeopardised the entire operation, DI Marsh!'

Gillian blinks rapidly. She is at a loss for words, and frankly, no words can fix this conundrum. She is better off listening – Scarfe, having vented his spleen, may just get down to the nitty-gritty in a minute. He does. 'Because of your untimely intervention,' he throws his arms up in the air, 'and who asked you to stick your nose into it, I dare not speculate! Because of you, SFO are forced to bring forward the next step in the operation – before Papariakas panics and goes under the radar. We're getting a warrant to search Cox Properties' premises. As soon as we've got that, we're moving in. I'm now in charge of the operation. And you... you -'

Gillian's body stiffens into a boy-scout salute. 'Yes, sir?'

'You do only what I tell you to do! Understood? From now on you do not exercise any initiative of your own.

Understood?'

The boy scout salutes again and marches out, tail between legs.

The lunch is in a cosy tearoom in the heart of Sexton's Canning. Gillian is not afraid to flaunt her affair. The word *affair* has a strange ring to it. She would much sooner call it a *relationship*, but it may be too early for that. She is wearing her high heels with the silver buckle – the only pair of high heels in her possession. Borrowing Tara's shoes is not an option as Tara is two sizes up on Gillian. Feet like flippers, poor Tara! Gillian makes a mental note to stop at Clarks' on her way back to the office, after lunch with Sean. For now, she pauses at the display window of an upmarket boutique and takes in the contemporary style of a lady's shoe, the blocky shape of the heel and the eye-watering prices. For so long has she lived in the land of casual wear that the inflation rates of the past twenty years have passed her by. She will have to get used to the real world of fashion, style and desirability.

On second thoughts she will pop over here after lunch, and splash out.

Aptly named The Tudor Tearooms, the establishment is housed on the ground level of a period building with windows overlooking the market square. There are a few small chambers, tiny and snug, each with two or three tables tucked away in private corners. The wooden floors creak underfoot as the waitress leads Gillian to a table by a delicious period mantelpiece. Sean hasn't arrived yet, but then it is still five minutes away from noon. Gillian orders a bottle of sparkling water, which arrives swiftly, accompanied by a glass full of ice and the menu. Two menus because, Gillian informs the waitress, someone will be joining her soon.

She remembers Mark's face when she told him she was having lunch with a friend. 'What friend?' Webber pulled another one of his silly faces. It is his day for silly faces. 'A boyfriend,' Gillian told him, to which words had failed him. She smiles. No one suspected her of being able to pull a man, get a boyfriend, have sex in the night (or day, as the case may be) and still be able to be a good copper. Perhaps being a good copper has temporarily taken a back seat! The world won't come to an end if she takes a couple of hours off policing and leaves it to others. Scarfe appears keen to take charge of the police work, for a change. And good luck to him. Gillian is in such high spirits that she has already forgiven him for all the abuse he threw at her earlier. It's all water under the bridge. Because she has a date.

The waitress is staring at her from behind the bar. Gillian takes a look at her wristwatch – it's ten past twelve. She buries her face in the menu to avoid the waitress's gaze. The room has filled with customers. She is becoming painfully conscious of the fact that she is occupying a table all by herself. This table could easily sit four. Sean seems to be running late. Perhaps he doesn't believe in watches. It's just him and the cows on the farm, neither party being in particular need for time-keeping. She is trying very hard to picture his wrist – does he even wear a watch? Not that she can recall. Her attention was never on his wrist. Though last night he was on time, so what's keeping him now?

She pours herself another glass of water. It froths, and bubbles burst on her hand and her face as she drinks it, even though she isn't thirsty and will soon need to find the toilet. But that may happen just as Sean walks in and looks for her. A loo trip is not on the cards. They could easily miss each other.

She looks at her watch. Thirteen minutes past twelve. She calls the waitress. 'I think I'll start with…' her eyes catch the first item on the Starters menu, 'the Welsh rarebit, please. We'll order main courses later.'

The waitress smiles – it's more like a smirk, like she already knows more than Gillian does, like she already knows that no one is joining her. When the waitress deserts her, Gillian's eyes skim across the room. She watches other customers, who casually perform tasks one normally does in a restaurant: eat, chat, scan the menu, put their elbows on the table, take them off because it isn't polite, pass salt to one another, laugh… She shouldn't be staring. Gillian turns to the wall above the mantelpiece. Lots of old photographs of the town, dating back to Victorian days: ladies in long black dresses with trails, gentlemen carrying umbrellas over the ladies' heads, horse carts carrying beer barrels along the sleepy street. The waitress returns with Gillian's order. She is wearing a dainty silver watch with an old-fashioned analogue face, Gillian reads the time: half past twelve.

'And I'll have the bill when you're ready,' she tells the waitress.

He is early. Mother won't be ready and she will take a lot

101

of convincing to get her on the move. She'll drag her feet, take hours in the bathroom, ask a lot of questions and debate for hours whether she should sit in front or in the back of his car. She might even choose to walk to the surgery so that they are late and miss the appointment. She's been digging her heels in just to make life difficult for Liam. She is only making it difficult for herself. The farm has to go – it is losing her money, and it's Liam's money at the end of the day. Besides, it isn't just about money – it's about Mother. She needs to be in a home, taken care of by professional people, kept warm and out of trouble, because Liam has more pressing matters on his mind than keeping an eye on her and her antics. Dimitri is breathing down his neck. Liam has decided to shake him off once and for all. He has had enough of the Greek's control over his life, his affairs and his mind. This will be their last enterprise; he will get his blood money back, and then they will go their separate ways. Liam is suffocating with the Greek's foot on his throat. The partnership has hijacked him. He's been neglecting his family, and when he finally finds the time to be with them it only leads to arguments. For one, he could've handled Esme better. Even Stella deserves better, though she can be an obstinate cow in her own right, as bad as Mother. But Mother leads the pack! And to make matters worse, she holds all the cards. Does she even realise she has the power to make or break her son's future? Perhaps he should tell her that.

Every day he reminds himself to treat her gently. He needs to tip-toe around her and gradually earn her trust. He wants what's best for her, she needs to be told that.

The problem is that she won't listen and she has her own ideas, ridiculous ideas, totally off the wall, about what's good for her. And when she drags God and His divine God-damned will into it, Liam sees red. Bloody irrational obstinacy! That's when he is forced to take action. He doesn't want to. As that God of hers is his witness, he'd much rather she went with him voluntarily to spare them both the grief. Maybe she will. It looks like he has Grace on his side. The old bag was easy to convince. Mother may take a bit more time to finally see reason. Except that time is a luxury Liam cannot afford right now.

He pulls up with a screech of tyres in the courtyard, sending a bunch of random chickens into panic, feathers flying, loud clacking setting his teeth on edge. He steps out of the car and finds himself in a Mexican standoff with the farmhand's dog – that huge and nasty German Shepherd. It is blocking Liam's way, its head low, its eyes fixed on his. He's heard somewhere that you should not look a wild dog in the eye – it will see it as a challenge. He doesn't like the sodding beast, which is a euphemistic way of saying he is shit scared of it. Challenging it is the last thing he wants to do. He escapes with his eyes, seeking help from the direction of the house. Perhaps Mother is watching from her rocking chair in the window, as is her habit. Perhaps she is letting him sweat a bit.

'Mother! It's me, Liam!' he shouts at the top of his voice. 'Can someone get that bloody dog away from me? Mother?'

The dog growls and pads a couple of steps closer towards Liam. He backs off, feels the metal of his car door against his back.

'Mum!'

Only now does he realise the place is empty. The door to the house is standing ajar. Mother never leaves the door wide open. She wouldn't let the warmth out, not on a cold day like this. She is not at home – she would've come out by now, even at her pace, even though she may be pissed off with him. She is not home. No one is home.

The cows are crying. No one's milked the cows. Something is wrong.

The hair is bristling on the dog's neck as it readies itself to pounce. Liam takes no chances; he pulls the door open, slides into the seat and slams the door shut just as the dog leaps up at him. Its teeth are ivory white against its purple gums. White foam drips onto the panel of the wound-up window. Liam starts the engine and takes off, the dog's paws sliding off the door. In the rear view mirror he can see the creature tailing him. It won't keep up for long. Liam slams his foot down on the gas pedal and puts some distance between them.

In the safety of his car, he retrieves his mobile and dials 999.

He is like a bull in a china shop. As soon as the nurse at the reception desk confirms Mother's whereabouts, Liam pushes by nurses and ghostly white patients, fury foaming at his mouth. Nobody has bothered to let him know!

He reaches the Cardiac Ward; storms along a clinically white corridor. Colleen gets up from a chair as soon as she sees him.

'Liam!'

She runs to him, her purple cape flapping behind her

like a broken wing.

'No one's told me! Why has no one bothered to contact me?' he pulls her arms from his neck. 'I have to call the bloody 999 to find out my mother's been taken to hospital with a fucking heart attack! How did you know?' It is more of an accusation than a question.

'Don't you want to know how she is?'

The bloody Irishman speaks even though he hasn't been spoken to. He is sitting in a chair next to the one freshly vacated by Colleen. He's wearing a fancy suit. His gaze is insolent. Liam can't hold back his emotions. He hits the wall just above the Irishman's head. 'Your fucking dog went for my throat! It should be put down! I'll see to it!'

The Irishman doesn't as much as flinch. He says, 'In case you do want to know, she's out of the operating theatre and the prognosis is good. A minor heart attack, we're told. A small blood vessel burst -'

Out of steam, Liam slumps into a chair next to the Irishman. He is breathing hard, as if it is his turn now to suffer a heart attack of his own. Colleen gazes at him, concern in her gentle eyes. 'They think she'll be all right. Of course, at Mum's age, they can't give any guarantees.'

Liam has recovered his breath, but the anger hasn't left him. 'A heart attack, of course! Do you know why?'

'Why what?'

'She's old. She's not coping. No one's out there to take care of her.' He glares with open disapproval at the Irishman. Liam really must make this point now – while the iron's still hot. 'She was lucky this time, but her luck won't hold. Not next time! If we don't do something about it, next time we'll be meeting at the funeral parlour. She has to go into a home, I know that and you know that.' His eyes are fixed on Colleen who cringes under the pressure of his words. 'We have to be on the same page, Colleen…'

'But Mum won't have it. She's so happy on the farm! If we force her to go to a home – it'll kill her…' It's a weak argument, weakly delivered. He can tell Colleen is wavering.

'Staying on her own at the bloody farm will kill her, for God's sake, Colleen, can't you see that?'

'Oh, I don't know… She won't have it. You know how stubborn she is.'

'That's why we have to go against her will. We'll have to do it for her. She doesn't know what's good for her anymore. The farm will be her end. Do you want to take that risk?'

'What can we do? I mean, it's her wish -'

She has caved in. At least, Colleen is now on his side. They are her children – the best people to make the right decision for their mother. Perhaps, in a way, this heart attack is a blessing in disguise. 'She can't go back to the farm from here, you realise that?'

Colleen nods, her big eyes glistening with tears.

'I'll organise a smooth transition from here to a home. I found a lovely home – top notch. In Werton. It's expensive, but we should spare no expenses -'

'No, we shouldn't,' Colleen echoes. 'Let's make it as comfortable for her as possible.'

'I'll deal with the legalities.'

'She'll never forgive us…'

'But she will be alive.' No arguing with that. A sense of achievement washes over Liam. He is calm at last. 'When can we go in and see her?'

A man is approaching from the far end of the corridor where a vending machine attracts a small queue of hospital patients and visitors. He is carrying three paper cups with plastic lids on top. He is heading in their direction. There is something familiar about that man. Something unsettling about him, too. He's about Liam's height, his build; he has his hair. Liam recognises him from the church. He is the man who sat in the back pew, on his own, during Father's remembrance mass. The man's eyes lift briefly from the cups and meet Liam's gaze. The man stops. Liam's heart sinks to the bottom of his guts.

'David,' he says.

'David found Mum. If it wasn't for him, God knows what would've happened!' Colleen speaks from inside a deep tunnel.

Mark is pulling another stupid face: a cross between Austin Powers and Inspector Clouseau; his left eyebrow is pressing down whilst his right one quivers over the bridge of his nose, his pinkie wedged into the corner of his mouth. 'Sooo, how was the date with the mystery boyfriend?'

Burying her head behind the partition separating their desks, Erin is failing to hold back a chuckle. 'Sorry, boss, I shouldn't be laughing, but Webber has been going on and on about your entering the dating scene – everyone, duck!' Webber bursts out laughing and Erin tries to stifle her own amusement.

'Don't you have *things* to do, you two?' Gillian burns Webber to a crisp with her fiery glare.

'He didn't turn up!' From the ashes, Webber manages to utter his disbelief.

'Bastard!' Erin concludes.

'Men for you, DC Macfadyen! Best kept at arm's length. And that's the end of the matter.' Now that Gillian has it off her chest, she is able to return to the line of duty. 'Right, we're on standby. The SFO are in the process of obtaining a search warrant for Cox Properties. There is an international search out for Papariakas, so it's only a formality. As soon as we have it, we go in. I don't know what the exact confines of the warrant will be, but we'll be looking to seize any documentation pertaining to Dimitri Papariakas and Greek island property exchange deals. Detective Superintendent Scarfe is in charge of this operation and he needs to be briefed every step of the way.'

Webber's desk telephone rings. 'DS Webber. Oh, Kate? What you doing calling me on my work number – everything all right?' He listens for a split second. His face drops. 'Take it easy, Kate. Take it slowly, OK? Have you called an ambulance? OK… No, that's not OK. Call the ambulance. I'm on my way.' His complexion turns truly ashen as he puts the phone down. He pushes papers on his desk without a clear purpose. 'Where's my house keys? I need to borrow a car…'

'I'll drive you.' Gillian can tell he's in no condition to drive. 'We'll get there before the ambulance.'

Their feet are clattering down the empty staircase,

Webber's Italian shoes with pointy toes and Gillian's high heels with their silver buckles. Her ankles twist and bend. She is finding it impossible to keep up with Mark. This reminds her why she should be wearing decent boots to work. They take a police car. Straight away she slaps the emergency blue light onto the roof. She shoots through the sleepy lunch-hour traffic, focusing on the road. To her left, Webber sits silent as a ghost. She can't even hear him breathe. He hasn't put on his seatbelt.

There is blood – too much blood. It has soaked through Kate's light-grey coloured joggers. It's all over her hands. It appears that she is trying to obstruct the flow of fresh blood – she is jamming her hands into her groin while sitting on the stained carpet, her knees pressed together. Her face is contorted in either pain or panic. 'I'm having these cramps, like in labour...'

'Don't speak! You'll be all right, just don't do anything!' He kneels beside her and attempts to lift her. She puts her arm around his neck – touches his face and leaves a bloody imprint of her fingers on his cheek. He gets hold of her body and heaves himself up with Kate clinging on to him. 'Gillian, get the door!' he shouts.

The paramedics meet them on the doorstep. Overcome by shock, Webber refuses to pass Kate to them and he strives to carry her – and his unborn son - all the way to the ambulance. They make way for him and wait until she is laid on a bed. That's where one of them firmly pushes him out of the way and the other one gets into the driver's seat. The door is shut and the ambulance takes off. Gillian follows, the blue light still frantic on the roof of her car.

Gillian watches them disappear behind double egress doors. Kate is in safe hands, they'll do what's necessary, she tells herself. Perhaps it isn't as bad as it looks – sometimes that is exactly the case. Kate has had three healthy children, if anyone can handle this, she can.

Gillian stands in the A&E admissions area for a while, wondering what to do with herself. She ought to wait for him. He has no way of getting back and will need a lift home – him and Kate. She decides to find a place to sit, a cup of coffee to settle her nerves. Only now does she notice that her hands are shaking and her mouth feels pepper-dry. She can't begin to imagine how Mark is feeling. She will have to find him first to tell him that she's waiting to take them home. She ventures through the pair of doors, down a long corridor devoid of colour. A man is heading her way – she will have to ask for directions to… where? The Maternity Ward?

It's Sean!

Of all the people she could bump into in the corridors of the Western National Hospital… They stare at each other, both equally puzzled and bemused.

'Bloody hell! I forgot our lunch date, didn't I! Have you been looking for me? I'm sorry!'

'No, of course not!' Gillian finds herself in defensive mode. 'I mean – yes, you forgot the lunch, but no – I'm not looking for you! I'm here with a colleague,' she points vaguely to an empty space next to her. 'His wife suffered…' She doesn't want to say the word *miscarriage*, and in any event, she may be wrong to call it that. She takes in his unshaven, drawn face and the same clothes that he wore last night, but less crisp and rather dishevelled with his shirt flowing out of his trousers and a few buttons undone. 'What are you doing here?'

'It's Mildred.' It takes Gillian a few seconds to recall who Mildred is: the old lady from the farm, Liam Cox's mother. 'She's had a heart attack. While I was out with you… His son found her.'

'Liam Cox.'

'No, not Liam. David. Her stepson. Just returned from Canada. Imagine that, the bloke has come all the way from Canada to find Mildred having a heart attack. He probably saved her life. While I was with you…'

It sounds like a regret. Gillian stiffens, yet she is civil enough to deliver her commiserations, 'I'm sorry to hear that. Will she be OK?'

He sees Gillian's face. 'It's not your fault! Sorry, I'm not good at expressing myself. I guess I feel guilty I wasn't there when it happened, but I'm not unhappy about being with you last night.'

Gillian tries to smile. It comes out a little rueful, a little resigned. It seems like the magic between them has burst – an overinflated soap bubble, gone in a blink of an eye. 'I'd better let you go then.'

'She isn't awake yet. We're waiting for her to come to after the operation. Frankly, I don't fancy sitting there with those… people. Her family. No love lost between them… and I'm not part of the equation. Do you have a minute? I haven't had lunch, as you know, nor breakfast. There's a place here where we can grab something to eat, downstairs.'

'I've eaten.'

'A cup of tea then? I feel I need to explain…' He

reaches for her hand, and it feels soft and gentle, and well-intended. A warm current travels through her body in response to his touch. The magic is still around and it kicks in again like a low-voltage electric nip to the tips of her fingers.

In the hospital cafeteria Gillian succumbs to a tuna jacket-potato and to Sean's natural charm. He is disarmingly genuine, and it would be such a shame if they lost each other because of a missed lunch date – missed for a very good reason. 'You don't have to explain anything,' she tells him at last, 'I'd have done the same thing. Let's forget the blinking lunch and start again.'

She is very pleased with herself for saying that. She has never been on such high moral ground – it feels great to be magnanimous. Not to mention that it is also a brilliant excuse to act on her desire for him. She is forgiving and she gets to keep him.

But Sean insists on explaining, and since she has nothing better to do while waiting for Mark, she allows him. 'I know Mildred and I aren't related, but she is like a mother to me.'

'You did say that.'

'And I can't say it often enough. She took me in and trusts me unconditionally – I have to live up to that.'

'I know. You've appointed yourself to be her guardian angel – that much is apparent. You have a lot in common, I guess.'

'True... We're both Irish and she reminds me of home and... and I never thought I'd hear myself say this, but she reminds me of my... real mother. I can't make up to her because she's gone – been dead for twelve years now-

'What do you need to make up for?'

'I haven't been the model son you may think I am. To be honest with you, I've been a shit. She was a simple woman – uneducated, hard-working - and there were times I was ashamed of her. I shunned her.' He smiles apologetically at Gillian, as if she had the power to confer forgiveness on him. She is thinking of saying something appropriate, but he doesn't wait for her to verbalise it. 'I was good at school and she pushed me to better myself; she sacrificed a lot so that I could be somebody. And when I got there, I just didn't want to know her. She was a bit of a liability for the sophisticated man that I had become. She wouldn't go down well in my new circles, my girlfriend from a well-to-do family and my pals from the city, so I... I shunned her. Hardly kept in touch – on the quiet, you know, a flying visit once a Flood.' He exhales his confession like a prolonged sigh. 'Not that she complained. She was proud of me, telling every Tom, Dick and Harry what a bloody God's gift I was. She worshipped me, and I... well, I didn't bring her to my graduation and she wasn't invited to my wedding. I told her it was a low-key ceremony, showed her the photos afterwards, but she wasn't there... my own mother. Because I was ashamed of her.'

Gillian is slightly disconcerted by the mention of a girlfriend from a well-to-do family, followed closely by the revelation of a wedding, but she quickly realises that it would be even more disturbing if Sean didn't have a past to speak of.

He is oblivious to her musings and continues with his

confession, 'And then she passed away as quietly as she lived – slipped away, as they say – and it was then that it occurred to me what a shit I had been. Too little too late, and I sort of glossed over the guilt and went on with my life until it all went wrong a few years ago... When Mildred took me in, it was like I was given a second chance to make it up to my mum, you know? Take care of her. Be there for her. All that...' He swallows the words that probably would sound too sentimental if spoken out loud, but Gillian gets the meaning nevertheless.

'I can see where the guilt comes from, but you have nothing to blame yourself for about last night. Mildred is fine. Someone found her in time -'

'I know. I know.' He lifts her hand to his lips and kisses it, his eyes fixed on hers. 'I just wanted you to know that it was something important – something very important to me – that made me forget our date. Because I really want to give us a chance.' And this is where Gillian's heart leaps for joy and performs a frantic somersault in her throat. She can only croak back, 'Me too.'

A phone call from Scarfe saves her from saying anything else. Her phone pings thrice. She answers it. 'DI Marsh, where the hell are you? No, don't tell me! We're going in. In my office in five minutes! We're bringing in Papariakas – I need you in the interview room.'

She gets up from the table, mechanically, abandoning her potato and a mini Bakewell tart she had lined up for afters. 'Duty calls,' she says and takes off. On reflection, she pauses and turns to shout across the cafeteria, 'Come for dinner tonight. My place! Eight o'clock!'

She's a pretty girl, that Stella Davies, pretty as a doll, even though her face is swollen with crying, her eyes red and puffy, and the bit of black make-up girls use these days to make them look like Cleopatra is running down her cheeks in dirty rivulets. She is still pretty – prettier than most girls. It isn't just her youth – it's her pale complexion and dainty bone structure, all so delicate and precious you want to look after her, protect her. No wonder the boys are fighting over her. No wonder it has come to this…

Reginald has left the house and won't have anything to do with it. He's off to his horses and pigs, keeping his hands occupied with something – anything. Mildred can see he is too upset to speak. What can he say anyway? He can't choose between his sons, between his eldest, David and his favourite, Liam. He would be damned if he made that choice, so he leaves it to Mildred. She is closer to God, he always says, God can tell her what to do. But God is silent on this occasion, and Mildred's heart is torn to pieces. Why did Liam have to prise those two apart? Stella was David's girl!

They'd been courting since she was fourteen – five years now. Mildred remembers the day when she first saw those two from the window, timidly holding hands under the apple tree in the orchard – David, almost a man at eighteen, Stella just a girl. That was the first sign that they were dead serious. Until then it was just horse-play: fooling around, chasing each other in the fields, all that clowning teenagers do when they first fall in love and don't quite know how to deal with their feelings.

When did Liam get interested in Stella? Girls weren't his thing to start with: football and motorbikes were, and experimenting with cider. Of course, girls would enter the scene at some point, but why Stella? Why couldn't he go into the world and find himself his own girl? Why did he have to steal David's? Mildred knows the answer to that: Liam always wants what David has. Being his older brother, David is his role model. But it isn't admiration that drives Liam – it is envy. Liam has told Mildred that. One day when he was in a strop over something or other, he just blurted it out. 'It's always David! Always first! I don't matter to you, do I? David this – David that – David everything! Not me! Is it because his mother is dead and you're still alive? You making it up to him, aren't ya? Never mind me! I'm more of an orphan than he is!'

His exact words. It had really stung when he said that. Mildred always tells herself to treat them all equally, love them the same because – deep down in her heart of hearts – she harbours a shameful secret: that blood is thicker than water, that Liam and Colleen have come from her womb, and David has not. Not very Christian, but true.

If someone had told her, she would've never believed that it would come to this. It was only a few months ago when Mildred noticed Liam's sudden interest in Stella. It started innocently enough: him teasing her here and there (brothers do that to their sisters, and sisters-to-be, nothing extraordinary about that). Then he turned. He'd be like a restless dog, sniffing around her, suffocating her. He was open about seeking her company, especially when David wasn't around, putting his arms around her a bit too much, too tight, taking her for walks... Alarm bells should have rung loud and clear, but Mildred turned a blind eye. Because she loved her boy and she didn't believe, not in a million years, that it would have come to this.

How it happened – where it happened, when - she dares not ask. It happened. Stella is crying. She thinks her life is over. She isn't nineteen yet. She wants to finish college. And what's worse: she cares for David! David is on her mind and she is on his. They've been sweethearts for five years. They are meant for each other. She loves David, even though Liam can't bear to hear it – it's how it is. She loves David, but she carries Liam's child.

It can't be David's, they all know that. Those complications after David had German measles when he was eleven mean that the baby she carries can only be Liam's. It should be a happy occasion. Liam wants the baby, and he wants Stella, except that Stella wants David. And she wants to finish college, to graduate. And David, despite everything, wants Stella back. That won't do. God doesn't have to speak to Mildred for Mildred to know what is right. She won't hear of abortion. A dirty word, like murder. Stella knows it too; hence the tears – because she knows she can't go ahead with it. She just needs to be reminded.

'I'll speak to Father O'Leary,' Mildred declares. 'It'll have to be a quick wedding, before you start showing.'

David stands up, kicks his stool back. He is angry. It's not often you see him angry. 'Didn't you hear her, Ma? She doesn't want the baby! She doesn't want to marry Liam!'

'God forgive you, David Cox, for your blasphemies!

You don't know what you're sayin'!'

David turns to Stella. 'You don't have to do as they say. You don't!'

Stella bursts into more tears – more rivulets of black mascara.

'Leave her alone, David,' Liam speaks without getting up from the window seat where he sits, calm and smug. 'She's made her choice. Leave her alone.'

David storms towards his brother, his fists tight as bullets. They will come to blows! Mildred steps in and stands between the two young men, facing David. 'You won't fight your own brother – not under my roof, you will not.'

David lowers his fists, looks at Stella. She can just manage to shake her head, and sobs some more.

'Damn you all!' David runs out of the house, past Reginald who's been standing in the courtyard, pretending to be doing something of importance, past the gate, into the road.

'Sorry, David! I'm so sorry!' Words come to Stella, but it's too late. He cannot hear her.

'He'll be back,' Mildred says. 'He just needs to clear his head. And he'll do the right thing and make way for the new baby, you'll see.'

And here he is, looking older, bulkier, a bit unfamiliar, but it is David all right. And Liam. And Colleen between them. Mildred smiles. She was right. David would be back.

Colleen, forever the exulted one, throws herself at Mildred and puts so much pressure on her chest that it hurts. 'Mum! Thank God you're awake! You gave us such a fright!'

'Stop it! You'll smother me!' Her voice comes out weak and squeaky. Only now does she realise she is lying in bed, connected to a drip, with a big, annoying plaster on her arm holding a needle attached to her veins. She is groggy and very thirsty. She is old – much older than she thought. So is everyone in the room: David, Liam, Colleen and Sean. Of course, Sean! He brings her to the present.

'So you're back,' Mildred smiles at David. 'At long last!'

'He found you, Mum! If it wasn't for David, I dare not think,' Colleen attaches herself to David's sleeve. He looks uncomfortable and embarrassed.

'He could be the reason why you're here in the first place.'

Liam can be so unkind! She didn't bring him up to be like that. 'Shush, Liam!' she tells him. 'You shush!'

She remembers now: the dreadful pain in her chest, the fear in her heart. 'What was it,' she asks, 'heart attack?'

'David found you and called an ambulance. It's a good job I gave him my number, he called me first thing,' Colleen said.

'Never called me,' Liam mutters under his breath, but Mildred can hear that. Is he surprised that David wouldn't call him?

'I'm glad you came back, David. Come closer – let me take a look at you.' She attempts to raise herself on her pillows, but she has no strength, no feeling. She collapses back in the bed.

'Mum, don't move. You've just had surgery. Rest! That's what you must do. You gave us such a fright!'

Mildred is catching her breath whilst Colleen carries on. It's more a wheeze than a breath. Her body is a broken vessel, full of cracks and holes. Maybe Colleen is right – maybe she's lucky to be alive. Time to sort out a few things. 'I think... think you're right. I must rest a while.' Something is missing, she realises. She is helpless without it. 'Where's my rosary? Can someone bring me my rosary?'

'Will do.' It's Sean. She can trust Sean to do that. He's such a good lad!

She can rest now. Almost. 'Just a word with you, Liam, and then I want to sleep.'

Good! There's hope yet. She'll have to listen, she has no choice. She must have realised what a stubborn old fool she has been. She knows this is the end of the road: time to go to a nice, comfy home, time to leave the serious business to Liam. It won't take long to tie up the loose ends, to re-zone the farmland and get started with the planning permission. And then he will have Papariakas out of his hair. It's high time. Their association would sooner or later bring trouble. Papariakas is up to his eyes in dodgy deals – something is bound to catch up with him. But not with Liam – because Liam will be out of this mess.

'I'm glad you're all right, Mum. You gave us all a fright.' He sits on the edge of her bed, mindful not to disconnect the tubes that run across to the drip stand. He pats her hand – a very pale and bony hand, dried up. He wishes he was brave enough to kiss it. He loves this stubborn old fool. But he isn't one for displays of affection, wouldn't know how to go about it. His mobile squeals in the inner pocket of his jacket. Mother winces. 'It's nothing. It's only my phone.' He knows this offers her no consolation – she has no concept of mobile phones, and the fact that they can travel with you and make sudden noises in your pockets puts the fear of God in her heart. And Mother is as God-fearing as they come. He fishes out the phone. It's only Stella. He presses the red button to ignore the call. The squealing stops and Mother relaxes.

'You'll be rushing off, won't you?' she says.

'Nah, not yet,' he assures her, though deep inside he battles the urge to step outside the room and call Stella back. She never calls him for no reason. She never calls him, full stop. Why did she?

'We need to make plans, I need to make plans,' Mother says.

'Yes, I know. I've been telling you, haven't I? Don't worry – I've already made plans. It's a lovely residential home in Werton. You'll love it. It has huge grounds, three acres – I'm told it's like a farm. Beautiful gardens. As soon as the doctors give you a clean bill of health -'

'No, no, no...' Her voice may be weak, but her intentions are clear. Liam has to swallow back his frustration. 'No residential homes. No. I'll be going home. That's not what I want to talk about.'

'I can't let you go back there. It's too far for me. No one will look after you!'

'Grace will. And Sean. And now David...'

'No. I'm your son!' He is hurt. People might think Liam has no feelings, but they are wrong. He hides them away – he's good at that – but it hurts when his own mother mentions the names of three people above his. Especially David's. It hurts like hell. It feels like a betrayal. 'You can't go back there and rely on strangers for a glass of water. You must see that, you must understand that, or I'll have no choice. I'll get the capacity assessment going. Don't force me down that route.'

She is blinking. She doesn't understand a word. That just about proves his point.

'David is no stranger. He's your brother.'

'I don't want to talk about David, Mother. I want to talk about your well-being. David's been gone for nearly thirty years – I was here all that time, OK?' He is unable to conceal the irritation in his voice.

'He was gone because we had forced him out. Now that he's back, we have a chance to make it up to him.' When did she become so eloquent? So forceful?

'Mother, forget David. He's a big boy, can look after himself.'

'He'll be staying with me -'

'You'll be staying in a home.'

'And I've decided to do right by him, before it's too late. The farm, you see, it was your father's – that's David's father too. And Colleen's. It must go to you three, to all his children. In equal shares. When I'm gone. I'd better make a new will then, hadn't I? That's what I want to talk to you about. Getting a lawyer, getting it all sorted out. That is really pressing, that is...'

Liam is staring at his mother. His telephone has started

squealing again, but he has not energy or willpower to reach for it. So it goes on and on, grinding on his brain.

'Do you think you can sort it out for me?'

He is staring.

Having stopped, the mobile rings again.

'What's that noise? Can you hear it?'

Without thinking, Liam picks it up. It's Stella. 'What the fuck do you want!' he shouts into the phone. 'I'm in hospital with Mother! Give me a fucking break!' And he rings off without listening to her reply.

Half of Sexton's bloody Canning has now gathered outside Mother's room: Colleen, the farmhand, bloody David of course, and now Grace with her husband and some other old geezer from the village. It's like a bloody Christmas dinner party! Liam waves them all away like flies.

The old geezer appears to be the new parish priest. Liam recognises him by his dog collar and the expression of martyrdom on his face.

'Can I go in now and see Mildred?' the priest asks. 'I know she'd like a priest by her side.'

'She isn't dead yet!'

The priest looks horrified. Colleen does too. 'Liam, you know how important it is to Mum! You can't turn away a priest from her sickbed. She wouldn't like that.'

'She doesn't want to see anyone. She's asleep. Leave her alone.' He pushes by the priest and by Colleen, and doesn't even spare a glance at the rest of them. *Fuck them all!*

Stella is running towards him. What the hell does she want? He asks her exactly that across the echoing corridor. 'I've been trying to get hold of you – the police are in the office, with a search warrant, confiscating papers, packing everything in boxes... That's why I've been calling... What's wrong with your mum? Is she -'

'Why didn't you -' he starts and realises that what he is about to say won't make sense. She did try to tell him... He focuses his mind, clenches his fists. He can deal with it all. He is good at that. He just has to stay focused. One thing at a time. He brushes past Stella.

'What's wrong with your mum?' she repeats.

'Nothing. She's OK now.'

'She's had a heart attack.' Liam hears David speak. He'd forgotten about him. How could he forget about him?

'David? Is that you? Is it really you?' It is, Stella. Who else could it be? Only she can ask such an obvious question. Never mind, Liam reminds himself, one thing at a time. He has to handle the cops in the office first – before Dimitri gets wind of the raid. Then he'll deal with Mother. And David. And Stella. The whole fucking world damned to hell!

Dimitri Papariakas arrives armed to the teeth. He is accompanied by a tight-arsed lawyer, a female with the appearance of Mary's little lamb and the attitude of the big, bad wolf. It is only an interview, but it is enough to make Papariakas sweat. It is taking place simultaneously with the search of Cox Properties' premises. A totalitarian offensive on two fronts. The chap from the SFO is sitting quietly next to Gillian, letting her fire the questions at Papariakas. If something goes wrong, it will be on her head. Nothing new about that. She is the foot soldier at the frontline; he is the James Bond – sleek and detached, operating in the shadows. If push comes to shove he will disappear in a puff of white smoke and Gillian will take the flak.

'The value of the retirement homes you sold in Greece is incommensurate with the value of the properties the complainants here traded in for them. The complaints we've received indicate that many vulnerable elderly people had been duped into exchanging their properties for something... virtually worthless. Would you like to comment on that?'

Gillian looks him straight in the eye. Papariakas doesn't flinch. He is a big, flabby Jabba the Hutt of a man, the kind that is used to this game and knows how to bide his time. He puts on his best poker-face, and waits.

'My client acted in good faith,' retorts Mary's Little Lamb on his behalf. 'At the time of the transactions my client had every reason to believe that the respective values were comparable, and that the buyers, elderly or not, were in no way induced into contracting with my client. My client strongly objects to your flippant turn of phrase – no-one was *duped*. That's not how my client conducts business. The property market fluctuates – it's a common occurrence. My client cannot be held responsible for the subsequent change in circumstances, such as the economic crisis in Greece and the influx of Syrian refugees to the islands which no doubt has affected the real estate values on some of those islands. These are passing circumstances, but they do not invalidate the original transactions all parties entered into freely and in good faith.'

'Our independent advice indicates that at the time of those original transactions the properties that were traded-in had already been considerably undervalued.' Gillian won't be played for a fool. She has done her homework. 'In some cases the true value of those properties was understated by more than half by Cox Properties Real Estate Agents and Surveyors.'

'Why don't you take it up with Cox Properties then? Nothing to do with me,' Jabba the Hutt retorts in his distinct South African accent. His body shifts with slight discomfort in his chair.

'We are searching Cox Properties' offices as we speak,' Gillian tells him. She watches him carefully as she says that. A muscle twitches somewhere at the base of his jaw. It's a satisfying sight – Papariakas is nervous. She presses on. 'I put it to you that you have a direct financial interest in Cox Properties and that the value of the trade-in properties was deliberately understated so that undue advantage was taken of their owners for your benefit. In short, the property exchange transactions were based on fraud. That's where we come in.'

'Do you have any concrete evidence to back up your allegations?' Mary's Little Lamb comes to her client's rescue.

'We intend to produce it as soon as we go through the business accounts which are being seized and examined right now.'

'You intend?' Papariakas asks, his eyes bulging in sheer disbelief. 'The road to hell is paved with good intentions. If that's all you've got, I want to go now,' he is looking at his lawyer. 'I think I'm done here.'

The lawyer rises from her chair. 'Unless my client is charged with anything?'

'He's free to go,' the chap from the SFO suddenly regains his power of speech.

Liam is too late. He watches the cops carry boxes of paperwork out to a police van parked conspicuously in front of the shop. The Indian guy at the newsagents' across the road is glued to the window, watching as the scene unfolds. He has probably never seen so much action since he took on the premises last year. Robert Wilcock from Tiles for Life next door has come out to fish for information.

'What's that all about?' he asks.

'I'll be damned if I know. One big cock-up, is my guess,' Liam tells him with the bravura of the innocent. Inside, he is experiencing that sinking feeling that gives him the distinct impression of his guts hitting the floor. He is too late. His risky association with Dimitri has caught up with him.

As the police van rolls off the pavement, Liam's telephone rings. He gawps at the lit screen of his mobile with Dimitri's name splashed across it. He can't bring himself to answer it. His hand is too heavy to lift the damned thing to his ear.

'Aren't you gonna answer it?' Wilcock points at the mobile in Liam's hand. He looks concerned. 'You all right?'

'Yeah… if you don't count the fact that my mother is in hospital,' Liam feels compelled to explain himself.

'Heart attack.'

'I'm sorry to hear that.'

He nods. That feels better. He deserves sympathy. The sodding phone goes off again. He should smash it against the wall.

'It may be something important… The hospital?'

'Yeah… I'd better take it inside,' he tells Wilcock. 'See you later.'

'If you need anything…'

'Yeah, thanks.'

Pressing the green button is like pressing the trigger of a gun held to Liam's head. 'Dimitri, what's up?' He tries to sound casual. It could be an innocent call.

It isn't. 'Have they been, the cops? What have they taken?' Dimitri sounds surprisingly calm.

'Books, contracts, shedload of papers.'

'And?'

'Nothing incriminating, Dimitri. Trust me.'

'Trust you? You fucking joking.' He still sounds calm. His voice is low and steady, but it oozes menace. 'Tell me as it is. I need to know exactly what they have on me, precisely what they took away.'

'Nothing! I swear – nothing!' That much Liam is sure of. 'Do you think I'd keep any sensitive documents in the office? They've got nothing. Found nothing.' Sweat forms on his temples and under his arms. He has to hold it together. He is nearly there. He is convinced that he is on the right track – now more than ever. Getting Papariakas out of his life is his first priority. 'Look here, Dimitri, my mother's in hospital -'

'Should I give a shit?'

'You should, actually. She's going into a home – all has been arranged. Bear with me, all right? Give me time. It's only a matter of time. I'll get you your money – all of it.'

'Where do you keep them?'

'Keep what?'

'The papers. You said they found nothing in the office, so where are they?' Papariakas sounds as if he hasn't heard him, as if he doesn't care about his money. That's a first!

'The papers? Don't worry – I've got them all at home, safely tucked away where they'll never look. Never in the office. At home, yeah? Hear me? Relax, all right? Just trust me, yeah?'

'Yeah.'

Papariakas rings off. Liam tunes into the engaged signal to make sure the man is gone. It's like a lifeline. He has bought it! It's unbelievable! Papariakas is appeased – for now. Liam has time to act.

A team of financial experts from the SFO wades through the books and documents seized from Cox Properties. They have taken over the whole of the first floor of the police station, as well as some of the staff members. Erin has volunteered to help. Good on her – someone had to, and rather her than Gillian. They've been at it for several hours. The vending machine is out of coffee. Polystyrene cups litter the floor – Mrs Clunes won't be impressed. And yet nothing has been found, not the thinnest trail of crumbs leading from Cox to Papariakas. This cannot be. It's too tidy, too clean, too perfect. It can only mean one thing: the search isn't over; Liam Cox has stashed documentation pertaining to his dealings with Papariakas somewhere else – somewhere private. Probably at his house. It will take another search warrant and a much more convincing argument to get the magistrates' consent to invade the sanctity of the man's home. But it can be done – it has to be done. Gillian is sure there is a paper trail to be found and when she is sure, she won't give up: she will find it.

Detective Superintendent Scarfe bursts out of his office, looking efficacious. He is conspicuously present today, all day, not very much like him, but he needs to be seen while the SFO people are here. He wants to come across as the good shepherd of his flock, the type of boss who rolls up his sleeves and gets his hands dirty – the type of boss he is not. This could be a propitious moment to get the ball rolling on Liam Cox's house search.

'Sir!' Gillian calls out, 'May I have a word?'

He glances at her absent-mindedly and when her small frame is finally in focus, he points a finger at Gillian and barks, 'DI Marsh, a word!'

I asked first, Gillian feels like protesting, but instead, meekly as a sheep, she follows him to his office. The moment may still be here to mention that search warrant for Cox's house.

'Have you found anything?' Scarface sounds accusatory, and before Gillian has a chance to disappoint him, he jumps to his own conclusions. 'You'd better find something – anything! You understand? We must look like we acted on strong and reliable clues. There has to be something in those bloody boxes!'

Gillian manages to shake her head slowly from side to side and to form her lips into a shape that would normally, were she given a chance to speak, produce a decisive NO.

'You look again! Start from scratch! I want something on my desk by tomorrow morning.'

This is the right moment. 'Sir, I'm convinced we'll find something at Liam Cox's house. I've no doubt whatsoever – I'll stake my career on it-'

'I wouldn't toy with your career so flippantly if I was you, DI Marsh. I've just received a phone call *from the top*,' he shapes inverted commas in the air with his fingers, 'regarding your handling of Mr Papariakas. It wasn't most professional.'

Gillian scowls, trying to remember where exactly she drifted off course when interviewing the Greek. For her dear life, she can't remember.

'Let's just say that unsubstantiated allegations have been made by you and let's just say that you didn't make the best impression. But then you're not known for your sensitivity, are you DI Marsh?'

Gillian is inclined to agree.

'So let me remind you that Mr Papariakas is a respectable businessman until proved otherwise. He is a member of several trade guilds in the City, where he has invested heavily in a number of government schemes -'

'I thought he was a big-time crook, wanted in South Africa for -'

'You thought wrong. From now on, tread very carefully indeed, DI Marsh. If you find something, bring it directly to me.'

'If we could organise that search warrant for Cox's

home,' Gillian begins tentatively.

'We could not. We will not. Haven't you heard what I just said?'

She is out on her face and joins the SFO team on the floor, looking for something she knows isn't there. It is now an exercise in laying papers in boxes, rather than examining them. Having produced nothing, the search is over. It's ten past six. Most people have already gone home, including Erin. Gillian is left behind with all these glorified paper-pushers from the SFO who, in their thick spectacles and black ties, look much more important than they really are. Her heart jumps for joy when she sees Webber arrive, but she takes one look at him and remembers: Kate, the baby, the blood.

'How is Kate?' Gillian besieges him at his desk. He has slumped into his swivel chair, his long legs outstretched, his hands bound on his stomach. He doesn't look good and it isn't just tiredness. It is something else, something that goes much deeper.

'She's lost it.'

'Oh, I'm so sorry, Mark.' Gillian knows how that feels: the empty, stupefying sense of bereavement without a corpse to prove the loss. The disbelief that hangs in the air stubbornly because there is no dead body to make it final and definite. She has been there once, a long time ago, but every so often it grips her all over again. Occasionally, when she is tired or a bit down, it rewinds in her head back to the day when she tried to make sense of it the only way she knew how, by asking for a reason: *what did I do wrong? Why?*

'Nothing we could do.'

'You shouldn't be here.'

'Kate's asleep. They're keeping her in hospital – she's lost too much blood. Where else was I supposed to go?'

'Go home,' Gillian states the obvious. 'The girls need you.'

'My mum's taken them to her place. I can't face them. Don't know what to say to them. They were making plans for their little brother, making up names for him... How am I gonna tell them? I can't. Not today.'

'Still, you need to rest. You're no good hanging around here.'

'I need to keep busy.' He lifts himself in his chair, attempts to look interested. 'What's happening? Who are all these people?'

'SFO. They're packing up. We've found nothing on Papariakas, no connection to Cox Properties.'

His gaze is glossed over. He clearly doesn't have a clue what she is talking about.

'We're all going home, Mark. It's been a long day.'

'I can't...'

Gillian relents, 'Let's go for a drink, all right?'

She has lost count of the pints they have downed in quick succession between the time they arrived and the time when a bell rang to invite them for the last round of the night. It's now a few minutes past eleven and Webber's glass is empty and with no hope for a refill. Gillian is struggling with hers. It's not like her – historically she can drink any man under the table. But today Webber isn't any man.

They haven't said much to each other, either. Drinking in silence is when the beer tastes the best. You can focus on the creamy froth and the cold and bitter bite of the drink, cold and bitter like the frost which has a numbing effect on the senses. After a few pints the taste blends with the background. You could be drinking concentrated cat piss and wouldn't be able to tell the difference. That means that they've had at least six, seven pints.

'I was angry with her, when they told me she'd lost my son,' he mutters under his breath. His bloodshot eyes drift on and off Gillian's face. 'Can you believe that? What sort of a cold-blooded bastard am I?' He picks up Gillian's glass and drinks it. Slams it on the table. 'Another round?' he asks.

'That's it for today. Time to go home.'

The chill of the night breathes some life into them. Mark staggers off the pavement, into an empty street. Gillian pulls him back and hooks her arm over his, guiding him like you would a blind man. He trips over an empty beer can, kicks it and the effort of tottering on one foot sends him off balance. He slumps to his knees. Gillian is fighting against the bulk of his body on its downward trajectory.

'Come on, Mark, you can't stay here. Get your sorry arse up... Come on, let's go to my place. It's only round the corner. You can sleep it off at mine, go and pick up Kate from the hospital first thing in the morning. You need your beauty sleep.'

He allows himself to be heaved up and leans on Gillian like a dead weight. They stagger to her front door. The key... It is in the pocket of Gillian's jacket, which for some reason, isn't where it should be. Only now does she realise that she has left the pub without it. Wearing only a thin blouse she feels no cold. It's the alcohol – you could give her open-heart surgery and now she wouldn't feel a thing.

She wedges the weight of Mark's body into the doorway and, supporting him with one hand, searches for the spare key under the pot plant. Mark leans forward and doubles over her. She groans under his weight. 'Get off me! For God's sake, get hold of yourself!'

She recovers the spare key, flings Mark upwards and pins him to the wall with her knee. Something white and flimsy is hanging on the door. It's a note. Gillian pulls it off and tries to read it in the light of the street lamp. It says: *Waited till 10PM. Did you forget our date or is it a payback for lunch? Sean the Sheep XXX*

Gillian curses out loud and shoves Mark into the hallway. He retches and throws up. She steps gingerly around him, heading for the comfort of her own bed.

Liam is pacing the length of his study, wall to wall, unable to settle his emotions. He has been doing this for hours. The grandfather clock struck three o'clock a few minutes ago. The three gongs resonated through the room, kicking Liam in the head, bouncing off the book-lined walls and spilling onto the landing. He never hears the clock though it must invariably announce every hour of the day and night. He is acutely aware of it today – tonight – this morning. He heard the relentless midnight pounding three hours ago, followed by the one o'clock singular strike, then the couplet of two am, and now three dongs. The acoustics seem to intensify with every strike, rippling through his brain, scattering his thoughts so that he is forced to gather them together all over again.

He can't sleep. He hasn't even tried. There is no way he could close his eyes – his head would explode.

After the noise of the clock dies away, the silence becomes even more oppressive. The whole house seems wrapped in silence, suffocating on it. That reminds him that Esme is gone – another reason for his raging disquiet. Has she made it to Harare? What time did her plane leave – did she tell him the exact time? Didn't he ask her to let him know when she got there? He did. She is not there yet. Probably waiting somewhere in Dubai for a connecting flight. What has possessed her? Isn't life good enough here? Is she not comfortable, warm, fed, bloody-well loved!?

His pacing forces the wood panels to creak in the same spot, by the strongbox. The papers are there: his copy of the loan document in which Liam has signed his soul away to Papariakas, and their silent partnership deed stipulating Papariakas' lion's share of Cox Properties. Is it possible that the cops will come looking here? Should he relocate the documents? Or should he pay Papariakas off here and now? It isn't that much that he owes him – it's just the compound interest that is driving the debt up. He could pay it off – he should... He could get the money from the bank, secure the loan against the value of the farmland: bridging finance. It can be done and once it's done, Dimitri Papariakas will be a distant memory. Of course, Mother is in the way and her bloody outrageous antics with re-drafting her will have thrust Liam into a frenzy of activity. He can't let her ruin it all! She has to be contained, or...

She is his mother. Perhaps there is time. Dimitri seems to be appeased for now. He might even stay away for a while, keeping a low profile. That whole police hubbub might yet prove to be to Liam's advantage. If Dimitri lies low...

But he knows the bastard and he knows he won't leave much to chance. The cops have spooked him. He might become irrational and that is where Liam cannot anticipate his next move. Papariakas is unpredictable. That is as much as Liam has learned about him in those few rocky years of their association. He winces at the memories of recurring humiliations. He has to get out – now!

The first strike of four o'clock makes him jump.

He opens the strongbox, takes out the papers and spreads them on his desk. Right, he is going to work out how much he owes Papariakas. It all boils down to money. Everything, in the end, boils down to this one question: how much? He is pouring over the ledgers, the percentages, the dividends he has paid so far to the bastard. He doesn't hear the clock strike five. Or six.

The final figure isn't as daunting as he has thought. It can be done. He can raise that much against the land. He will.

With his mind cleared of the clutter and made up once and for all, Liam is in charge again. He looks at the clock – it's almost seven in the morning. He's been up all night. Never mind – the adrenaline will keep him going. He needs a shower, a good hearty breakfast. He's hungry, he realises. Shower first, breakfast second.

He will wake up Stella – get her to cook him scrambled eggs and bacon, some toast. He could do with a cup of strong coffee. Their bedroom is just across the landing.

'Stella!' he bellows, 'rise and shine! I need something to eat! Bloody starved!'

He has unbuttoned his shirt and is tearing it off his back as he enters the bedroom.

The bed hasn't been slept in.

Perhaps she got up early and made it up already? 'Stella, where the hell are you?'

His voice, like the ding-dongs of the clock, resonates through an empty house, rattling between the walls. Stella is not home. She never came home from the hospital.

The first strike is like pulling the lid from a pressure cooker. It brings relief. Liam's fist has landed on the bridge of David's nose, satisfyingly smashing David's head against the wall. It ricocheted against it, back at Liam's fist. He strikes again. And again, but David ducks the third blow and locks Liam in a wrestling vice, his ribs cracking. He binds his hands, aligns his forearms and rams his elbows into David's back. His grip on Liam's ribcage loosens.

Stella is screaming. She is naked, her hair wild, her face flushed, her lips swollen with sleep. Liam has found her asleep in David's arms, curled into him like a baby in its mother's womb. She never does that with Liam. She turns away from him and rolls to the far edge of the bed. And she is never naked – never as beautiful as she is now.

Unattainable.

David regains control and pushes him back. His nose is bleeding. He extends both his hands, palms out, towards Liam. 'Stop it,' he whizzes and spits blood.

'Stop it, Liam, please,' Stella echoes. She steps between them, facing Liam.

His first instinct is to cover her nakedness, protect her from lecherous eyes, and then hold her in his arms and make her realise that the choice she made all those years ago still stands. He wants her to bury her face in his chest and cry, let go of her betrayal – he will forgive her. He is craving to feel the warmth and the trepidation of her naked body. He wants to cry with her – God knows, he needs to bleed out those thwarted sobs.

He picks up her clothes from the floor, throws them at her. 'Get dressed. We're going home,' he tells her.

David pushes forward. 'She's staying.'

Liam charges at him. He'll kill him –

With her clothes bundled on her breasts, Stella stands between them. They will have to go through her before they kill each other.

'Let's go home. Please.'

'Stella, don't let him -'

'Let's go home and talk about it calmly. You can do this much for me... Did you know Esme has left? Gone to Zimbabwe.'

'I know.'

'Stella, don't let him -'

David doesn't seem able to move beyond that. He has always been a drifter, never knew how to put up a decent fight. No staying power. Liam passes him his handkerchief. 'You're bleeding. Clean yourself up.'

Stella is getting dressed. Liam is taking charge. What doesn't kill him will only make him stronger. 'Let's go home.'

In the car, Liam tells her, 'We don't need to talk about it - ever. It's all forgotten. I have been a crap husband of late – I probably deserved it. We need to start again. I've got a few things to sort out first, then we can take a holiday. Your choice. Spoil yourself rotten.'

She stares at him. He can feel her eyes fixed on him, not unlike David's wrestling lock on his ribcage a few minutes earlier. 'It's too late to talk.'

'I agree. Let's not. Let's -'

'I am leaving you.'

'We're both too emotional at the moment.' He has to play it down, even though he is frozen to the bone with the fear of losing her. 'Look, you haven't seen David for what? Nearly thirty years? Neither have I. It came as a shock to both of us when he turned up, just like that. We both overreacted. I'm sorry I hit him – I'll apologise to him if you want me to. But let's go home for now...'

'I just want to pick up my things.'

'You need to calm down. Think about it calmly.'

'I don't want to think. I'm tired.'

'Exactly. You need some rest, gain some perspective. Me too, believe me! I haven't slept all night wondering what happened to you! I was beside myself with worry.'

'I'm sorry. I haven't played it right. I should've told you I was leaving you.'

'No, you're not. You're tired.' He is relieved when she

averts her gaze towards the window on her side. It is as if she has conceded defeat. She is not challenging him. Her body language is submissive – like she said, she's tired. Liam doesn't want to contemplate her exulted night, her lovemaking with David, her feelings reaching such highs that she is exhausted now and out of steam, allowing him to take her home – *allowing him*, not choosing him.

His mobile rings. He has to take it – it's Dimitri. 'No follow-ups from the cops?'

'No, it's all quiet. They have nothing to go on.'

'So you keep telling me. The papers are at your place?'

'Yes, I told you. Look here, Dimitri, I think it's time we parted ways.' He needs to do it – do it now. His marriage is in tatters, his daughter is gone – he can't afford to be buried in business while his whole life is falling to pieces. 'I'll buy you out of your share. I've my ways -'

'I'll see you at your place – tonight. Be sure to be there.'

The phone goes silent. It seems like Papariakas is on the same page. They have to finalise matters and draw a line under their association. Tonight.

He pulls up in front of the house – his family home. It's worth saving. They're worth saving: his home and his family, wife and daughter. Nothing else matters. He opens the door for Stella, throws her fur over her shoulders. 'I've got a few things to sort out, OK? I must do it now – it can't wait. One last time, then I'm all yours. Go in, have a rest. Don't worry about anything.' She is walking slowly towards the house, staggering slightly as if drunk.

'I love you!' he shouts after her, but she doesn't even

141

look back.

Gillian drops Webber at the hospital. Wearing a crumpled old shirt, unshaven and still quite unsteady on his feet, he is a poor replica of his former self. For the fifth time he offers a grovelling apology for his vomit stuck in the cracks between the floorboards in Gillian's hallway. As he leans over her car window, Gillian can smell his breath – a mixture of beer fumes and stale vomit. She really should keep a spare toothbrush in the house.

'Take a few days off. I don't want to see you in the office. You need to be there for Kate. Take as much time as you need, I'll explain to Scarfe.'

'Thanks, Gillian.' He makes a mock salute and wanders off towards the revolving doors of the hospital's public entrance. His steps are heavy and reluctant. She watches him go in before she leaves.

The inside of her car stinks of Mark: his sweat, his vomit, the beer fumes and his misery. She wishes she could have done more for him, but what? What could she have done? Getting him drunk to drown his sorrows was the best she could achieve. Gillian's interpersonal skills are pitiful and the repertoire of her Good Samaritan deeds very limited. Getting drunk with Mark was her personal best. And it cost her a date for the evening!

She'll have to explain herself to Sean. She braves the morning traffic on her way to Nortonview Farm. It sits on the northernmost outskirts of Sexton's Canning, a couple of miles off the single carriageway to Grayston. It will be mission impossible to make it back to town by nine.

As she swerves onto the bumpy cobbled road leading

to the village, she is almost mowed into by a Toyota Hilux driven by Liam Cox with his ear to a mobile phone. He doesn't stop in the small lay-by on his side of the road and instead nearly forces Gillian's car into a ditch. Her wheel on the passenger side hits some invisible boulder and she sails up in the air, like a boy-racer on a joyride, cursing Liam Cox as her car touches down and the engine dies.

Brilliant! She's stuck in the middle of nowhere.

The car won't start. She has to abandon it squatting across the road, and she starts walking towards the farm, the word *fuck* gracing her lips along the way.

A man is leaning on the gate of Nortonview Farm. When he sees her, he runs towards her, fast at first, and then, as he begins to distinguish her features, he slows down and ultimately stops. He turns on his heel and sets back towards the farm. Gillian quickens her pace and soon catches up with the stranger. She hasn't seen him before. Could he be perhaps one of the farmhands? But he is wearing only a T-shirt and a pair of joggers – not quite the attire for a chilly March morning, not quite the milking man's uniform.

'Hi there!' she calls after him. 'Are you from Nortonview? I'm heading there!'

He stops, turns to face her. 'David Cox,' he says and waits for her to catch up with him.

'Oh! You're related to Liam Cox then? His brother? Just saw him drive off…' She is huffing as she draws level with him. 'In fact, it was him – well, his car – that drove me off the road a few hundred yards up that way,' she points back. Her car can be seen in all its glory, sprawled across the road. She outstretches her arm to the

143

man to shake his hand. 'DI Marsh... Good grief, what happened to your face?!' Only now can she see the gushing cut at the base of his forehead and the blood caked on his nose and swollen lips.

'Nothing. Family business.'

'No wonder he drove like a maniac!' She looks closely at his face. 'You need that seen to.'

'I'll be all right. Do you need help with that car of yours?'

'Well, yes... Well, no... I was on my way to see Sean... Mr Corrigan,' Gillian stammers and rolls her eyes at her own awkwardness. 'Police business.'

He raises an eyebrow as if to say her *police business* sounds almost as alarming as his *family business*. Is she that transparent?

'Nothing serious, really. I might as well talk to Mr Corrigan first, then yes, perhaps we could look at the car. Probably nothing serious.'

'Let me know when you want help with that... I'll be inside.'

As they part company and David Cox climbs the steps up to the house, Corky runs up to greet Gillian. It seems at least the dog has forgiven her and is happy to see her. He jumps on her, runs one circle around her and returns to his master. Sean is standing in the yard, wearing overalls and boots, his head cocked to one side, his hand guarding his eyes against the weak winter sun. For the benefit of David Cox, who may be lurking in the shadows of the porch, Gillian calls out, 'Mr Corrigan, may I have a brief word with you?'

'Any time, DI Marsh!' he responds.

Third time lucky, Gillian tells herself as she unpacks her shopping on the kitchen table: mince, pasta, Bolognese sauce, a bottle of rich and oaky – whatever that means - Bordeaux. She chops and fries the onions and garlic before going for a shower – onion and garlic smell delicious in a dish but revolting on your fingers and in your hair. Gillian wants to smell like a goddess, not like a French onion seller from *Allo, Allo!*

She smothers herself in body lotion and puts on what she considers daring lingerie: a matching set of see-through bra and thong, so skimpy and revealing that it is more a strip of cling-film than lace. It indeed clings to her skin by its sheer willpower. It is her nipples and her hips - more than anything else - that keep it in place. But Gillian likes it and the mere idea of Sean peeling it off sends her twitchy with excitement.

She browns the mince with the onions and garlic, wearing nothing but her clingy underwear. She doesn't possess an apron and wouldn't wish to splatter her little black number with cooking fat. A few burning droplets of hot oil pierce her skin as she tosses the meat in the frying pan. She wriggles and arches over the stove – thank God no one is here to witness her incompetence, no one but Fritz who watches her, impassionate and disdainful, from the window bench. Finally she pours the sauce into the saucepan and sets it on medium gas. It will need twenty minutes before it is ready – perfect timing! Sean is due to be here any minute and twenty minutes is what they need to settle at the dining table. Which is ready: cutlery laid out, candles burning, salad tossed to perfection. The water for the pasta is boiling. All under control.

Knock on the door. OK, he is five minutes early – it isn't quite seven o'clock. Gillian hasn't reckoned with that possibility. Her heart jumps to her throat. She cannot afford to make him wait at the door – she's done it once already! She races to the door and flings it open, a grand smile lifting her face and crumpling it into a network of happy wrinkles.

'WOW!' he says and stares at her, mouth gaping. It is here that she realises she forgot her little black number. It is still hanging on the door, clean and un-splattered with cooking oil, while Gillian is wearing nothing but some cling film and a few oily patches on her bare skin.

'I… I meant to wear a dress, I swear!'

'Don't bother on my account. I prefer you this way.' He pushes her in and shuts the door behind him with his foot due to the fact his hands are already all over her and his fingers are peeling the cling film off her skin, just like she has imagined they would. Except that she thought it would occur after dinner.

Too late. He sweeps her off her feet and carries her upstairs. She means to tell him to mind his head as the ceilings are very low – it's an old house, dating back to the times when people were half the size of him, but she is too engrossed melting into his strong hands and peering into his eyes. So he bumps his head on the landing, and swears – and that is damn sexy too.

She leads him to her bedroom: freshly made bed, crisp sheets, not quite silk, but will do. His dexterous fingers have disposed of her bra and her knickers, and are now circling her nipples, which cry out for more: to feel his skin pressing into them. 'Don't you think you're a bit overdressed?' she purrs into his ear and helps him undress, relishing the size of his engorged erection that grows under her touch. She wants him to lift her and impale her on it –

'Can you smell that?' he asks.

'The Bolognese sauce!' She races downstairs. He follows. As she flings the kitchen door open, the smoke and the burning odour envelopes them and a feline creature shoots out like a bullet. She grabs the first thing that comes to hand – her little black number from the door – and waves it over the gas hob. It catches fire. The smoke alarm screams, deafening her. She is already blinded by the smoke. Sean tears the burning dress from her hands and tosses it into the sink and opens the cold tap over it full blast like a fire extinguisher. The smoke alarm is going berserk. Gillian grabs the saucepan – it stabs her hands with blistering heat. She drops it – remnants of the sauce splash onto her. She is crying in pain. The smoke alarm screeches louder than her. Sean pushes the window open and the smoke begins to clear, revealing his naked torso in her kitchen window which overlooks the street. The smoke alarm must have alerted the entire neighbourhood. It is still going. She grabs a tea towel and brandishes it like a banner under the alarm. It stops. She drops her arms. 'Bloody hell…'

'Good Lord,' he pounces towards her. 'You're covered in blood!'

'Oh, that?' She is glancing at the red patches on her body. '*That* was our dinner!'

'Ah! It looks like I'll have to eat it off you.'

147

'Care for a sprinkle of Parmesan?'

They burst into laughter so hard that she stumbles and has to hold on to him to recover balance. They are close – skin on skin. He goes down on her, following the trail of Bolognese sauce across her thighs and stomach. 'You're one spicy lady,' he murmurs. Automatically, she opens her thighs -

The telephone rings in the hallway.

'Keep that thought,' she tells him and goes to answer it.

'Roaming Security here, madam. I believe you have a fire on the property. We're about to call the fire brigade -'

'NO! No, don't. It's nothing, it's under control. Thank you.' She hangs up. Last thing she needs is a bunch of firemen joining in the party. She wants Sean all to herself, and probably he wants the same thing. 'You can feast on me in the dining room, the kitchen is a bit messy,' she calls him from the hallway.

They move next door. He doesn't have any patience left in him and lays her on the table, pushing the salad bowl out of the way. The cutlery tumbles to the floor, clanking in protest. Fritz yodels and emerges from under the table, looking distinctly annoyed. He leaves the room in a huff.

The bloody telephone rings again. This time it's her mobile. It could be work. It is.

'Gillian, it's Erin. Hope I'm not interrupting anything. We've been called to an explosion at number 3 Blue Orchid Close, Liam Cox's house. I'm here already, the Emergency Services have arrived… It looks like we have casualties.'

'I'll be there in ten minutes.'

SEPARATING THE WHEAT FROM THE CHAFF

The place looks like a scene from the Blitz: rubble everywhere, gaping eyeholes of windows, roof caved in with supporting beams hanging down at unnatural angles like broken tree branches. Firemen are packing up their equipment though smoke is still rising from the ruin. Forensics have gone in tentatively, using large halogen lamps to light the scene. They are treading very carefully – the place is a death trap. Walls wobble and creak unsteadily, floors are torn, and gaps are filled with loose bricks. The staircase in what must have been a large square hallway ends abruptly as if it was sheared off with blunt scissors. The banister is swaying in the wind, threatening to collapse altogether.

Uniform have cordoned off the entire area. Two officers are guarding the main gate; a hundred yards beyond it the house lies dismembered. A group of onlookers have congregated outside the police tape: local residents, some still in their pyjamas, dressing gowns and slippers. DC Macfadyen is telling the paramedics to stay put. Tall and powerfully built, her high ponytail bouncing in the wind, she looks very much in charge.

'Doing a good job, Erin!' Gillian approaches her. By contrast, she looks small and rather insignificant, and therefore doesn't inspire the same confidence. 'What do we know so far?'

'Thank God you're here!' Erin rejoices. 'Not much yet. They finished putting out the fire half an hour ago or so, and have just given us the all-clear. Two bodies, both badly charred, have been found, but there may be more. Forensics are having a thorough sweep as we speak.'

'Who lives – lived here?'

Erin checks her black notebook. 'The Coxes – Liam and Stella Cox, with their daughter Esme.'

'*Our* Mr Cox?'

'Looks like it.'

'It can't be a coincidence.'

'We'll know soon enough, I hope.'

Gillian shakes her head. It isn't a coincidence – she doesn't believe in coincidences.

The first body is being carried out of the rubble. She stops the stretcher bearers and takes a peek. Black, contorted in extreme temperatures, the human remnants cannot be identified by sight alone. She covers the corpse and nods to the men to proceed. Another stretcher with another body bag follows hot on the heels of the first one – equally damaged beyond recognition. 'We can only presume it is the Coxes. Should we expect the third one – the daughter?'

'They're looking.'

'We'll have to notify the family.'

'The Family Liaison Officer went to Nortonview Farm

about quarter of an hour ago. It's a couple of miles up north, on the outskirts of town. That's where Liam Cox's mother lives.'

'I know, except that she isn't there. She's in hospital – heart attack. Any family on Stella Cox's side?'

'Family Liaison said her parents are both deceased. No other immediate family in the area. They're checking further afield, but that may take a while.'

'I think there's a brother, David, Liam's brother, living on the farm. Funny enough, I met him this morning. Small world…'

Gillian leaves Erin to carry on with the housekeeping and ventures to track down the leading firefighter. She finds him co-ordinating the post-operation tidy-up. He is in his mid-thirties, muscular, with a square jaw and a Nordic-blond short crop of hair, the male stripper prototype you would expect any minute to take off his Velcro-ed trousers and start thrusting his pelvis forward. Of course, that expectation could have something to do with Gillian's freshly aroused and still unfulfilled libido. She keeps it in check when identifying herself, 'DI Marsh. I'll be assuming the SIO's responsibilities for this incident.'

'Station Officer Palin.'

'Any light you can shed on the causes of this? Was it accidental or was it arson?'

'I can't be definite at this point.' He sits down on the step of one of his engines. Now he is on Gillian's eye level. He unzips his fireproof jacket; Gillian wonders if the trousers are coming off next. He wipes his forehead, leaving a black smudge on it. The trousers stay firmly on.

'It doesn't look like arson, more like an explosion. Gas explosion. Whether that was deliberate or not, I can't tell as yet. Based on my provisional inspection, I'd say there were two explosions – if you look at the damage to the entrance hall and the staircase, the fire occurred consequently. So no arson, I'd say. But that's just my provisional assessment, like I said.'

'But we can't eliminate foul play?'

'I wouldn't, no – not at this stage. I'll have more in my report.'

'When is that going to be available?'

'I'll need forty-eight hours.'

'Tomorrow then?'

'Forty-eight hours,' he repeats firmly. There is no way she can bend him to her will, but Scarface may invoke his fast-track channels to expedite matters.

She has donned a full bodysuit inclusive of a face mask since the fumes inside may still be toxic, and is treading over the rubble in search of Bobby Hughes from Forensics. He may be able to tell her more than the firefighters. He is collecting fragments of plastic scattered on the floor around the stairs, and bagging them each separately. Gillian trips over a blackened letterbox flap from the front door, or at least that's what it looks like.

'Careful, Marsh!' Bobby shouts at her. 'It's a crime scene!'

'You think it was deliberate?'

'Almost positive. Someone blew this place to smithereens!'

'Sure? The fireman was talking about a gas explosion.'

'That too. From that end,' he points in the direction of what must have been a kitchen going by the distorted double sink lying upside down in the company of a charred boiler. 'The fire would've claimed lots of evidence, I'm afraid. The bodies for one…'

'Just two?'

'Two for now.'

'Are you saying -' Gillian is prevented from finishing the question. A man, followed haplessly by two Uniform, is running towards the scene, clearly with every intention of breaking into it.

'Stella! Where is she? Stella!'

It's David Cox.

It takes a while to settle the poor man. The paramedics wrap him up in a thermal blanket and give him something hot to drink, possibly with a mild tranquiliser. He is in shock and is trembling, his complexion ghostly white. Just like this morning, Gillian observes, he is wearing only a T-shirt and joggers. His face doesn't look any better although he is no longer bleeding. The gash on his forehead bears a dark scab and his nose and left cheek look painfully swollen and discoloured. There is blood drying in his beard.

'Did you find her body?' he keeps asking and sooner or later someone will have to answer.

Gillian says, 'We found two bodies, but we can't tell whose bodies they are. They are yet to be identified.'

'It's Stella… I shouldn't have let him take her… It's her. I can identify her. Let me, please…'

'You couldn't, Mr Cox. The damage is… extensive.'

154

'What do you mean? Has she burned alive?!' His bloodshot eyes are pleading for a merciful assurance, one Gillian is unable to provide at this point. 'My God, I shouldn't have let her go with him! What have I done! Why did I let her go!' He drops the cup with his hot drink in it, and buries his face in his hands. His sobs shake his whole body.

Gillian picks up his cup, refills it from a flask, and waits patiently for him to look up. He doesn't. He's curled up inside the blanket, covering his face. Erin is talking to Bobby Hughes. The three fire engines are leaving the scene. The crowd outside parts to let them through. David Cox goes silent and still. Gillian puts her hand on the man's shoulder. 'Mr Cox? This morning, when I met you outside the farm, was that after Stella had left with her husband? I saw them on the road. Is that what you mean?'

He lifts his eyes, frowns at Gillian. 'Was that you? Yeah…' He takes the cup from her and drinks a small sip, scowling as he burns his lips. He tosses the rest of the drink on the grass. 'What was the question?'

'Did Stella spend the night with you? This morning, did she leave with Liam in his car?'

'She did. Because he came for her and wouldn't take no for an answer. She wanted to stay with me, but he wouldn't have it. He treats her like his possession. And I let her go with him. I assumed she'd come back, she made me think she would… I shouldn't have…'

'The black eye?' Gillian probes further. 'Did you have a fight with Liam?'

'A scuffle. He hit me.'

'It looks more serious than a scuffle. He must've made

155

you angry.'

His eyes round with disbelief. 'What? Angry enough to come and kill him? And Stella too? Is that what you're saying?'

'I'm only asking.'

'I wouldn't hesitate to kill the bastard, trust me, I wouldn't. But not Stella... I loved her, I came back for her... to save her from him.'

Why has Sean come back?

He visited her only this afternoon, shortly after Liam had left. He said he'd be picking her up tomorrow; he said not to worry, she'd be going home, she was being released. So why is he back? Truth be told, Mildred is a bit drowsy and would appreciate a bit of peace and quiet. Liam tired her out this morning, having her sign all those bank forms on all those dotted lines. That did her head in. He insisted she had to know what she was doing in case someone came and asked her. He kept explaining and she was trying very hard to comprehend what it was all about. She told him she understood everything just to get rid of him. And when, on his way out, he said he'd be taking her to that old people's home in Werton tomorrow, she told him outright to leave her alone and be off with himself. Oddly enough he listened, perhaps because he was in a hurry. He left but she was already unsettled and filled with anxiety, finding it hard to sleep. Until Sean came and told her not to worry. She could trust Sean. Thank God for Sean!

She has been nodding on and off since they gave her dinner, at seven it was. They say sleep is good for her so she gets as much of it as she can, little cat naps through the evening until she drops off for the night. Why have they woken her? Mildred struggles to stay focused.

Sean is here with that policewoman whose name Mildred cannot remember. All manner of trouble started when she turned up on Mildred's doorstep, going on about investigating Sean and fussing over accounts. Mildred thought that had been sorted out. What is Sean doing bringing this woman over here to her hospital bed in the middle of the night? It is already quarter to ten and Mildred has been asleep. Sleep is good for her, the nurses tell her. Why wake her? What is it that can't wait until tomorrow?

Sean sits on her bed and takes hold of her hand. He is squeezing it way too hard – it hurts – but she doesn't have the heart to tell him that. The policewoman speaks.

'Mildred, you may not remember me…'

'Oh, I do. You've been snooping around the farm, throwing all sort of accusations at Sean here. I just can't remember your name, that's all,' Mildred informs her and stops short of asking her why she is here. Something stops her, some sharp twist in her chest.

'I am DI Gillian Marsh.'

'I see, so you are.' Mildred wishes DI Gillian Marsh would go away. She doesn't like her being here and she doesn't like Sean squeezing her hand so hard. It hurts.

'I am afraid I've bad news for you.'

Mildred blinks at her. The sleep is all but gone now thanks to her. Alert, she notices that lovely young doctor who told her yesterday she had the constitution of an ox. He is also here by her bedside, hands in the pockets of his blue uniform, watching silently with a grave expression on his baby-boy face.

'There has been a gas explosion at your son's house, Liam's house. Two people have died and… we can't find your son or his wife Stella anywhere. Esme is also missing.'

'Esme is in Rhodesia, fighting poachers,' Mildred begins to wonder if Gillian Marsh has her facts right. Just because she can't find someone… People don't have to report to her, do they? Her brain whirs, as if it wanted to fend off something that is yet to come – something Mildred should not be hearing. 'Well, in that case we have even more reason to believe that those two people found dead are Liam and Stella. I'm very sorry.'

No, that's not true. She didn't hear that.

Sean leans over her and tries to put his arm around her, his other hand still clutching hers like a vice. It isn't very comfortable – his arm behind her back forces Mildred up, away from the warmth of the pillow. She is feeling cold, really cold. The young doctor has stepped forward and grabbed her wrist, his thumb pressed into her protruding blue veins, strained and taut like guitar strings. What are they all doing to her?

'What's this all about? Why is he man-handling me?' she asks Sean.

'You'll be all right, Mildred. The doctor's just checking your pulse.'

'This is not very comfortable, your arm behind me,' she musters the courage to tell Sean. Hastily, he removes his arm and lets her collapse back on her pillow. She needs air – she needs all these people to go away and let her breathe. She is trying to.

'I may have to ask you to leave,' the young doctor seems to read her mind. She is grateful to him. Her breathing is shallow, it's like the air doesn't have enough strength to get past her throat and into her lungs. It swells in her throat, making her retch. She overcomes that impulse and swallows the air. 'Pass me my rosary,' she frees her hand from Sean's grip and reaches out to her bedside table where earlier today he left the rosary for her. She feels around for it, her fingertips make a brief contact with the beads – the rosary tumbles to the floor with a clank. Sean doubles up to retrieve it and places it on the palm of her hand, closing her fingers over it. That's better! She still struggles to comprehend why they are here. What this Gillian Marsh is saying cannot be true. Didn't she once accuse Sean of stealing from Mildred – and that wasn't true either. 'What's she saying, Sean? You tell me. I don't know what she's saying…'

'Liam is dead. Gas exploded in his house. They're both dead – Liam and Stella. An accident…'

'You're lying.' God wouldn't do that to Mildred, wouldn't put that cross on her shoulders because she can't carry it. She is too weak – she's in hospital with a heart attack! Liam was here only this morning. What sort of talk is this? She is dreaming. It's a bad dream.

The rosary beads between her fingers feel real.

Sean doesn't lie. He never does.

The air fails to travel to her lungs. Like a fish out of water; her chest is compressed. There is no air. They've stolen all her air!

The young doctor stabs her with a needle. It may be

time to sleep. Sleep is good for her, so they tell her.

'Thanks for coming with me, most obliged.' Gillian's smile drowns in the shadows of her car. She hopes he can hear the gratitude in her voice even if he can't see it. 'It's always better if it comes from someone they know. Well, *better* is a relative word here. The poor woman! As they say, no mother should ever have to bury her own child. It's against nature.'

'I wouldn't let her endure that on her own. I'm grateful you included me in this.'

'I had no one else to come with me. David Cox was in no state to break the news to her. He's in shock himself – mainly because of Stella. They were lovers, did you know?'

'Yes, I knew. Poor Stella, just as she was finding her feet... I am sorry about her.' Sean is staring into the funnel of headlights sweeping through the blackness of the night. Gillian is driving. They are near the Poulston turn-off. She's contemplating whether she should drop him off at the farm, or whether... She is about to ask him when he says, 'I didn't know about them until this morning. Well, David only came back a few days ago – from Canada... There was something between them in the past – they just rekindled the old flames. This morning I found Stella in the house with David – went to check why the lights were on at the crack of dawn. I didn't realise she'd been staying with him – don't know for how long. She looked well settled in. David told me she was there to stay, they were together. I nodded. Not my place to ask any questions. They went back to bed... I thought she was

160

there all along, I didn't know she had gone back with Liam.'

'Not of her own free will, or so David claims. Apparently Liam came and dragged her back home.'

'I can believe that. That's very much his style.'

'They had a fist fight, Liam and David. Clearly no love lost between them.'

'Heat of the moment, I'd say. I wouldn't draw any conclusions from that. Just because a chap has a punch-up doesn't mean he's capable of killing...' He is looking at her. They are approaching Sexton's Canning and the turning to Nortonview Farm is only a couple of hundred yards away. She really should be offering to drop him off at the farm. She should be but she doesn't want to. Neither does he, it turns out, because he says, 'So, should we be going to yours and finishing what we started before we were so rudely interrupted?'

Their lovemaking is gentle and tender, with a touch of melancholy to it. It may be because of what happened, because of how jaded they both feel in the aftermath of that, particularly Sean – he is so devoted to Mildred that her pain is his pain. Gillian detects it in the slight tremble of his fingers as he caresses the skin at the back of her neck, before he turns her over, aroused and breathless with anticipation, and makes love to her, their hips pressed together, his eyes fixed on her face, savouring her every reaction, every moan, every twist of pleasure. He goes on for a while, prolonging the moment as far as his need allows, until he can hold back no longer. They collapse in a heap and tumble into the righteous sleep they both deserve.

Fritz joins them in the corner of the bed – his corner, which he won't relinquish for anyone.

'Mum, I'm home!' The front door is closed with a spectacular thud. It is that and Tara's cheery greeting that bring Gillian and Sean to an abrupt awakening and send them scuttling around the room in search of their clothes. Fritz watches them with a mixture of disdain and bemusement. *Oh, just wait for your daughter to find you in this state of moral disintegration,* his narrowed eyes seem to be saying. He is smiling the Cheshire cat smile. No, it's not a smile – it's a vicious smirk.

Tara's footsteps resonate on the wooden stairs. She is heading straight for Gillian's bedroom. Where the hell is her bra?! Too late for the bra – she pulls on a T-shirt and folds her arms across her breasts. At least Sean has found his trousers.

Tara bursts in without knocking.

'Oh, sorry! I... I didn't know you...' She flushes and backs off onto the landing, an expression of embarrassment and disgust etched into her poor little face. 'You could've told me!' she scolds her mother just as her back hits the banister and there is nowhere further to run.

'Um... oh... well,' Gillian is explaining as lucidly as she can under the circumstances.

'You knew I was coming today!'

'Did I?'

'Can he please get dressed? His zip is undone.' Tara averts her eyes.

'Oh, I am sorry,' Sean apologises. 'My zip seems to be

162

stuck.'

'This is Sean, by the way,' Gillian feels it's time for formal introductions. 'And this is my lovely daughter, Tara. Back from uni… for some reason or another?'

'Easter holiday, Mum! You knew I was coming. I texted you yesterday.'

'Oh well, yesterday, ha!' She now remembers Tara's text, which she had every intention of reading in full at some point. 'That was yesterday, and yesterday was one hell of a day, believe me!'

'It always is with you.'

'Nice to meet you,' Sean steps forward to seal the new acquaintance with a handshake. 'Sorry it's a bit unexpected.'

Tara snorts, but takes his hand. 'Hi,' she mumbles.

'That's sorted, then,' Gillian chirps away. 'Breakfast time! Who's for scrambled eggs on toast?'

'I must be off to milk the cows. Didn't realise the time!' Sean says, and Tara speaks at the same time: 'I've had breakfast. I'm full.' Gillian doesn't believe her. She still has many misgivings about Tara's diet, though looking at her, she surmises that the girl might have put on an ounce or two since they last saw each other at Christmas time. Every ounce matters, Gillian reminds herself, all those ounces add up to a pound and pounds will add up to a stone. She lives in hope.

'Are you coming back later?' she asks Sean. 'You two should really get to know each other.'

'If you will have me, and if Tara doesn't mind…' he looks pointedly in Tara's direction. Her imperceptible shrug and even less discernible nod give him encouragement. 'The same time as yesterday? I'll let you know if I can't make it. I was supposed to be bringing Mildred home today, but now… who knows they may keep her for a bit longer. I'll see how she's getting on.' He kisses Gillian, but because it is in front of her disgruntled daughter, it is only a kiss on the cheek.

Gillian relishes the moment and no, she doesn't mind telling him this, 'I told you so… Sir!'

His scarred lip twitches and she basks in her momentary glory before she goes on, 'I knew Papariakas was up to his eyes in Cox's business affairs, and I recall mentioning it to you, sir… Now my every instinct tells me he is behind the arson. It was intended to bury all the incriminating evidence Cox kept in his house. What better way than to blow it all up, together with Mr Cox himself. He can't talk now, can he?'

Scarface recovers some of his considerably wounded pride, enough to ask acridly, 'Do you have anything else to go on apart from your every instinct, DI Marsh? Something called *reasonable grounds*? Maybe even, dare I suggest it, a morsel of hard evidence?'

'The experts agree that it wasn't accidental. The gas explosion was preceded by another one somewhere in the hallway of the house, and that one could've only been deliberate. I don't have any formal report from the Fire Service or Forensics yet, but informally they both say the explosion in the hallway was the originating cause. We don't know what exactly it was – a petrol bomb or something similar, I guess, but we know enough to treat it as suspicious. So the second question is that of motive:

who had a motive?' Gillian glances at Detective Superintendent Scarfe with an air of superiority.

'I'm sure you already know, DI Marsh, and will enlighten me as soon as you're done with your dramatic pause.' Scarface is rapping on his desk: a rata-tat-tat of frustration.

'You see, when we found nothing at Cox Properties premises – nothing to link Liam Cox to Dimitri Papariakas, my first instinct,' Scarface rolls his eyes. He doesn't have to say it: Gillian knows what he means. He is sick and tired of her *instincts*. He wants *reasonable grounds*. She carries on, intent to provide just that, 'was to extend the search to Liam Cox's house. Any potentially compromising documentation would be kept away from prying eyes – what better place? As far as I could tell Cox Properties was only a vehicle for their dealings, to lend them a veneer of legality, but the real deal was done behind closed doors.'

'Remind me how we know there was a deal?'

'Liam Cox in his capacity as a property surveyor and real estate agent was tracking down elderly people with large houses on their hands; he would understate their value – seriously understate, but those people hadn't a clue about present day property values. Most of them haven't bought or sold a house since the sixties... A glossy brochure about a Greek retirement paradise was shoved under their noses with a simple deal – exchange one for another. Naturally the Greek homes had only a fraction of the value of the British homes, which were promptly sold at their market value and the profits split between Cox and Papariakas. Their erstwhile owners were shipped off to the Greek islands too quickly to realise they had been conned but were too ashamed to admit it to anyone.'

'That's your theory, I take it.'

'Not just a theory, sir. We have a number of complaints from family members of those duped into those transactions. The SFO felt they had enough to step in -'

'They stepped in because you started meddling in it and they *felt* you'd spooked Papariakas.' The satisfaction from pointing out this simple fact brings a healthy glow to Scarfe's cheeks.

'Whatever their reasons, sir, they had reasonable grounds to expect to find material evidence of profit-sharing between the two men. Since they didn't find it at the business premises, the only sensible thing was to extend the search to Cox's home. He apparently conducts – conducted - most of his business from there. That's when *you* stepped in and told me to pack it in.' Gillian duly notes the lightning crossing Scarfe's face and before it turns into full-blown thunder, she finishes on a conciliatory note, 'So would I have your permission, sir, to bring Mr Papariakas in for an interview under caution and can I have a warrant to search his house in Wensbury? What I mean is, can I pursue the bastard or is he still off-limits to me?'

This isn't just a house – it's a stately home. In a prime position, overlooking an idyllic bridge arching over the River Avon, it sits on an elevated river bank, fortified and inaccessible other than by an electric gate with an intercom. The house is of white stone, three storeys high with three rows of tall, airy rectangles of Edwardian windows – a residence that could easily house the entire population of a medium-size village.

Gillian and Erin are armed with four uniforms, and a search warrant obtained by Scarface on the back of a single phone call. She rings the intercom and lets Erin exchange the pleasantries and formal greetings with the residents, 'DC Macfadyen, DI Marsh. We have a warrant to search these premises. Mr Papariakas? Can you open the gate for us, please?'

'Mr Papariakas is not home.' It's a male voice and it sounds foreign.

'Open up, please.'

They go in.

Two shady – though vaguely familiar - characters are in occupation of the premises. They both look like they have seriously overdosed on steroids. One of them in particular seems to find it impossible to drop his arms or draw his legs together. He is an updated version of the Michelin Man. Those two aside, neither Mr nor Mrs Papariakas are at home. The good thing about it is that no one has the presence of mind to call the nasty lawyer Gillian had the misfortune of meeting once before, and the Uniforms are free to roam about and turn the place inside out. The bad thing is that it appears Papariakas has given Gillian the slip.

'So where are they?'

The less inflated man responds in halted English. 'Persa – Mrs Persefina Papariakas – gone to South Africa.'

167

'I see. Is Mr Papariakas there as well? When did they leave?'

'Only Mrs Papariakas. Mr Papariakas is joined her later.'

'Where is he, then?'

The man shrugs his shoulders to indicate that he is guessing. 'Business trip?'

'Where to?'

'I don' know. He doesn' say.'

'He only say he have business to do and then we all joined Persefina in South Africa.'

Gillian and Erin exchange knowing glances: looks like Papariakas is winding up his affairs and getting out of the picture, at least until the dust settles. The Michelin Man contradicts his counterpart: 'We go to South Africa every year for Easter. Lots family!'

'Visiting family in South Africa?'

'Every Christmas and every Easter, we go. Mrs Papariakas stay longer, Mr Papariakas come back for business, like I say.'

'Who are you? May I have your names, please? DC Macfadyen will need to take your full details for the record.'

'Christos Panayiotou,' the man points to the Michelin Man. 'My name Taki Georgianou.'

'And what is your… in what capacity are you here?'

They both gaze at her blankly.

'Do you work here? What are you doing here, in their home? Are you relations of Mr Papariakas? From Greece?'

'Yes, Greece,' the Michelin Man smiles, revealing

stained teeth.

'We cousins. For Persefina – Mrs Papariakas,' the other one says, and then adds on reflection, his turn of phrase surprisingly improved as if it has been rehearsed, 'We are Dimitri Papariakas' business associates.'

Gillian produces an appreciative nod. 'In that case you may be able to answer a few questions about your dealings with Mr Liam Cox. You've heard of Mr Cox, I assume, considering that you are Mr Papariakas' business associates...' But just as things start looking promising, Gillian hits a wall of silence for it turns out the two men have never heard of Liam Cox and have no idea of Mr Papariakas' connection to him. In other words they have caught up with her.

'I think I call our solicitor,' Taki informs her and reaches for the phone. The honeymoon is over.

The two of them are sitting by her bedside: David and Sean. David looks pale and worn out. His hair is a mess, his beard stained. In the bright light of the hospital ward, Mildred can appreciate that he has gone grey around the temples and on top of his head his hair is thin and lifeless. He looks like Reginald did when the illness first gripped him. He needs a good rest – she ought to tell him that – any good mother would, but somehow she can't bring words to her lips. She is tired, so tired that her lips feel wooden, as if she has been to a dentist and he has numbed her gums with injections. Her whole body is stiff; she can't lift her hand – it weighs a ton. Her brain isn't much better. It is hiding something from her, she knows that. It is filled with haze, like a smoke screen. She is too weary to venture beyond that. Her eyes are droopy. She doesn't want to be rude, but she wishes them gone so she can at last close her eyes and sleep.

David could do with some sleep, it occurs to her. His gaze is glazed over and absent. He is here in body but not in mind. And how did he get that blood on his beard? Has someone hurt him?

If she could speak she would tell him how sorry she is about everything that happened, but that there are things greater than love, like duty, righteousness and God's will. She was duty-bound to protect the unborn.

Poor, poor David! She will pray for him. A prayer will bring him release – if only he believed in it… She knows his pain intimately, but she doesn't want to remember hers. She must put his above hers, because hers she cannot bear. She pushes it out of her mind.

Thank God, Sean has a lot to say: trivial, meaningless facts that keep both her and David within the realm of sanity, because even though they can't reply, they're too polite not to listen to what Sean has to say. He means well – full of good intentions, that boy. He would love to take Mildred home today, but the doctors want to keep a close eye on her for another couple of days. So she'll stay for a bit longer. He, and David, will pick her up on Friday. Today is Tuesday, so two days from now make Friday. She'd be excused for forgetting what day it was, but that's what it is – it's Tuesday. She's doing really well, the doctors say – Sean thinks she should know that, because she mustn't give up. She is strong as an ox (the young doctor said the same thing; Sean must've got it from him). They want to monitor her progress for another two days, and then it's home-time. He goes on and on – droning. It's like a distant sound of bombers, coming closer and closer but never quite hitting the target. His words swirl around her, adding to the merciful smoke screen of that haze in her head which, in tandem, keep her pain at bay.

Colleen bursts in and makes quite a spectacle of herself. Everyone's looking at her, and in all fairness, she is something else! Like a big fancy bird – a peacock – she flies into the room, her purple cape fanning behind her, the look in her eyes wild and untamed. A runaway peacock.

'Oh, Mum! I'm so sorry! My God! I can't believe it! I'm so sorry! Mum?' She swoops on Mildred and hugs and kisses her, and presses her cheek against Mildred's, and sobs, and sobs, and sobs. It is a bit like an out of body experience for Mildred, for she watches her daughter's antics without feeling a thing. She can't allow herself to feel so she doesn't feel Colleen's kisses or her hugs, doesn't feel her daughter's arms around her. She's numb. It is an odd sensation, a paralysis. Mildred is incapable of returning any of those hugs and kisses.

'Is it true? Is it really true?' Colleen demands to know. 'I can't believe it! How did it happen?' And so Sean tells her about an accident, or is it an explosion? Yes, it is an explosion at Liam's home, and Liam is dead, and so is Stella. The police are working on it. What can they do? Can they turn it all round? Bring Liam back from the dead?

Liam is dead.

Colleen gazes at her mother with anguish, as if she's checking that Mildred herself is still alive. She is talking

171

through her. 'How is Mum taking it? It must be killing her?' she says, her voice dropping to a hardly audible level, but funny enough, unlike everything else, Mildred's ears are performing at their best. They bring it all home. A tear, her first tear, burns the back of her eye and bubbles up like acid, and then rolls into her gaping mouth. Mildred is drinking her chalice of penance. *My God... Oh Father, why have you forsaken me?* She wants to cry out, but she remembers that she can't speak so she swallows the tear.

You can't teach an old dog new tricks, Gillian doesn't have to remind herself of that. Guiltily, she is peering at her dining table freshly laden with Chinese takeaway containers, a trail of irrefutable evidence piled up against her. She is back to her old ways: cooking comes last. Always has, even after she had told herself to make an effort for Tara's sake, because – let's face it – her erratic eating habits have to come from somewhere. From someone: her mother. Gillian has only herself to blame.

She was late. The team meeting with Detective Superintendent Scarfe heading it couldn't be snubbed. She had to be there. Decisions had to be taken and they couldn't be taken without her. Gillian couldn't have that. It's her damned case! By the time she picked up her coat and was seen off the premises by the reproachful glare of Mrs Clunes, the shops were closed and the choice was rather straightforward: Chinese or nothing. So she ordered Chinese and wasted another twenty minutes waiting for it. When at last she arrived home, she found Sean and Tara sitting opposite each other at the two far ends of an empty table, standoffish like a pair of territorial tomcats.

Obviously the conversation hadn't been running smoothly. They both looked constipated with discomfort. Gillian unpacked the Chinese and they dug in, stabbing at the silence with chopsticks. Only Fritz was prepared to openly express his dissatisfaction by yodelling in a resentful crescendo, trapped on the window sill, watching Corky ruling supreme over *his* garden. Sean had brought Corky with the intention of introducing him into the lap of the family – big mistake but one Gillian wasn't going to point out, considering her own guilt-ridden conscience.

'We found enough to go on.' In a last-ditch attempt to justify herself, Gillian tells them about the search in minute detail, 'a loan agreement between Cox and Papariakas, eye-watering interest rates if you think of the rates we have today…'

'Five per cent?' Sean says.

'Ha!' Gillian raises her chopstick triumphantly. 'It was twenty-one per cent, an extortionate rate even by 2008 standards! Papariakas had Cox under his thumb. However you look at it, Papariakas controlled Cox Properties. It was a very elaborate scheme – it took our men a while to get to the bottom of it – like a pyramid of corporate shareholders, inter-dependent, all ultimately controlled personally by Papariakas. I don't think we uncovered everything, and they are still working on it… they'll be working on it through the night…'

She glances around the table to gauge their appreciation of the effort she has made to abandon it all and come home to them. She sees none of it. Sean is struggling with the chopsticks and Tara watches him with a bemused frown. She has hardly touched the food on her plate though, unlike Sean, she is proficient with chopsticks. 'Oh my, do you want a fork?' Gillian inquires.

'That'd be nice.' Sean looks relieved as Gillian presents a proper piece of cutlery from the drawer. 'You too?' she asks Tara, glaring pointedly at her full plate.

'No, thanks. I'm fine.'

'Something wrong with your food?' Asking this question makes her feel cold inside. Is she heading for a confrontation? Has she grown neurotic about Tara all over again? She promised her that she would trust her. She must stop treading on her toes. Leave her be. The girl has just got home!

'No, it's good, but I had a sandwich at seven. I was hungry.'

'That's great!' Gillian beams. She will take the sandwich answer in good faith, and this gives her a way out of the impasse. 'Yes, so as I was saying, we've got it! We got Papariakas stamped, sealed, but not quite delivered!'

'It's a bit reckless,' Tara says, 'that your guy would hang on to all that compromising documentation while he was so desperate to destroy it at the other bloke's house... That's a bit inconsistent, don't you think?' She is a clever girl, Gillian fills to the brim with pride.

'It crossed my mind,' Gillian agrees readily, 'but that's arrogance for you. I don't think he ever expected we'd dare to go and search his house. He's got all those sharp lawyers covering his rear at all times. Except now! He got out of town and we sneaked in during his absence. And now I'm obliged to follow the scent. We can't give him a moment to think, which-' Gillian falls silent. She will have to break it to them sooner or later.

'Which?'

'Which means that I'll have to go away for a while.' The words don't come easily. The guilt grows on her conscience like rapidly rising damp. Gillian screws her face into an apologetic scowl. 'I'm sorry, Tara angel - you just got here for Easter, and I've had great plans for us, all three of us... I was hoping you two would have a chance to get to know each other a bit; we could do a few fun things together – that's what I was counting on when I was planning this...' her eyes shift earnestly between Tara and Sean. She's such a crap liar! But what can she do? She has to soften the blow before she drops it on them: 'But I have to travel to South Africa. Short notice, I know! We have every reason to believe Papariakas has holed up in South Africa to weather the storm, and he's not coming back. There is no chance in hell he'll take the risk of walking right into our arms... He isn't stupid. He must know by now we will have seized the evidence. He knows that we know he had a motive to kill Cox. He won't be back of his own free will, and that means I have to go and find him there. It shouldn't take long. It won't! We know where he might be staying – he has relatives in Kwazulu-Natal... We're having an international warrant for his arrest wired to the South African authorities overnight. The sooner I go... Well, we must take him by surprise so he won't have the time to rehearse his lines and get his brief to cover his flanks. That's why I have to go now! Tomorrow, I mean... I'm leaving tomorrow.' She sighs and drops her chopsticks on her plate. She isn't hungry any more. An absentee mother, and now an absentee lover. No wonder her life is always on ice – never quite consummated in full. 'I'm sorry…'

'Brilliant!' Tara looks positively enraptured. Is she really this delighted to be rid of her mother? That hurts a little. Gillian would much prefer a touch of the old resentment in her daughter's tone.

'I didn't know it would make you this happy,' Gillian takes umbrage.

'No! You're so silly, Mum! I'm coming with you. I've been thinking for a while to go and see Dad, but I didn't want to leave you on your own. It's brilliant – we can both go! I'll give Dad a ring to let him know we're coming!' Tara pulls out a phone from some invisible pocket in the skinny jeans stuck to her skinny backside as if they were painted on it. She scrolls down her Contacts list. She puts the phone to her ear. 'It's ringing,' she announces, her face bright with excitement.

'I'm not sure it's such a good idea,' Gillian attempts to reason with her. Staying with Deon after all those years seems like the greatest, and most undeserved, pain in the neck she could bring upon him.

'Nonsense, Mum!' Tara is heading out of the room as she chimes a cheery, 'Hi Dad!' into her mobile. 'I hope you don't have any plans this week? Mum and I are coming tomorrow. I know! It's always unexpected with Mum, you know how she is!' Her laughter echoes from the stairwell.

Gillian looks at Sean. 'Tara's father lives in South Africa, did I tell you? It doesn't mean anything, but for Tara's sake I may as well… Nothing to do with my investigation, but I have to go. No one else can. Sorry…'

She bites her lip.

'It's not for ever,' he shrugs it off. 'You'll be back. Unless some lion has its way with you...'

'That's not very likely. Too gristly, me!' She perks up and kisses him across the table. She'll still have him tonight, and all the nights after she comes back home.

'I didn't know how to tell you but I won't be around that much in the weeks to come. I'll be spending every minute I can with Mildred. She's coming home on Friday, and she'll need me. I want to be there for her – I owe her this much. It looks like your trip suits all of us just fine.'

Gillian begins to feel very pleased with herself – she's done them both such a favour!

The commotion occasioned by the two stewardesses offering breakfast and a choice of tea or coffee brings Gillian back to the land of the living. As soon as she recovers her senses, she realises that her head rests on Tara's shoulder and a dribble of her saliva is making its way down to Tara's chest where it has created a small pool in her top pocket button. Gillian clenches her slack jaw and, discreetly, wipes her chin. With her one eye open, she notes that Tara is watching the newest James Bond movie, headphones hugging her ears. Gillian ascertains further that the stewardesses and their trolley are only three rows of seats away. She doesn't want Tara to know that she is awake. She doesn't want to be parted from her chest – it feels incredibly, soothingly good to be so close to her child that she can hear her heartbeat: para-boom, para-boom, para-boom... She hasn't been this close to her since Tara was a baby, and then the roles were reversed: it was Tara's head buried in her mother's chest and it was Tara's ear listening to her mother's heartbeat, drawing comfort, her lips gaping and dribbling down Gillian's cleavage. Good old days…

'Mum, wake up,' Tara breaks the spell. 'Smell the coffee!'

Over scrambled eggs which remind Gillian of silicone breast implants, due to their grey complexion and wobbliness, she ventures deeper into her daughter's life. She had a go at it last night while they were sitting in the heavily air-conditioned Dubai airport, waiting for their connection to Johannesburg, but she is hungry for more of Tara's jealously guarded secrets. They are more interesting than the scrambled eggs by some considerable margin! 'So… that new chap who moved in with you, what's his name?'

'Charlie.'

'Charlie, right. So, where does he sleep? There's four of you now in a three-bedroom flat – is that right?'

'Lauren's leaving in May, after her graduation.'

'And until then? Sleeping in the lounge, is he?'

'No, he isn't.' Tara is spreading her triangle of processed cheese over a cracker. This procedure seems to have totally absorbed her. She doesn't appear to be able to find a place for her plastic knife – she rearranges it on her tray several times, knocking a teaspoon to the floor in the process. 'Damn it! D'you have any room? I don't want half of this stuff!' She points to her tray and the disarray of napkins, salt, sugar and pepper sachets, transparent plastic lids and items of food which have mysteriously grown in size and are spilling out of their allocated spaces like rising dough. By comparison, Gillian's tray looks methodically organised: most of her food is gone and empty containers sit in a neat stack in the style and likeness of matryoshka dolls. 'Do you want my custard slice? I can't manage that as well as everything else.' Tara pushes her pudding box onto Gillian's pull-out table.

'I can swap your slice for my peach segments,' Gillian offers.

'No, thanks, but I could do with more coffee.' Tara waves her empty cup to the stewardess, miming the word *coffee* to her.

Gillian attacks the custard slice. It goes down nicely with the peaches – they complement each other really well. Tara receives her coffee refill and borrows Gillian's teaspoon to stir in the powdered milk. She drinks it with relish. 'I needed this coffee – my tongue feels like sandpaper.'

'Touch of jetlag... I always develop a headache on long-haul flights; can't shake it off for days.'

'Nothing Dad's Sauvignon Blanc won't be able to cure.'

'Wine is the last thing I'll need. Nah... a good-night's sleep in a horizontally oriented bed – that's what my old bones need! And a bath.' She is interrupted by the captain announcing in a crumbling voice that they are approaching O.R. Tambo International Airport, their estimated arrival time being 8:20 am local time, the temperature on the ground at 26 degrees Celsius denoting a pleasant start to a sunny late summer day.

Tara hangs herself on her father's neck, her feet dangling

above the floor. She is a tall girl but he is even taller. Gillian used to think of him as a galleon – big, wide-chested, and with sails rounded by the wind. He is still tall but no longer larger than life. Somewhere along the line the wind had been taken out of his sails, leaving him deflated and his wide frame sunken in. He has lost plenty of weight since she saw him last, but that was fifteen years ago. He is no longer thirty-four, he's now middle-aged. He doesn't spin Tara in a fit of joy; he stands her down on the floor and takes her into his arms. Over Tara's shoulder he peers at Gillian – smiles, and quickly returns his attention to his daughter. 'My God, you got skinny! No meat on the bone!' he comments.

'So did you!' Tara retaliates, and they are even, and hug again. If Gillian had said that to Tara, her head would have instantly been bitten off.

Gillian steps forward, hesitant as to what manner of greeting to proffer. Fifteen years ago they parted on bad terms, without a backward glance. But that was fifteen years ago. They have grown up since then, or rather grown out of resentment. She extends her hand to him. 'Thanks for having us both at such short notice. You're sure you want me around? Tara -'

He embraces her. It comes naturally to him, as if time and grievances have not passed between them and pushed them to the far ends of the earth. 'Of course! It'd be daft any other way. You can't be staying at a hotel while the two of us are sat over the *braai* on the farm on Easter Sunday!' His face is weather-beaten like it always was, but it is also drawn and sagging around the eyes. He's lost so much weight! It must have been recently since his clothes seem way too big for him and his trousers are hanging on his hips, looking like they belong to his older brother. Or a rapper. Or an older brother who's a rapper.

'Right! That's settled then. Let me grab your cases and then we can be on our way.'

He bundles Gillian into the back seat of his Land Rover while he and Tara sit arm in arm at the front, Tara chirping away, putting on a babyish Daddy's little girl voice Gillian has never heard before. They are chatting, their voices projecting forward, away from Gillian and soon she switches off, and lets those voices be swallowed by the hum of the engine. She leans on the bags next to her, her head flops and her heavy eyelids surrender to gravity. She makes an attempt to *inventorise* the facts of her case – she has arranged for a meeting with Andreas Botha, a retired detective who has had plenty of dealings with Dimitri Papariakas in the past; she's meeting him tomorrow and has questions to ask, but that's tomorrow. The safety of the back of the car sailing across the African plains, the draining warmth of the car interior, the awareness of Tara sitting within easy reach, inches away from her, next to her father – all of that sends Gillian to sleep. This trip is going to take five long hours.

Some hard, angular object in the bag digs into her ribcage on a curve of the motorway which Deon takes with his trademark bravura. Gillian shifts the weight of her body to find a better nesting spot, but everything seems to be bloody uncomfortable and her arm has gone to sleep. She, on the other hand, is now fully awake if slightly disoriented. She sits up, massages her arm to force the crawling ants out of it. She must have slept for a good two-three hours, for the increasingly rocky and uninhabited landscape outside the window reminds her less of the rolling plains of Transvaal and more of the ragged stretches of Natal. She winds down her window and warm, sultry air floods in. The speed of the car pushes the air into her nostrils in an attempt to throttle her. She closes the window. From behind the glass the sky is pale, distant and worn out with age. She remembers now how she used to love this place.

'And how's Charlie?' she hears Deon ask and she smirks under her breath – he doesn't know that Charlie is ancient history; he doesn't know he dumped poor Tara at the airport a year ago almost to the day, just as they arrived back home; he doesn't know, but Gillian does, because mothers know everything and distant fathers, don't. She may even tell him later today, when they have a chance to talk, that she holds that bloody, good-for-nothing Charlie Outhwaite responsible for Tara's battle with anorexia over the last year; she may have to tell him that Charlie Outhwaite is better left out in the cold – unmentionable. No one wants him back in the equation, stirring bad memories.

'Yeah, he's fine,' Tara says. 'Moved in with me last week. He says *hi*.'

'You must bring him with next time.'

'I will.'

Gillian isn't sure whether she is actually hearing this conversation or whether she is still dreaming. She sits up to attention, her whole body tenses. Are they talking about the same Charlie – Charlie Outhwaite, the little shit who broke her daughter's heart? It can't be, she tells herself, but then she remembers the mysterious Charlie who is now flatting with Tara and her friends, the same damned Charlie whose precise whereabouts around the flat remains veiled in obscurity! That could explain Tara's sudden preoccupation with cheese and crackers when Gillian inquired about the new sleeping arrangement in the flat. Fucking Charlie Outhwaite!

'Are you seriously back with that Outhwaite character?!' she bursts out from the back of the car. 'Please tell me I'm wrong!'

Tara turns to face her. She is smiling a silly, puppy-eyed smile of a woman doomed. 'That's why I *don't* tell you anything, Mum! You always make such a big deal out of everything. But if you really must know, then yes, we're back together,' she announces without losing her charmed smile. The pupils of her eyes are large and wet, and shiny, like she is high on something. She must be!

'But he dumped you last year! You were devastated!'

'Thanks for reminding me, Mum.' Tara turns away in anger. 'Can't tell her anything, honestly! She's impossible,' she informs her father.

'Yah, I know what you mean,' he nods.

Deon has sold some of his land and invested the profit to convert the rest into vineyards. It is odd to see a typical French countryside landscape in the heart of Natal –

'It is Kwazulu nowadays,' he tells her, 'Get used to it – that's what it's called now.'

'Yes, I know. Keep forgetting.' The name suits the place; the vineyards don't. Where are the stretches of

183

maize fields, leafy and tall, with their yellow kernel heads? Don't they eat mealie anymore?

'Course we do! Hortensia grows our own at the back of the house.'

'Hortensia is still with you?!'

'Where else should she be?'

And there is she – waddling out of the house: ageless, cuddly Hortensia in her immortal washed-out blue apron and a headdress of elaborate construction. Her face is grinning, wide and chubby, her whole body is toy-toying as she tumbles towards them with astonishing agility for someone of her stature. And age... How old is Hortensia?

'Madam Gillian, it been so long! I couldn't believe you coming, not till I saw you!' She opens her arms to draw Gillian into them. The warmth of her body could melt the entire Arctic Circle. She smells of cooking: spices and onions. She releases Gillian from her grip and turns to Tara. Her grin is as wide though there is a tear she needs to conceal so she wipes it off her round cheek with her thumb. 'And young Miss Tara! Is she growing or am I shrinking?' Her chuckling is as warm as her body.

Deon has taken their luggage out of the boot, one case in each hand. Hortensia charges at him, finger wagging, 'Oh no, you won't!' she scolds him. 'Put them cases down! I get Sunny to bring them in.' She scans the horizon with her hand shading her eyes. 'Where is he? Sunny! He never here when I need him. That boy needs seeing to. Sunny!'

A young man, wearing a guilty expression, emerges from a concrete outbuilding Gillian's never seen before. Hortensia clasps her hands in despair, 'He's been at the wine again! I'll give you a clip on the ear, boy!' She makes an attempt to deliver on her threat, but the boy ducks, and grins.

'I asked him to stick the labels on the bottles.' Deon comes to the boy's defence.

Hortensia shrugs, but looks appeased. She tells the boy in a regal voice, 'Take the cases to the house. Then go back to the labels, and don't you touch the wine!'

'I wasn't!'

As he is weighed down with the suitcases, she manages that clip on the ear this time, 'Don't talk back!'

Deon laughs. 'Sunny's Hortensia's grandson. From Botswana. Earning some money on the farm before he starts university next year.'

'Smart devil but needs a firm hand. He be studying for a doctor.' Hortensia watches her grandson as he moves ahead of them, laden with suitcases. Pride brings another tear to her eyes, and that tear too she wipes out with her thumb.

Unlike the fields, the house hasn't changed. The cold, polished stone floors feel exquisite underfoot. Gillian has left Tara and Deon frolicking in the pool with his two Irish wolfhounds watching over them. She is drawn indoors, curious to see how much she can remember of it. The memories flood back with every step. The grand piano still stands, dominant but silent, in the living room. Deon's mother used to play it, a tiny, frail woman in charge of this powerful instrument. It was a sight – and a sound – to remember. Now the lid is down and though it has been dusted and polished to perfection, it is obvious that no one has played it in years. Photographs have been arranged on top of the piano. Plenty of photos of Tara when she was a baby, then a toddler, and then the stream of images stops at the age of four when Gillian left and took Tara with her. She is looking at a picture with Tara in a conical birthday hat, the elastic cutting into her chubby chin, chocolate smeared around her lips and stuck between her teeth as she grins at the camera, wielding a yellow fluffy duck in her hand. Her fourth, and last, birthday on the farm. And then many years away...

A guilty sensation tingles in Gillian's fingertips as she puts the picture down. She has deprived Deon of watching his daughter grow, lose her milk teeth, learn to ride a bike, break her arm when she fell off the trampoline, wear that beautiful frilly dress to her prom. She never thought he would forgive her, but he seems to have done so. Thankfully. After the long break on Tara's curriculum vitae, she returned to her father last year and there are more photos to testify to that: Deon and Tara with the vineyard in the background and the cloudless sky bleached by the February sun. Last year Deon was still a big man, filled with *boerewors* and mealie to the brim. How did he lose all that weight?

Another picture catches her eye, and brings on a heavy sigh: it is that good-for-nothing, skin and bone Charlie Outhwaite, caught carrying Tara towards the pool, his red hair held by a Rambo-style bandana. Bloody Charlie Outhwaite! Gillian pushes the picture behind another one – out of sight, out of mind... The other picture is that of a young boy, dark-headed, dark-eyed, wearing a Spiderman outfit – it must be Deon's son from his second marriage. She knows so little about his life after their divorce. The boy is a spitting image of his father. There are no photos of his second wife; neither are there any of Gillian. Fair enough.

'Dinner is on the table and no one's ready!' Hortensia proclaims, irritation in her voice. 'It's no good eating cold pies!'

Gillian rejoices when Hortensia piles up food on Tara's plate and doesn't take *no, thank you!* for an answer. The pie is rich with gravy and huge chunks of beef. The mashed potatoes are as smooth as a baby's bottom. And naturally, she has served corn on the cob. 'That's a feast and a half,' Gillian beams.

'As we always do, but for Mister Deon.' She insists on calling him *mister* despite having been with him on the farm for over thirty years, being his house-keeper, child-minder, nurse and mother after his own mother died when he was a lad of eighteen.

'Why is Dad not having the same as us?' Tara inquires, indignant, and points at Deon's plate daintily holding a lean slice of grilled chicken and a few salad leaves. 'Can't I have what he's having?'

'No, you can't. You're young and healthy, and you need to add some meat to the bone,' Hortensia eyes Tara critically, 'but Mister Deon is not a well man. We've had a big scare, didn't we, Mister Deon?' He opens his mouth to speak, but she won't let him. 'Three months ago... No, I lie – four months now Mister Deon gave us a big fright with his heart attack and what not. Good thing I had Sunny to take us to hospital, or he'd be as good as dead.'

'Hortensia is exaggerating a bit -'

'Not one bit, no!' She fixes him with a steely glare. She means business. 'The doctors brought him back from the dead, if you must know. And they tell me he must lose all that fat on him, if he wants to live. All them arteries clogged up, all the way to the heart. Next week, straight after Easter, he be going for that *bypast craft* on his heart.' Her expression changes. It is tender now and anxious at the same time, as she puts his plate in front of him. 'So that's what he eats – healthy food, no fry-ups. I keep an eye on him.'

'Why didn't you tell me, Dad?'

'What's there to tell? I'm all right now.'

'He will be when that *bypast craft* is done on him. But-' Hortensia pauses, and unlike herself, is unable to finish the sentence. Her thumb is back in action wiping another stray tear. 'That's why I am so happy when he tells me you two coming. So happy!'

The guilt that has been ebbing and flowing in Gillian's fingertips washes over her from head to toe, and leaves her cold. Has she returned Tara to her father that tiny bit too late? Had he been missing her? Was he lonely? Did the thought that it was the end for him cross his mind four months ago – did he want a chance to say goodbye to his daughter? It wasn't Gillian's right to withhold Tara from him, and that's not even a question.

A LAMB TO THE SLAUGHTER

She must be in her cell: the walls are white and bare but for a large wooden cross hanging above the bed. The walls in her cell were also whitewashed and she also had a large wooden cross: dark wood, with a silver-plated figure of Jesus, blackened by time, growing into the wood and blending with it. The floor in her cell was made of stone tiles and when Mildred woke up with the first sound of the bell at sunrise, she would drop her feet to that floor and feel its electrifying cold travel to her brain to kick-start it, like a bucket of ice-cold water.

She sits up, her body tenses in memory of that old sensation, but when her feet make contact with the floor they are surprised at the warm touch of a woolly carpet. Mildred's brain doesn't quite spring into action like it used to. It is in fact a bit muddled up. She has to make sense of things – they aren't all as they should be. The carpet for one – where did it come from? Mother Superior doesn't believe in all those mod cons; they kill the spirit, she says. It looks like nobody listens to her anymore. Mildred surveys her cell. It has changed a lot while she was away. She remembers now – she has been in hospital, God knows how long. They must have decided to make it

189

more comfortable for her on her return. They fitted the new woolly carpet over the stone tiles. They even installed a radiator under the window – now, that's extravagant by any standards! What convent could spare the expense for such a pointless luxury as central heating?

No, this isn't Mildred's old cell. The window is large – they wouldn't have changed the window. What for? No, this is a different cell altogether. A modern cell. Apart from the carpet and the radiator, there is a digital radio-clock on her bedside table. It's showing nine fifteen in the morning. She is late for morning prayer! Instinctively, Mildred reaches for her rosary and kisses the cross with trembling lips. Mother Superior would have frowned at her for missing morning prayer – she was a stickler for discipline. But she is no longer around to exact punishment, Mildred realises this now. Mother Superior is long dead. This is the twenty-first century.

On the sideboard, plain and square, someone has placed photographs. It was very thoughtful of them. Mildred is reminded of her wedding day – she is standing next to Reginald, her head cocked gracefully towards his chest. She is only a small woman; her shoulders are lifted in a defensive pose, her bouquet held upright like a shield. She wasn't used to tailored dresses then, ones that cut into her waist and opened up around her bust to reveal her whiter than white cleavage. A nun's habit had been her shell since she had been sixteen, so when she put her wedding dress on, it was like being prised out of that shell and held out naked for the whole world to see. Thoughtfully Reginald had offered her his arm – without his support she would've folded in half and toppled to the floor. She managed to trip over the train of her own dress as she turned away from the altar and made her first step into her new married life. That had made a few guests chuckle. Mildred chuckles too. Now she can laugh, then she was mortified and in no mood for chuckles.

Photographs of Liam and Colleen stand in a double frame, both taken at their First Communion. Liam looks a proper little man in his black suit with a white bow tie. Colleen is the Lord's little angel in her white tulle dress and lace gloves. Her blonde ringlets had given her plenty of trouble; Mildred remembers like it was only yesterday. Colleen had to sleep with rollers in her hair, fixed so tightly that the poor child woke up with a raging headache. *In the name of beauty,* Mildred said, but Colleen still cried and her little face was crestfallen. It shows in the photograph despite Mr Smith's efforts to distract her with a fancy doll. Good old Mr Smith – he took these pictures in his very prestigious studio in Sexton's Canning High Street. Even Liam's wedding photo. By that time Mr Smith was a grey old man, well into his seventies, but he loved his job. He used to say it was art, like painting or making sculptures. And it definitely was – not everybody would know how to position Stella for the camera so that her bump wouldn't show. He is dead now and his photographic studio is long gone. Esme's school photo with her two front teeth missing – that wasn't Mr Smith's work. He would've made her close her mouth and smile without showing the gap.

There are no more photos to look at. Mildred's attention drifts to the window. It's raining. Raindrops tap on the glass. Rivulets of rainwater roll down the windowpane. Mildred follows their paths with some interest. They don't travel in perfectly straight lines. They wriggle and stray; sometimes they merge, sometimes they part company. The view outside the window is fuzzy. Mildred wonders what's up there, beyond the sheet of water. The children loved to play in puddles outside on a rainy day like this. They would go out with their bare feet, and splash, and scream their heads off. On a warm spring day.

A knock on the door puts a stop to Mildred's memories, like someone pulling the gramophone needle off the vinyl record to stop the music. An unfamiliar face addresses Mildred by her first name. 'Someone here to see you, Mildred. You have your first visitors – how good is that?'

'Who are you?' Mildred asks, but doesn't listen to the woman's reply; Sean and Colleen burst into her cell. Colleen – the exulted, loud Colleen, smelling of strong perfume and cold air – squeezes the living daylights out of Mildred's lungs. 'Oh, Mum, I'm sorry you had to go through this! There was a big mix-up. Liam had organised everything before he... before... And –with everything going on – I forgot to cancel this place! Of course we're taking you home! You don't have to stay here a minute longer!'

Mildred blinks. She has been quite content sitting here in her quiet cell, smiling to old photographs and chuckling at old memories. She was at peace, for five minutes, until Colleen opened the door and let in the cold air. And things Mildred prefers not to remember. Too late now; what's done is done. Mildred cringes, but puts on a brave face. 'Stop you squeezing me. You'll break my ribs!'

Sean has found the photographs. He is picking them up one by one, and without looking at them – really looking at them – puts them in a cardboard box which has STORAGE printed on one side in big letters. 'Careful so you don't break the glass,' Mildred tells him.

'I'll be careful, don't worry.' His gaze is searching as if he's trying to read her mind. *Don't do that,* Mildred feels like saying, *let sleeping dogs lie.*

It is dreadfully cold in the house even though the heating is on, or so they tell her. Mildred doesn't believe it. She is shivering all over. Her fingers are curled up seeking warmth in the bundles of her fists. Truth be told, she'd much rather be inside her cosy white cell than here. There she would have her peace and her prayers for company – the only company she cares for right now. Here she is crowded with all these people. They mean well but they keep scratching at her scabs and don't understand that scabs are best left alone; otherwise they won't heal.

Sean has brought in the priest. It isn't Father O'Leary – not that Father O'Leary would make any difference, but at least Mildred would be more at ease. This is the new priest, new by Mildred's standards. She used to know his name, but forgot it. What does it matter anyway? She makes no effort to recall it. He's plump and balding on top of his head – just as a priest should be. He does, and says, all the right things, just as a priest should do, but Mildred isn't listening very well. She is a sheep that strayed away from his flock and she doesn't particularly want to be found. Thankfully, Grace is here to entertain the priest with conversation and a cup of tea with biscuits. Shop biscuits, not Grace's own. Mildred won't touch them, but the priest has been slowly making his way through them, with some help from Colleen. Colleen has taken time off school to stay with Mildred until the funeral, and then, she says, it's the Easter holiday so that will be another two weeks. What happens after that she does not say. But Sean is here. Sean will always be here. As for David, Mildred doesn't know and she doesn't ask. He probably doesn't know himself. He is standing with his back to them, looking out of the window at the rain. Sinfully, Mildred wishes he were Liam. It's a sin she will not confess.

'It'll be a closed casket, for obvious reasons,' the priest says.

'Oh, yes!' Grace concurs. 'Goes without saying!' *So why say it?* Mildred wonders. Scab-picking, that's what it is.

'Would anyone be willing to do the Readings?'

'I'll do one,' Colleen says bravely. 'And you, David, would you do the other one?'

'Count me out,' David says to the window. He doesn't even look back. He never liked Liam – why should he start now? *Out of respect for the dead,* Mildred admonishes him, but only in her head.

'I'll do the other Reading, no problem.' It's Sean. He always steps in to save the day. He's a good man, Sean is. He means well. All that rumpus he has created bringing her back here from that nursing home! Though frankly, Mildred would've much rather stayed there, like the olden days, in her small white cell.

'Mum, drink your tea. Just one sip for me.' *Where did Colleen get that tone from?* They do say that old people regress into their childhood the older they get, but Mildred isn't there yet, she doesn't get any comfort from being spoken to like that. She has lost her son, not her marbles. She ignores Colleen on purpose even though she was just thinking of having her tea, now that it has cooled down a bit. She was thinking it might warm her up a bit. It is dreadfully cold in this house.

'As soon as they return Liam's remains, I'll confirm the date for the service. I've pencilled it in for next Tuesday. I could squeeze it in on Wednesday at a push. Thursday may be harder. I'm doing confessions all day – in Sexton's Canning and then at St John the Baptist's in Horseacre. Their parish priest has taken ill; he's in hospital with a stroke.'

'Didn't know that,' Grace informs everyone. 'Such a nice man. But old. Age is a cruel master. How old is he?'

'Going on eighty. Should've retired years ago, but he isn't the type to give up the ghost.'

'I'll be in touch, Father,' Sean tries to bring the conversation on track, 'as soon as the police release the body.'

Mildred makes a strange noise. It's not a squeal, it's not a wheeze – it's something in between. It has sneaked into her breath. She didn't know she could make noises like that. The priest takes hold of her hand, pats it. 'You must be strong, Mildred. God had his reasons to take Liam. He's in a better place now. Pray for him. Prayer is all he needs at this time.' He says all the right things, this new priest. His gaze is earnest and soulful. Mildred does as she is told – she unfurls her fists and prays, but her fingers, stiffened with the cold, struggle to take hold of the rosary beads.

Andreas Botha is a man with a crumpled face and concave posture that once upon a time may have been compelling and authoritative. He has long arms, a long torso and pinched lips. His thick glasses belie the size of his eyes – make them tiny, like Piglet's beady eyes. He strikes Gillian as a canny man, someone who has seen it all and knows what to make of it.

'Thank you for your help,' Gillian shakes his hand and sits down in a chair he has pointed out to her.

'It's the least I can do. Quite excited, actually, to hear what has become of my *old friend*, Dimitri.' His accent is thick with Afrikaner's guttural undertones. 'Help yourself to the cake.'

'Please do,' his wife chirps in. She is wearing a broad, delighted smile, almost rubbing her hands with glee at the prospect of someone trying her homemade strawberry sponge cake. She has brought tea in a beautiful Royal Albert tea service, one the Queen wouldn't be ashamed of. For a fleeting moment Gillian feels like she has travelled back in time to early Fifties rural England. She won't say no to the cake. It's moist and fluffy; the strawberries are bursting with flavour.

'It's delicious!'

Mrs Botha beams; her cheeks flush bright pink. 'Have another piece, why don't you?'

Gillian doesn't have to be asked twice. She obliges.

She is a vulture when it comes to food. She could polish off this entire cake in half a minute, given half a chance. It's an ability she has developed in the line of duty. You never know when your next meal will come when you're in the middle of an investigation, so you have to grab what you can on the go. She hopes her greed doesn't become too obvious as she stuffs her face with another mouthful.

'I've fished out Papariakas's records, not that I need any notes,' Andreas Botha informs her. 'We've been very closely acquainted in our time.'

'Anything you can tell me about his modus operandi,' Gillian manages to mumble with her mouth full.

'He started an honest man – a small Greek tavern in Durban, family-run. It was his life. It went up in smoke. Arson. There was an extortion racket in Durban at the time – an Italian mafia, you could say. They offered small businesses so-called *protection* for a fee. Papariakas refused to pay. They taught him a lesson. Unbeknown to them, Papariakas is a fast learner. In no time he'd become the Godfather of the Greek mafia in his own right. We had a gang war going on for several years, and at the end of it Papariakas and his bunch were the ones left standing. By that time, he had built an empire – on the surface it was a franchise of Greek, and funnily enough, Italian restaurants and takeaways; beneath the surface, it was an elaborate money laundering and extortion operation.'

'You mentioned arson. This is exactly what happened in the case I'm investigating back in the UK. It fits.'

Botha slowly shakes his head. 'No, Papariakas doesn't do arson. Like I said, it was done to him, but arson isn't his style.'

'How can you be sure?'

'I followed the man's scent for ten years, when he operated here, on my patch. I know his methods. You can't prove anything with Dimitri. Nothing sticks. He's got the best lawyers, but I know his *modus operandi*, as you've put it. Arson isn't his way of doing business. Knee-capping, beatings, kidnap, even shooting people dead, but never arson. Bad memories for him, I gather. Too much heat...' Botha chuckles at his own half-hearted joke.

'Dreadful business!' Mrs Botha shivers and claps her hands over her bare shoulders. 'I never liked Andreas's job - glad it's behind us. Another cup of tea to wash down the cake?' She hovers over Gillian's vintage tea cup with her vintage tea pot.

'Yes, thank you!' Gillian tries to smile at her appreciatively, but finds the woman a nuisance. Once there is business at hand, cakes and tea – not to mention intrusive hostesses – need to back off. Absent-mindedly she throws several lumps of sugar in her cup without counting. Mrs Botha stares at her in horror. Gillian's attention is on Andreas. 'I wonder if he could diversify into arson... It'd really fit my case. He had every reason to get rid of his silent business partner, together with the evidence the man was bound to be hoarding at his house. Papariakas blew the whole house, including his erstwhile partner and his wife, sky high. And now he's hiding -'

'No, no...' Andreas Botha keeps shaking his head, now with more conviction. 'Dimitri wouldn't have dirtied his hands. He has people to do it for him, and he would have a cast-iron alibi for the time of the incident – he wouldn't have to run and hide. How do you think he got away with all his antics over here? Even the best lawyer wouldn't have saved his skin if there was a shred of evidence pointing in his direction. Dimitri knows how to use other people to do his deeds. I tell you, he wouldn't need to go into hiding. You've got the wrong perpetrator for your arson.'

'Even if it was to destroy evidence?'

'Dimitri Papariakas would've simply taken it from the man in question and destroyed it in his own time. Why blow up the whole house? No, not his style. I'm telling you, you've got the wrong man.'

The place is a Little Greece, a parody of what a typical Greek house on the coast of the Aegean Sea would look like: thick, whitewashed walls, small windows with blue shutters, a flat roof doubling as a balcony – everything as it should be, only bloated out of size. Aunts, uncles and a multitude of twice-removed cousins are making enough noise to bring forward the resurrection of all the family dead. The Michelin Man, Christos, and his more eloquent version, Taki, are also here, adding to the vibe of homeliness.

'We meet again!' Gillian grins as she approaches the front step, but neither of them reciprocates her cordiality. Taki stares, definitely taken aback to see Gillian in this remote corner of the Southern Hemisphere. Christos positively scowls, which after all, is a form of facial expression that renders him more human than his steroid-packed body would imply. Gillian is undeterred by their hostility. 'Glad to see you again. Could you please take me to Mr Papariakas – police business, I have a warrant for his arrest.'

A woman steps out from the dark interior behind the two bouncers. She says something in Greek. It sounds like a question. Taki responds, and all Gillian understands is her name: Marsh. She's impressed he remembered it. The woman pushes forward. She is a Mediterranean beauty: thick black hair weighing down on her bronzed, round shoulders, an ample bosom bursting out of a tight top and voluptuous hips moving with a fluidity that could hypnotise a man. She faces Gillian on the step and only now does Gillian recognise the anxiety in her eyes. 'Have you found my husband?'

Either she is an excellent actress, or indeed she hasn't got a clue about Dimitri's whereabouts, and it frightens her. Gillian can't make up her mind. 'I thought I'd find him here with you,' she says. 'I was told he was joining you here.'

'He isn't here! Can you see him anywhere?' A hint of hysteria sneaks into her voice as she sweeps her arms over the backdrop of the house and garden. 'He hasn't arrived. He should be here... should've come three days ago! It isn't like Dimitri!' She bites her cherry-red lips. 'Does his disappearance have something to do with you?'

'Can we sit down somewhere private, and talk?'

'Has something happened to Dimitri? My God, something *has* happened! Tell me! Tell me what you've done to my husband!' she screams, her voice travelling up an octave, and suddenly the rumpus of Greek conversation on the roof balcony stops; they are all looking down at Gillian, an expectation of an answer in their stony silence.

'Can we sit down somewhere?' Gillian repeats, but that isn't what they all want to hear.

'Where is he? Where is my husband!' That's what they want to know!

'I'd like to know that too,' Gillian snaps. She refuses to be the one under interrogation here. If the woman won't sit down then let her hear it standing up. 'I'm looking for your husband in connection with a double homicide. Two people are dead as a result of arson – Mr Liam Cox, and his wife, Stella Cox. Do you know them? Your husband has had business dealings with Mr Cox. We have reasons to believe -'

'Liam? Liam and Stella?' Persa Papariakas interrupts. 'What are you saying? What arson? Are they dead? Where is Dimitri?' Is this part of some elaborate act? The woman goes weak in her knees, stumbles and is caught by the Michelin Man just before she slumps to the ground.

'Can we sit down *somewhere*!' Gillian insists.

They lead her inside the house, into the kitchen. It's a huge room, a culinary armoury filled to the brim with pots and crockery. Whoever lives here treats cooking with all the seriousness it deserves, like a military manoeuvre. Persa Papariakas is seated at a table and given a glass of water. Gillian isn't offered one. She waits patiently for the woman to come to her senses. Is it really an act? It probably is – so over the top! The twice-removed cousins from the roof balcony have poured into the kitchen, crowding over Mrs Papariakas. What a performance!

'This is a police investigation,' Gillian says it slowly

and firmly. 'I travelled this far to speak to your husband about his relationships with Mr Cox and his whereabouts on the evening of Tuesday last week. May I please speak to your husband?'

'He not here!' Taki tells her while Persa Papariakas gazes at her without comprehension. 'We do not know where is Mr Papariakas, OK?'

'OK... Tell him I need to speak to him, urgently – as soon as you see him. He must present himself at Sexton's Canning police station. There's a warrant out for his arrest.'

'For what?' asks the ever sharp Taki.

'You must find my husband,' Persa Papariakas speaks in a small, plaintive voice. 'He was going to see Liam on Tuesday, he was... But he wouldn't... I mean, arson! It's awful. Dimitri would never... We were good friends, Liam and Stella, and us...'

'Were you aware of their business dealings?'

'No. Dimitri doesn't involve me in his business, and I don't want to know... But he said he'd be joining us here on Friday. I haven't heard from him. I don't know where he is. You must find him.'

'As soon as he gets in touch, please let us know.' Gillian is wasting her time. Even if he is hiding somewhere in the depths of this house, he won't come out and hand himself in. She has to find a way to smoke him out. It is such a shame she is way outside her jurisdiction and all she can hope for is Dimitri's goodwill, a very rare commodity indeed.

Tara and Deon went to the Drakensberg for a couple of

days to do some father-daughter bonding on horseback. They will be back tomorrow so for now Gillian is in sole charge of the farm, with Hortensia hovering in the background. Sitting in the rocking chair on the veranda, her legs stretched on the banister, gazing at the large red ring of sun sinking on the horizon, Gillian remembers how this place was once home. It still feels right. It is ancient and primeval. It is endless; it could never oppress – it allows room to breathe, more room than her mind can embrace. It exists on a different plane, way above her earthly concerns. It puts everything into perspective and makes it all seem utterly pointless and insignificant, like finding Dimitri Papariakas... Even if he's found, the course of events will remain unaltered: his lawyers will get him out on technicalities, two people will still be dead, a mother would have lost her son and another mother would have lost her daughter.

The sun dips quickly into the depths of the horizon and darkness fills the vacuum it has left behind. Night descends unexpectedly, like a raid. Gillian could easily fall back into this rhythm of life. Perhaps she could take redundancy, pack up and return – leave the rat race behind. It's comforting to know that she could do that, just like that, any time she wanted. It's good to know she has something to fall back on, but she won't do it, not yet, not for a while, maybe never. But it's good to know. Meantime, she has Fritz yearning for her on the other side of the world. And Sean. Hopefully, Sean is yearning for her too. Because she misses him.

He answers the phone on the first ring – he's been waiting for her to call, his finger on the trigger of his phone's touchpad. 'And how's our intrepid traveller? Been thinking about you…'

'So have I about you.'

'Small world.'

'Not small enough. I wish you were here.'

'I don't cope well with the heat,' he tries to sound carefree, but she detects a tiny quiver in his voice, and then a snap: 'Damn it! Get yourself back here!'

Gillian basks in his yearning. 'I will - we will, straight after Easter. We'll be flying on Monday, home on Tuesday morning. You'll manage just a few days, won't you?'

'Will try.'

'How is Mildred?'

'In one word? Shell-shocked. But she'll get over it. She's back home – she'll be fine. Give her time… How you getting on with your investigation?'

'Getting nowhere.'

'How's that?'

'Nothing fits, nothing sticks together… Not to mention the fact that Papariakas is nowhere to be found. I spoke to his old nemesis here, a retired detective. He could pull a few strings for me to get a warrant to search Papariakas's family home here, but he thinks Papariakas wouldn't be stupid enough to hole up there. In fact, he thinks Papariakas has no reason to hide, and that he had nothing to do with the arson – not his style, he tells me. And I'm inclined to believe him. And to top it all, Papariakas's wife is genuinely concerned about his absence. Either that, or she's a bloody brilliant actress.'

'Maybe something went genuinely wrong at the

Coxes's - an innocent accident?'

'No… Well, I'll get more information from Forensics when I get back, but so far they've led me to believe that it was some sort of explosive that started the fire. A deliberate act. We'll see. '

'You know what you're doing.'

'Course I do! And I never give up. Do you know what they call me at the station?' Gillian realises she must be boring him to death with her boasting, never mind the fact that right now she has nothing to boast about. The case has come to a dead end, and she is dumping it all on the man whom she's hoping to keep for life. Not a good start!

'Let's not talk about work,' she reverses quickly.

'OK…'

'How are you coping with Fritz? Is he behaving?'

There is a brief and troubled silence at the other end of the line. 'Ah! Fritz… Um… How shall I put it?'

'What has he done now?'

'Nothing serious… I'd say he acted in self-defence… Don't worry. Nothing to worry about, honestly! Let's just say him and Corky had a small misunderstanding.'

A bleep on her mobile alerts Gillian to someone trying to get through to her. It could be Tara. 'Sorry, Sean! Hang on! I must go… Someone else -'

'No problem. Talk later!' He rings off.

It's Webber. 'Mark, what are you doing back at work?'

'Working.' That sounds rather ominous.

'You all right? How's Kate?'

He ignores her questions. 'I thought you'd want to know straight away: we found Stella Cox, alive and well. She was staying with her sister in Scotland. Flew in this

205

morning.'

David is gibbering manically – Mildred can't catch a single word of what he's saying before he storms out of the house. What has he seen in that window? Mildred would like to know. He had been standing there for hours, staring out at the road. And he has scarpered, leaving Mildred to wonder what has possessed him. She shuffles to the window to see for herself. A taxi is driving away, splattering mud into roadside ditches. David is holding someone in his arms, someone of small posture, wearing a knee-length tailored coat. Mildred can't make out who it is other than it must be a woman. Esme? Esme must have heard and she is back from Zambia... Was it Zambia where she's been working, tracking down poachers? Or Zimbabwe? It's all muddled up in Mildred's head, but she soldiers on trying to work it out so she doesn't have to think of anything else.

They are walking towards the house, David carrying a small case in one hand and squeezing Esme's shoulder with the other. Mildred didn't realise how close those two were. She would've never thought David would care this much for Esme – after all, she was the cause of all his misery; she was the one person who stood between him and Stella. Her birth meant the end of his hopes. He has risen above that. David has always had a big heart.

Mildred has a spring in her step. She hurries to the front door to greet her granddaughter. To hold her tight. To tell her she's all Mildred has left of her son so no, she won't let her go back to Zimbabwe, or Zambia, or wherever it is that she puts her life at risk.

They are climbing the steps and at last Mildred can see their faces – can recognise them. 'Where is Esme?' she asks. .David and Stella stop dead in their tracks, halfway through a step.

'Where's Esme?' Mildred repeats.

'It's Stella, Mum... Stella's back. It wasn't her in the house... She's alive!' David sounds ecstatic.

Mildred nods. 'Good,' she says with little enthusiasm. 'I'm glad.' She can see for herself that it is Stella, but what she really wants to know is *where is Esme!*

'Mildred, I... I don't know what to say... I'm so sorry, I feel so guilty that I wasn't there!' Stella clutches at Mildred to embrace her. It is really awkward to endure that, together with the scent of perfume, not to mention the fact that for the first time in years Stella is addressing Mildred in the first person. That over-familiarity feels very uncomfortable to Mildred. She cringes. Not knowing how to respond, she clings on to her original question.

'Where's Esme?' Someone has died in that fire alongside Liam. Who?

'Let's go inside. It's cold out here.' David doesn't have any answers, or doesn't want to tell her. He shoves Mildred inside, pushing Stella's case at her; his hand is resting on Stella's back as he ushers her in as though she were royalty. Mildred can tell he's struggling to contain his puppy-dog excitement, probably for her benefit. Liam is still dead and no one knows – or wants to inform her – where Esme is.

David is all words, but not the ones Mildred wants to hear. 'Stella's been so incredibly lucky. We all thought you were at the house when it -' He gazes at her tenderly with his puppy-dog eyes. He looks at Mildred as he finishes the sentence. 'It turns out Stella travelled to Scotland, to Martha's -'

'To clear my head,' Stella adds, ever helpful.

They said she had died, but here she is standing before Mildred's very eyes, alive and in one piece. Mildred is happy for her and even more so for David, but, more to the point, if Stella is alive, would it be too much to hope that so is Liam? They don't know what they're talking about, those police people. They've got it all wrong. Stella is living proof... 'Was Liam with you? In Scotland, I mean. Was he?'

Stella frowns, shakes her head. 'No, he wasn't. He stayed at home. I'm sorry, but -'

No! Mildred doesn't want to listen to her sorrows. No! Why is it her? Why not Liam? What's better about her? What makes her life more valuable than Liam's?

Good Lord, forgive me, Mildred pleads, I don't know what I'm thinking. Her fingers search her pocket for her rosary. It isn't there. She must have left it somewhere. Her sense of bereavement grows. She is on her own. God doesn't wish to offer her consolation. She must bear her cross alone. Alone... Liam didn't die alone. Someone was there with him, if the police people are to be believed. They said there were two people in the house. Two people.

Mildred looks up at her daughter-in-law, and repeats her question: 'Where's Esme?'

Gillian is cold with contrition. The icy air-conditioning on the plane doesn't help matters. She was at pains to explain herself to Tara and Deon, not to mention Hortensia, who listened to her lame excuses, her mouth gaping in morbid condemnation. Hellish fires, that's all Gillian can expect in the Afterlife.

'There's been a new development in England. I really have to go.'

'It's Easter, Mum! No one'll miss you over there, get real! It's only a couple of days till Easter – we could spend it together for once in our lives!' Tara, flanked by Dean and Hortensia, wasn't taking any of Gillian's crap.

'I have to go,' Gillian repeated stubbornly. 'I'm in the middle of a case. Me being here – it's because of the case I'm on. This isn't a holiday for me. Please don't make me feel bad about it.'

'The *bypast craft* on Mister Deon's heart could be life-threatening, the doctor said so – told me himself, I didn't even ask,' Hortensia added fuel to the fire.

'You could stay here with me and Dad over Easter. Just make an effort. The world won't end when you're not there to run it for a couple of days.'

'I can't take leave in the middle of -'

'A case, blah, blah, blah...' Tara's expression was hard and unforgiving, her lips pursed, her gaze fixed on Gillian. 'I give up on you, Mum.' She lifted her hands in mock surrender.

'If I could...' Gillian shrugged – she had also given up on herself. There was no convincing them, she would take the flak. 'Look, enjoy Easter together. I wish I could be here with you, believe me, but I can't. I have to go. I'll see you on Tuesday – I'll collect you from the airport, all right?'

'No, I don't think so.' Tara oozed contempt. 'I won't be taking that plane home, I decided. Dad's op is on Thursday. I'm staying -'

Thankfully, Deon managed to open his mouth. 'You don't have to, really. Hortensia always exaggerates. I'll be fine.'

'I know you'll be fine, but I'll be here with you if it's all the same to you.' If only she could look so lovingly at her mother! Gillian squirmed with resentment.

In the end she decided on a change of tactics. 'It's a good idea. I'll rebook your flight for the following Monday then. It's settled.'

'No, I'll be staying longer – a couple of months, maybe more… I'll see how it goes.'

'You don't have to – really…'

'I do, Dad. I only have one dad… I intend to see you through this.'

That was the point where Gillian made her biggest mistake. 'What do you mean – a couple of months? What about uni? You're not telling me you're going to miss lectures… You'll fail the whole year. Get your priorities straight, Tara! For God's sake, you're an adult – take some responsibility-'

'Priorities?' Tara gasped. 'You ought to be ashamed of yourself, *Mother*. And of your *priorities*!' That was her child's parting blow – and a well-deserved one.

Gillian is still reeling from it. She hasn't slept a wink for the whole night's flight. She tossed and turned in her seat, her eyes wide-opened, burning with dehydration and that dreadful guilt of someone with screwed priorities, someone who brings nothing but shame to her family.

From time to time however, and with intensifying regularity, her thoughts begin to drift towards the case. She gives in to that trend (there is nothing she can do to exonerate herself in Tara's eyes anyway at this point in time!), and succumbs to *inventorising* the facts of her case. Stella Cox is alive. Two bodies. One must be Liam Cox. Who the hell is the second one?

Talk about being swept off her feet, Gillian reflects as she picks herself up from the floor – it was a knockout! Sean picked her up at the airport and drove her home at a speed which under normal circumstances would require emergency sirens. She remembers little of their conversation in the car – maybe she dozed off, maybe her brain was already burning with the anticipation of what was coming for her to give any conscious thought to civilised dialogue. In no time they were tearing through the door, Sean having the presence of mind to shut it closed with his foot. Their hands became momentarily entangled in their garments, each trying to undress the other faster than they could think, faster than their hands could act on their desires. When at last his hands cupped her breasts, they clawed them as if he had no control over them. That sent a current of pain to her brain – a bizarre pain that made her cry for more. She reached down to his groin and clutched him in turn, her fingers curled around his erection in some involuntary, primeval ritual of claiming her mate.

He pulled her into the convex bow of his body and clapped his hands on her buttocks, forcing her to arch her back to fit into his form. Her left leg went up to accommodate him. Destabilised, she bobbed on the toes of her other foot and grabbed the nearest surface for support. It was the coat stand. Wobbly and unstable as it already was, it crashed to the floor, taking with it all the coats and umbrellas, the little telephone table including the telephone, a stack of letters and a bowl with a bunch of clanking keys, and finally Gillian with Sean on top of her. The rumpus must have rippled across the neighbourhood in a powerful aftershock, but they went on with their business at hand, grunting and gasping, until, in one sharp thrust, it was all over and their appetites subsided as suddenly as they had come about.

'Bloody hell!' Having picked herself up, Gillian is now picking up the coat stand, and the coats, the keys and the telephone which appears to have been pulled out of the wall in all that mighty frenzy. 'You must stop smashing things in my house like that! I don't think I've insurance cover for this kind of risk.'

'An act of God – surely you're covered for that!' Sean laughs. He has found the telephone wire and is plugging it into the phone. He picks up the handset and puts it to his ear. 'As good as new,' he comments. He cuts a comical figure with a trouser leg wrapped around his left ankle and his shirt clinging to his right arm by one sleeve. His hair seems to have been subjected to an electric shock. Gillian ruffles it ever more.

'Look at yourself! You're a mess!' she chuckles.

'Look who's talking,' he retorts. She does. The mirror tells a sad tale of a woman afflicted by madness. There is even a red imprint of his fingers on her chest. Charming!

'Right, I think I may be ready for a cup of tea.' She

finds her top on the floor and restores herself to a semi-respectable state of apparel. Her breasts and her thighs ache delightfully, but she won't be sharing this with Sean. That would only encourage more destruction around the house.

'Stella's return has thrown her off big time, I must say,' Sean looks worried. 'She just can't get her head around it, no matter how much explaining we've been doing. She's totally spaced out... I'm afraid it's a setback for Mildred – Stella coming back from the dead...'

'Lucky woman! So what is she saying? Why did she go to her sister's without telling anyone?'

'Apparently she told Liam. She told him she was leaving him. Obviously, he was unable to pass on the message so we all assumed she died with him.'

'She was leaving him for David, is that right?'

'Yes, that much is clear. They're childhood sweethearts, those two.'

'So why didn't she tell David? In fact, why didn't she go straight to David? Why to her sister's?'

'You'll have to ask her that. I couldn't speculate. I mean, she had already spent a night with David – the decision had been made... But now she's saying she had to think it through. Women!'

'There's a reason behind every action – it's just a matter of finding it.'

'That's your job.'

'Yes, though the first thing to find out for me is who the second body belongs to. There's the daughter...'

'Esme, yes.'

'Could she have been in the house on that night?'

'No. She was gone. That morning she went to Zimbabwe.'

'Something to verify. I'll get Erin to check.'

'No need. Stella's already been in touch with Esme. She's coming for the funeral. Tomorrow. I'm collecting her from the airport, as it happens.'

Something catches Gillian's eye. It is a fluid movement at the periphery of her eye as if something has slithered across the floor. She follows it and discovers Fritz. At least, she thinks it is Fritz. Surprisingly, he's absolutely mute and stealthy, not his typical vocal self. In addition, half of his head is bandaged and he's wearing a strange funnel around his neck. She slumps to her knees and pulls the creature towards her, into her arms. 'What on earth happened to my cat?!'

Fritz makes a feeble attempt at a yodel, but the sound dies in his throat. He appears seriously traumatised.

'Um...' Sean mumbles, 'that's what I wanted to talk to you about. Before you hung up, remember? You had another call coming.'

'All right, all right. Tell me now!' She is cuddling poor Fritz.

'Like I was saying, Fritz and Corky had a misunderstanding. Corky was outside in the garden; Fritz was in the house – I knew not to mix those two together, but Fritz had other ideas. He sneaked out through the window to confront Corky. I guess he didn't like him on his patch... Before I saw what was going on, they were in... well... open combat.'

'What's wrong with Fritz's head?'

214

'Nothing. His head is fine – he had a scan. It looks worse than it is. It's just his ear – Corky took his right ear, most of it, actually. They couldn't sew it back on because... well... we couldn't find it. Looks like Corky ate it.'

'Ate my cat's ear?'

'Well, Fritz started it -'

'It's his house!'

'And he gave as much as he took. Didn't you notice Corky at the back of the car?'

'I wasn't looking. What's wrong with him?'

'Fritz bit him around the neck – real deep stabs. He clawed him too. Corky needed three stitches... nasty abscess... a series of antibiotics – you name it! They had to shave his neck. He looks like a turkey.'

Serves him right! Gillian triumphs internally, and gives Fritz a little kiss on his bandages. 'Poor Fritz!' she says out loud. 'He's the one without an ear.'

She doesn't try to stop Sean when he says he must go back to the farm. He shouldn't be leaving Mildred alone for any period of time. And she is alone – David and Stella have moved out; it was too much for Mildred to see them together right under her nose while Liam...

'Yes, I understand,' Gillian agrees readily. Her mind is elsewhere – back on the case. She can't wait for Sean to close the door behind him on his way out so that she can pick up the phone to call Webber. 'Mark, I'm on my way to the station,' she informs him without any preamble. 'Any other developments? Do we have the identity of the second casualty?'

'Hello, ma'am. And thank you – I'm fine, too,' he

215

snaps at her for no reason. She knows she should be more sensitive, but knowing is not the same as doing. Besides, it's no good having personal conversations over the phone. She promises herself to take him out for a drink – give him a chance to get it off his chest, whatever it is that's eating him…

She is trying to change into fresh clothes while holding the phone to her ear. It's not easy. 'Sorry, Mark. I'm a bit jetlagged.' The phone falls from her hand and hits the floor. She grabs it. 'Are you still there?'

A heavy sigh, then he speaks, 'Yeah. And no, we haven't identified the second body. But we now know it's a male.'

Gillian beams. 'Aha! In that case, we also know that male is Dimitri Papariakas. No doubt about it! I'll explain when I get there. Meantime we'll be contacting his wife in South Africa and organising DNA testing. I'm on my way.'

Scarface displays an unusually patient exterior. He's either listening to Gillian because she is making sense or – what is more likely - he is recovering from a particularly debilitating hangover. The fact that he is having his parents-in-law for Easter may have something to do with it as well. Under any other circumstances, he'd be out of that door by lunchtime, heading for the creature comforts of his pipe, slippers and creme eggs. Listening to Gillian's drivel must be an incomparably better proposition than a bunny hunt in the back garden with his in-laws. His black coffee, freshly delivered from Costa, is steaming on his desk. He has squeezed two pills of sweetener into it and stirred it with a plastic spoon. His calorie-free diet has done wonders for him: he has lost his double chin and can now button up his uniform without having to hold his breath. There are rumours at the station that Scarfe is having an affair – thus the general mellowing of his disposition, weight loss and a funky new haircut.

'I hope you're right, DI Marsh,' he says while blowing at his coffee after burning the zigzag of his lip with the first sip. 'This is a great leap of faith.'

'My instinct tells me I'm right -'

'Oh yes, your instinct…'

'His wife told me Papariakas was on his way to see Cox in his house on the night of the incident. She sounded genuinely concerned. And confused – she struck me like she honestly didn't know where her husband was. I bet she wasn't putting it on – she doesn't know where he is!'

'We're not in the betting business.'

'Call it an educated guess, sir. But I am in possession of facts to back that guess up. For one, Papariakas didn't take the flight out of the UK that he was booked on the next day. Granted, he could've left the country by different means, but why would he want to draw all that attention to himself? Act like a guilty man? I think I'm right, but let's test the waters – if it isn't Papariakas's body and he has indeed gone into hiding, she won't come here and she won't let us take a DNA sample. If on the other hand, she hasn't got a clue what happened to him, she'll be on the first plane to the UK. If nothing else, we'll know if she's lying.'

'Go for it. And keep me informed – any time of day or night… Easter, or not Easter. This is a high-profile case, as it happens. Some idiot from Sexton's *Herald* insinuated we were exploring the possibility of this being a terrorist attack. In Sexton's Canning of all places! God knows who he got it from. We need to wind this case up quickly and efficiently – with no loose ends and no room for speculation. The public are already stirred up by it. Call me the moment you've a result. And do whatever it takes to get one.'

'Thank you, sir. Will do!' Gillian turns on her heel and leaves his office before the man changes his mind.

In the briefing room, Gillian slides Dimitri Papariakas's mugshot from the *Suspects* side of the board to the *Victims* area in the centre, and draws a big question mark next to it. 'DS Webber, I'd like you to follow this lead – we've a green light from Detective Superintendent Scarfe. Contact Papariakas's wife in South Africa. Tell her we're investigating the possibility of the second body being that of her husband. Tell her that, with her permission, we'll be running DNA checks as soon as possible. See how she reacts to that.'

Webber nods. He doesn't look his best – still not back to his usual crisp self. The most alarming feature is his several-day stubble. Has he lost his razor or is this some kind of Lenten resolution? As long as his brain is in good order, it isn't really any of Gillian's business, though she must remember that drink after work; ask those grinding questions about Kate and their son, and how they're getting on. He probably won't like those damned questions, and she definitely won't like asking them, but it's the right thing to do – apparently.

'Anything else?' he asks.

'Yeah, one more thing. I want you to explore if the arson could be a hit by Papariakas's old business rivals. Apparently he has lots of enemies in South Africa, plenty of unfinished business there and probably many more all over the show here in the UK, and further afield, in Europe, Greece. I want you to call the SFO – find out what they have on him; any disgruntled associates or employees, any enemies from the criminal underworld, anybody who may have reasons to hold a grudge against the man. Let's make a list of those individuals, and go through them methodically.'

'Sounds good.'

'Anything for me, boss?' Erin looks dead keen. Clearly, she doesn't have a home to go to this Easter either. Bloody hell, they're a miserable bunch – the lot of them, Gillian muses for a split second before her focus is back on the case. 'You, Macfadyen, yes… A completely different line of inquiry. David Cox.'

'Right.' Erin is scribbling in her notebook. She and her notebook are inseparable, like Bridget Jones and her diaries.

'David and Liam Cox didn't see eye to eye: a decades-old rivalry over Liam's wife, who used to be David's childhood sweetheart until Liam forced a wedge between them. David was gone for over twenty years, living in Canada, I believe. He came back just a few days before the arson. What's more, he claimed Liam's wife back – they were seen together; she spent a night with him on the farm, and according to a witness they looked pretty cosy with each other. We need to dig deeper into the nature of

219

their relationship. I want you to find out everything there is to know about David's past, his life in Canada, any form – all there is to know. No such thing as a coincidence.'

'Should I run checks on Stella Cox, too?'

'It won't hurt if you do. Let's put them both under a magnifying glass. Something doesn't fit here. Her trip to her sister's – conveniently out of harm's way... Fishy!' Gillian drags Stella's photo from the *Victim* area to *Suspects*, and joins it with an arrow pointing to David Cox's name written in Gillian's scruffy handwriting. 'Do we have his photo, by the way?' she asks.

'I'll organise one, boss,' Erin is tireless in her enthusiasm.

'Good. We'll reconvene tomorrow, nine thirty. I'm off to Forensics to pay Riley a friendly visit.'

Jon Riley is wearing an Alice band with bunny ears to keep his long, greasy hair out of his face. He probably doesn't realise it but his resemblance to Buddha is uncanny. 'Like my Easter accent?' he asks, pointing to his bunny ears.

'Where's your rabbit tail?'

'I'm sitting on it. Want to see?'

'Don't,' Gillian hovers a steadying hand over his shoulders, 'don't get up on my account. I believe you.'

'Creme egg?' He pulls open his top drawer, where several chocolate eggs in shiny wrappers roll to the front in the hope of being picked up.

'I'll have one, thanks.'

He gives one to Gillian and takes one for himself. The

wrapper flies into a waste paper basket under his desk and the chocolate egg is swallowed in two gulps. Nibbling on hers, Gillian wonders if he as much as registered the taste of it. In Jon's case it is less about the taste and more about the force of habit.

'Lucky I found you still at work,' she tells him.

'I'm not in a hurry to get anywhere. I have my stash of Easter eggs handy and I've just downloaded this new version of *Crackdown* – what else does a red-blooded male need on a rainy day like this?'

Gillian can't possibly comment. She reins him in with the business at hand. 'The arson at 3 Blue Orchid Close – what have you got for me?'

'I'll have the report ready by… let me see -' He is such a teaser!

'Just give me the abridged verbal version, Jon. I want to go home, open my Easter hamper, and put my feet up. I just came off an overnight flight.'

'Where did you go?'

'South Africa.'

'Sunny, warm and dry… You never take me with you.' Riley puckers his lips and furrows his forehead. Honestly, with all these folds he could make a fortune as Buddha's body double.

'The arson?' Gillian prompts him.

'Technically speaking: a bomb, not arson.' He opens a file on his computer, reads and gives the short version. 'A small homemade bomb with a two-hour timer and two toggle isolating switches, mounted on a plastic lunchbox, *Thomas the Tank Engine* branded, it appears – I never liked Thomas the Tank Engine, always preferred

Noddy…'

'Thanks for sharing that, Jon. So, a bomb? Did you share this information with anyone, members of the press for example?'

'Who do you take me for?' The folds in his face deepen in an expression of his sorely tested professional integrity.

'Sorry, we've had a leak to the press, Scarface thinks. Carry on.'

'Power was provided by batteries housed within the box. Holes melted into the sides of the lunchbox to accommodate the major components and to allow for the output wires to leave the box for connection to the detonator. What else? The components and internal wiring were glued in place with hot melt glue. They used 9v batteries and an electrical resistor. It was all held together by insulating tape. Homemade stuff, like I said, a conventional, old-fashioned device. You can get most of the components in any DIY shop. But it wasn't exactly an amateur job, not the kind you can learn about on the internet – someone knew what they were doing.'

'OK. Two-hour timer – does that mean the bomb had to be planted two hours before the explosion?'

'Yeah. You're looking for someone who was in the vicinity of the property somewhere between six thirty and seven p.m., I'd say. What's more, the package was left in the house around the staircase in the hallway, so whoever it was had been inside the house. A friend, a family member, someone the Coxes must've known to let them in. And that would've been about half past six in the evening.'

'So at the time of the actual explosion...'

'They could've been sunning themselves in Ibiza. The thing would've gone off all by itself when the timer sent an impulse to the switch.'

'That puts a new complexion on the matter... Thanks, Jon.'

'Any time. You know I'm here for you.'

'Can you print what you have there for me, please?'

'Is that all?' He is scowling. Gillian wonders what his problem is now, but she doesn't bother asking – she has a number of alibis to verify for the period between six thirty and seven p.m. on Friday, the eleventh of March.

Reading through Riley's forensic report, she has the distinct impression that she has read it once before already. She can't quite put her finger on it: it could have been one of her real cases from a distant past or perhaps, more likely, a case study from the police academy. It sounds very familiar, but not quite immediate. Gillian's recollection is rather fuzzy, but she is sure she has seen it before. It's a classic. Increasingly, she becomes convinced that it is uncannily like one of the case studies from her detective training. The fact that a bomb was used to start the fire points to the criminal underworld. Papariakas's old enemies from South Africa have now become her prime suspects.

'Mark!' she shouts over the flimsy screen of their open-plan office.

'Ma'am?'

'What did you find out from the SFO?'

'Near to nothing. They aren't keen to share any

information.'

'It's a murder investigation.'

'I told them that.'

'OK, give Scarfe a call. He said to keep him in the loop. We need him to use his connections. I want a list of Papariakas's enemies here in the UK. Also, call Andreas Botha in Durban, get the names of those Italians who had an axe to grind with Papariakas – those that are still alive. Those Mafia feuds can go on for ever.'

'Will do.'

'Good. Then we'll call it a day.' She remembers how late it is, and that she really ought to have a little heart-to-heart with Webber. 'Feel like a drink before home-time?'

'Sounds good.'

Erin approaches from the far confines of the office in the south wing. Gillian forgot she was still here. It must be only the three of them still working at this late hour. Gillian should feel bad about it, but she doesn't. No time for pointless sentiments. 'Anything?' she asks before Erin delivers her bombshell.

'I ran checks on David Cox. The Canadians keep very tidy records, I say. So, here it comes... Would you believe it if I told you that David Cox was a civil engineer and spent the last twenty years building roads in Ontario.'

'And that involves using explosives?'

'Lots of explosives.'

'Well done, DC Macfadyen!'

'That's not all.'

'Go on.'

'I checked his travel arrangements. He came here four weeks ago,' Erin checks her trusty notebook, 'February

25th, on a one-way ticket with Virgin Air, but two weeks ago – 10th of March - he booked a flight back to Canada – for two. One ticket in his own name and one in the name of – wait for it! - Stella Cox. Flying out on 31st March. And this isn't a holiday trip – it is one way only.'

'Do you think the lovebirds have planned the whole thing?' Webber has joined Erin and Gillian at her desk.

'We'll have to ask them, won't we.'

It is rather fortunate that Erin decided to join them for a drink – the more the merrier, not to mention that any deeply intimate subjects will have to wait. They may even be able to hold an impromptu briefing to tie up a few loose ends of their inquiries before heading home. The three of them are sitting at a table which is way too big for them, but the pub isn't as full as it would normally be on a Saturday. After all, most normal people with lives of their own and families to go back to have gone home laden with chocolate Easter eggs and hot cross buns. The leftovers in the pub are all those sad individuals who have nothing better to do than drown their sorrows in a pint or two, either blissfully unaware of Easter or not giving a toss about it.

The first round was on Gillian. She is nursing her large glass of house red, sipping it slowly, contemplating whether this could be a good time to call them in South Africa and wish them a happy Easter or whether she should wait until Sunday morning. Sunday morning it is, she concludes. She looks up from her glass and finds herself staring at the face of misery. Webber is focused on his pint, his objective clearly to drain the whole glass in one go without coming up for breath. Erin is gazing at a coaster, her glass nearly finished too. Gillian takes a deep swig. She must keep up.

'Your kids with their dad?' Gillian takes a stab at some social talk around the table.

Both Mark and Erin scowl at her. She must've interrupted their deep meditation. It was a stupid idea to ask questions. She doesn't even know if Erin has any kids. She's divorced – that much Gillian knows. Her ex-husband is an Aston Martin dealer – useless bits of irrelevant information rattle through Gillian's head. She really doesn't know shit about her colleagues. And vice versa. This is going to be a bloody long night!

'Another round?' Mark gets up, his glass dry. 'Same for you?'

Erin nods, 'Thanks.' Gillian finishes her drink, and nods too. He heads off to the bar. When he is out of earshot, Erin says, 'I haven't got any kids.'

'I thought so. Wasn't sure.'

'We never got round to having kids. Cars were Matt's babies.'

'You're still young, you've time.' Gillian tries to sound neutral. She can't tell whether Erin does or doesn't mind not having any kids.

'Thirty-seven, and counting.'

'Yeah, that's a spring chicken by today's standards.'

'OK.'

'My daughter – Tara, her name's Tara – is with her father, in South Africa. I don't see her much these days…'

'Oh? How old is she?'

'Nineteen… no, hang on, is it nineteen or twenty? Let

me think -'

'Here we are!' Mark saves her the trouble of trying to remember when he thrusts the drink into Gillian's hand. 'Cheers!'

Gillian must ask about Kate. It's not that she needs to know – it's more to do with him knowing that she cares. 'Everything OK at home, Mark? How's Kate coping -'

'She isn't.' His reply is curt. He goes on to drink half of his glass before returning to the topic of conversation. 'Her mother's come over to look after the girls – to help out round the house... She blames me.'

'Who? Her mother?'

'Kate does.'

'For what? It wasn't your fault.'

'She obviously thinks it was.' He picks up his glass – drinks it all up – bangs the glass on the table. 'Your shout now,' he fixes poor Erin with a menace of a glare.

'Yeah – same for all?'

'Not for me. I'm still on this one,' Gillian points to her glass.

'I'll get you one for later.'

When she's gone, Gillian tries her staff leadership skills on Webber. 'Do you think... you should've taken a few more days off, spent time with Kate... You know, be there for her?'

'She doesn't want me there.'

'Still – just show her you care, all right?'

'What business of yours is that?' he snaps at her. 'Leave off, yeah?'

Gillian shrugs her shoulders and focuses her attention on her glass of red. It isn't really any of her business, she

227

concurs.

'Sorry, let's just…' Mark scratches his head, ruffles his hair, and taps his fingers on the table – a subtle indication that he's longing for his next drink to arrive. 'Oh yeah!' he perks up. 'I didn't tell you, did I?'

'What's that?'

'Papariakas's wife – she's on her way here. She was… what you call it? *Inconsolable*!'

'I thought she'd be. It's Papariakas's body we have on our hands, I knew it.' Gillian is relieved to be back on the terra firma of the case at hand. And she's delighted she's been proven right. 'The DNA test will be just a formality.'

'You didn't invite me, Gillian! I'm hurt, you know!' It's the familiar voice of Jon Riley. He's walking – waddling - arm in arm with Erin, carrying two glasses: his own pint and Gillian's red.

'Look what the cat's dragged in!' Gillian retorts. She's over the moon to see Buddha. He's bound to lift the mood a notch or two.

'I found Jon all alone at the bar. Couldn't leave him there on his own,' Erin explains.

'What's done is done. Come on, Riley, take a seat! The next round is on you.'

They are all here, attending the mass with Mildred on Easter Sunday – except Liam. He wouldn't be here if he could help it, even if he were alive. Liam was as stubborn as his father… like father like son… two men Mildred has loved and – no matter what anyone says – they loved her too. In their own way.

The communion wafer melts on Mildred's tongue as

228

she kneels and prays for their souls. At least they have each other for company, and Mildred will be joining them pretty soon. She can feel it in her whole body. And she knows it in her mind. She has no business lingering here while they're both there. She prays that God will call her soon; she's ready, eager to be with them. She isn't too sure if praying for her own death is a sinful act – it falls short of suicide but one can sin in one's thoughts as much as through one's deeds. At least she is honest and her deepest wishes are clear to God so He knows what's what.

'Gran, do you need help getting up?' Esme whispers in her ear, and puts her arm under her elbow. Everyone has already stood up and the whole church is ringing with the final hymn. Mildred loses the train of her thoughts. She smiles and nods, grasping Esme's hand on her left and Colleen's on her right. They lift her off her feet between the two of them, and Mildred feels airborne and free to go for a split second until they stand her on her feet – the moment is gone. Sean pats her on the back and when she turns, passes her the rosary – she must've dropped it on her seat or on the floor. Her fingers close around the beads. She will pray at home; she will pray some more – hours of prayer for her deepest, sinful, wish to come true.

'Shall we go and visit Grandad's grave?' Esme suggests as they head out of the church.

'Yes, we must. We're already here. We must.'

It's drizzling and the ground is soggy, waterlogged. It squelches underfoot as they cross the cemetery and weave amongst tombstones, heading for Reginald's grave by the well, under the cypress tree.

Mildred's arm is hooked over Esme's, and Colleen is

close by on her right. They are Mildred's flesh and blood – all she has left on this earth. David and Stella are coming as well. Stella has abandoned her atrocious fur and is wearing a long black coat. David plays the gentleman or a man in love by holding an umbrella over Stella's head. Secretly, they've been holding hands in church. Mildred noticed that from the corner of her eye but when she looked directly at them, they let go of their hands, ashamed of their happiness. Mildred doesn't mind. She will need to tell them that when they get home. Why shouldn't they be happy? They deserve every happiness in the world. She wishes them well. She doesn't mind.

They reach Reginald's grave. Sean wipes the water from the bench and tells Mildred to sit down. Sean is a good man – almost like a son to Mildred. But not quite. Liam was her son – she gave birth to him. For better or for worse, Liam was her son, her flesh and blood. Colleen sits next to her on the bench. Her daughter. For better or for worse. Mildred puts her hand in Colleen's lap and she cups that hand between hers. Her hands are warm and soft. Her flesh and blood... these words are swirling in Mildred's head as they all keep silent vigil around Reginald's grave.

The cemetery is empty and the churchyard has emptied, too, now that the holy mass is over. Two people walk through the gate, down the path; they cross the soggy ground, heading towards Mildred. Mildred's eyes aren't what they used to be. She squints. 'Who is that?' she asks.

'It's that policewoman, I think, and some other man with her,' Colleen informs her.

'What do you want now?' Mildred speaks directly to

the policewoman.

Out of respect for Mildred Cox, Gillian and Webber wait in the car until the service is over. Gillian's head is cracking with a hangover. So is Webber's, by his own admission. They drank two double espressos each before getting in the car and attempting to drive in a straight line. Erin is nursing her hangover whilst manning the station. She threw up in the night and this morning still looked like she was going to do it again. It was safer to leave her in the office, answering phones, rather than driving her up and down winding country lanes.

The first parishioners begin to trickle out of the church, the Easter service over and done with. DI Marsh and DS Webber step out of the car. They watch the priest shaking people's hands and exchanging cordial words. The Coxes come out last. It may have something to do with Mildred, who shuffles very slowly and painfully, supported on both sides by her daughter, Colleen, and a pretty young woman – Mildred's granddaughter, Gillian guesses. So Esme Cox has made it back home... Sean is walking behind Mildred, dressed in his best Sunday suit, looking dashingly handsome, if pensive. Behind are David and Stella. David has opened an umbrella, and they are both huddled under it.

'Shall we?' Webber is keen to get on with the arrest so the lovebirds can be interviewed, booked in and ready to go before a magistrate; so that he can go home to his wife and his girls, and make amends.

'Let's wait here. Not in front of the whole congregation.'

He rolls his eyes. 'Well, they're on sacred ground. They may yet withdraw back to the church and claim God's protection.'

Gillian looks at him closely, uncertain whether he's serious or just being his usual facetious self. All she can ascertain is that he looks crap, so no change from yesterday. She answers him nevertheless, in good faith, 'You'll find that particular law is no longer in force.'

'So let's go and bring them in.'

'Be patient, show some sensitivity. They aren't going anywhere, other than this way.'

But they prove her wrong. Led by Mildred, they proceed to the back of the church, towards the cemetery.

'What now?'

'Give her time. Looks like she's visiting the family grave. The woman's been through a lot of late. Let's not make it harder for her than it has to be.'

'Where did that correctness come from, ma'am?' Webber is genuinely baffled.

'It comes with age and breeding, DS Webber,' Gillian says, putting on an imperious tone of voice.

Webber laughs out loud and instantly winces in pain, clutching his temples. His headache must be worse than he lets on.

They watch the small group gather around a tombstone under a tall cypress. Sean cleans a bench with a handkerchief – he didn't strike Gillian as a handkerchief man – for Mildred and Colleen to sit on. He then steps back and stands next to the pretty young woman – Esme Cox. He puts his arm over her shoulder and she lowers her head onto his chest. Her arms are bound around his waist.

232

They look cosy together, way too cosy for Gillian's liking. She is struck by a pang of jealousy. It doesn't help to see that Colleen is also watching those two and her face is contorted in a mixture of horror and disgust. An old spinster with an overactive imagination, Gillian tries to convince herself, but the sense of discomfort stays with her. 'OK, let's not waste time,' she informs Webber briskly. 'Let's go and get those two.'

As she and Webber approach the group by the grave, she can't help noting that Sean shies away from the pretty young woman. Or perhaps she shies away from him. They're standing apart, their hands dangling aimlessly. Stella and David Cox have also moved away from each other, his umbrella raised between them, offering no shelter against the rain to either of them. Guilt.

'What do you want now?!' Mildred Cox sounds like a school mistress who's telling her ward off for some major transgression. 'Can't we have some peace? It's Easter Sunday.'

'I am sorry to intrude like this, but it can't wait,' Gillian is firm, her temporary display of sensitivity gone with the wind. 'It's a murder investigation, I'm afraid.' She turns to face her suspects, 'David Cox, Stella Cox, I'd like you to accompany me and DS Webber to the station. We've some questions to ask you in connection with the deaths of Liam Cox and Dimitri Papariakas.'

Sean frowns at her, 'Are they under arrest? Does it have to be now?'

'No, they're not - they're helping us with our inquiries. And yes, it does.'

They have interviewed Stella first and now she's brewing next door while Gillian and Webber are getting David's version of events. Both of them refused a solicitor. So far, David Cox says exactly what Stella said a few minutes ago. It means nothing. They've had time to rehearse their story. The interview is a formality because, at the end of the day, it will be the forensic evidence that will hopefully nail him and implicate her as an accomplice. The Prosecution will demand that in support of the circumstantial evidence Gillian has uncovered so far.

'Do you deny that on March the 10th you purchased two one-way airfares to Canada, for yourself and Mrs Stella Cox?'

'No, I don't.'

'Can you tell me what the purpose of your joint trip was going to be?'

He doesn't flinch when he says, 'Stella agreed to leave Liam. We were going to go to Canada to start afresh – the two of us.'

'Did you anticipate that Mr Liam Cox may object to this idea?'

'Of course we knew he wouldn't like it.'

'How were you going to deal with that? It wouldn't be easy – he was a wilful man…'

'Frankly, we didn't care. Stella was leaving with me – he'd have to live with it.'

'*Live* with it…' Gillian purposefully pauses on the word *live*. 'But he wouldn't just *live with it*, as you've put it, would he? You knew him better than I, but I'd say Liam Cox wasn't one to take his wife's adultery lying down.'

'No,' David says softly. 'He came the next morning – we were staying at Mildred's farm; Mildred was in hospital at the time... He raved, made his demands. We had words...He dragged Stella with him.'

'It was more than just words, I think... You must've been angry with him for taking her away? Again... I understand it happened once before. Liam Cox *stole* the woman you loved.'

'Obviously you know the story; I don't need to tell you. Stella told you already.'

'Never mind who told us. You were angry with Liam. You wanted Stella back, but as long as Liam was alive, you stood no chance. He had to go.'

'No, it wasn't like that. I was hurt, yes. I thought Stella knew what she wanted but then she wavered. I was disappointed she went with him without any protests, yes... But I wasn't angry. I just let her go – it was her choice.'

'Or maybe you let her go because you had a plan of how to get rid of your rival?'

'No.'

'Stella was in on it.'

'No.'

'Naturally she had to leave, to go away for a bit – out of harm's way.'

'No.'

'So you could get Liam when he was alone. Only you didn't count with the possibility of Dimitri Papariakas being there with him that night, did you?'

'No!' He exhales. 'I mean, I didn't do it.'

'Dimitri Papariakas was just collateral damage.'

'I didn't do anything. I don't know who did.'

'You told Stella to go away. Was she in on it? Did she know what you were planning?'

'No, no, no!' He is beginning to lose his composure. He's held on well so far, but he's losing it. Good!

'I find it hard to believe. She must've asked you why you wanted her to go away to her sister's. She knew, didn't she?'

'No! I didn't... We didn't do anything. Leave Stella out of it, for God's sake!'

'OK. Let's leave her out of it for now,' Gillian has cracked his defences, she's sure of that. She must strike while the iron is hot. 'You are a civil engineer by profession?'

'Yes. What's that got to do with anything?'

'I understand you used to work for Public Highways in Canada, building new roads. That involved explosives?'

'Sometimes. Why?'

'You see, explosives were used to kill Liam Cox and Dimitri Papariakas. Quite expertly prepared by someone who knew what they were doing – someone like you? What do you say to that?'

'It wasn't me.'

'This may be a good time to ask for a lawyer, Mr Cox, because I am about to charge you with the murder of Liam Cox and the manslaughter of Dimitri Papariakas. Would you like us to organise you a duty solicitor?'

'Yes.'

'Very wise. We'll get onto it now. Would you like a cup of tea while we're waiting?'

David Cox looks at her without comprehension. He's

shaking his head. 'I didn't do it,' he insists.

'You don't have to say anything else. Let's wait for the solicitor.'

'Liam was my brother. I couldn't kill him.'

The wait for the duty solicitor may be a long one – it's Easter after all. Erin has made tea and she's found some shortbread biscuits to go with it. The three of them are sitting outside the interview room, idly watching David Cox through a one-way window as he sits perfectly immobile, his elbows on the table, his face hidden inside his hands. Stella Cox is next door, crying, unable to compose herself.

'We gonna charge her too?' Erin asks.

'As an accomplice, yes.'

'I'm not sure about her,' Webber ventures an opinion. 'When she said she wanted David to fight for her, and he just let her go without a fight, she must've been confused about his feelings for her – I don't know. It rings true... I sort of believed her that she'd go away to think things through away from both of them. I'm not sure she was a party to this...'

'Neither am I. It's all circumstantial. It may well fall through unless she confesses.' Gillian puts aside the rest of her shortbread biscuit. Truth be told, she's unsure. She believed David Cox when he told her he wouldn't be able to kill his brother. They *were* brothers. And assuming he didn't know Stella had gone away to her sister's, he couldn't have possibly done it and risked her life... They were either in it together or they were perfectly innocent. Except that he is the only logical suspect – the only person in this equation who could handle explosives with such expertise… Yet, something doesn't sit right. She tries to dismiss her doubts – they are irrational. Scarfe could tell her a thing or two about her damned instincts! 'I'd better let Scarfe know we're about to charge them,' she says without conviction, and can't quite bring herself to reach for the phone. 'Mark, can you do that? Can you call Scarfe, please?'

'All right. You sure?'

'Yes! Look, if we let him go without charge, he's free to leave the country. We can't let him go. The solicitor will want us to charge him or release him. We've no choice.'

Mark gets up and takes his mug of tea with him to the office to make the call.

Erin says, 'This may be irrelevant now.'

'What?'

'Well, a man called when you were gone this morning.' She takes out her trusty notebook. 'Benedict Roulson. He lives two houses down from the Coxes, 5 Blue Orchid Close.'

'OK. And?'

'He's a pilot, just came back from a long-haul flight to Australia. He was responding to our calls for witnesses. Anyway, he claims that on the evening of 11th of March, at about six twenty in the evening – he was quite precise about the time as that was when he was reversing from his driveway to go to work… anyway, he claims he saw a man with a dog. It stuck with him because he'd never seen that man before. It's a small cul-de-sac, not much foot traffic there and the residents all know one another by sight. It's only seven houses in that whole street. I don't know how that may be relevant, but the time – six twenty p.m. – I think it may matter. He said he would recognise that man…'

Gillian is feeling slightly nauseous. She asks weakly, 'Did he say what breed of dog it was?'

'Yes,' Erin flicks through the pages of her notebook, 'a large dog – an Alsatian. German Shepherd.'

Gillian's guts are twisted into a knot, and it has nothing to do with yesterday's binge drinking. She remembers now why Riley's description of the explosive device was so familiar. She read that before, almost word for word: the same components, the same method of assembly, the same getup, except that this time it was a *Thomas the Tank Engine* lunch box! Still, a lunch box…

The dog gave it away.

She has Riley's provisional report in front of her and is tapping her computer keyboard feverishly. Her mind is in turmoil and her fingers slip so she has to start again, this time taking care to enter the details correctly. She is looking for the Omagh bombing files – the archived records and the Ombudsman's Report. She read them a couple of weeks ago when -

'The duty solicitors are here,' Erin informs her.

'Not now!' Gillian feels like throwing something at her. Erin doesn't know it yet but when Gillian is following a scent she can be like a rabid dog, and she can bite.

'They want to confer with their clients. They want to know what the charges are… Shall I tell them to wait or -'

'You can tell them to fuck off, thank you.'

Webber shrugs his shoulders when Erin gives him a questioning look. He says, aiming his words randomly into the ether, 'Scarface is on his way.'

Gillian mumbles something under her breath, which can be construed as another *fuck off* or possibly something much stronger. In response, Webber pulls Erin by the elbow and leads her away from Gillian's desk. 'Leave her when she's like that. She's a *pitbull*. Don't touch her bone.'

'What?' Erin is puzzled.

'Can you two have this conversation somewhere-bloody else?' Gillian snaps.

'Woof, woof,' Mark mimes to Erin, and drags her away.

The dog gave it away. A German Shepherd. Sean doesn't go anywhere without that dog. Corky is always by his side.

She found the Omagh records. She read them from cover to cover after Sean told her he had been one of the forensic scientists examining those bombings. He must have learned plenty about making bombs – learned from experts. Yes, she is right! Her eyes shift between Riley's report and her computer screen – the bomb at 3 Blue Orchid Close was a trademark IRA device with all the hallmarks of that era. It can't have been anyone else. Yet she finds it impossible to accept... She needs to find a way out for Sean. There has to be a logical explanation! Didn't Liam Cox do business in Ireland? There was something in the papers... Her hands are shaking as she dives into Cox's background notes. Yes! He invested in some property deals that went pear-shaped in the crash! He must've made lots of enemies – lots of Irish enemies. What are the odds that one of them had some deep-buried links to the old IRA, links that came in handy?

But then again, what are the odds that the mystery enemy of Liam Cox would have come to Britain, strolling in with a German Shepherd by his side? What are the odds…

'Webber!' she shouts across the office. It's astounding how a small woman like Gillian can be possessed of such a thundering voice. She is taken aback by the volume of her own voice. And by the tone of it – it sounds terrifying. Desperately terrifying.

'All right?' Webber materialises in front of her, looking genuinely anxious.

'Call Roulson, or whatever his name is – the pilot - the witness.'

'Who?'

She realises Webber knows nothing about it. 'Ask Erin for his details. Get him to the station ASAP. We need him to identify the man he saw that day.'

'Riiight…'

'Yes, right! You'll need to organise an identification parade. Here,' she is jotting down the general description of her lover, the man she trusted and came - almost came - to love in the last three insane weeks of her life. She should've known better – right from the start Sean was a potential suspect. Somewhere along the line she has lost her professional distance. Is she really that lonely, that desolate, that desperate? Her hands are still shaking as she tries to write down the approximate height, build, hair colour and physique of the man she is just about to arrest. 'There,' she passes her specifications to Webber. He takes the piece of paper and walks away purposefully, without any comments. He knows not to question her when she's like that.

She cradles her head in her hands. What time did Sean come to her place that night? She remembers he was a couple of minutes early – five-to-seven. He would've had enough time to plant the bomb and make it to hers by seven. Fuck! She has to go and arrest him.

A male voice sounds from behind her, 'DI Marsh -'

It grinds on her nerves. Webber should know better! 'Oh, just bloody well fuck off! Just do as I say!'

'I beg your pardon!' It's Superintendent Scarfe.

Gillian jumps to her feet. 'Sorry, sir! I thought you were someone else. I thought you were DS Webber. My apologies.'

'That's not a way of speaking to anyone!'

'I will apologise to DS Webber. Of course... I must go now, sorry.' She tries to push by him.

'We have two suspects, complete with two duty solicitors, waiting to be charged. This may be a good time to deal with that!'

'Erin!' Gillian shouts over her superior. 'Get a car. We're going to Nortonview Farm.'

Scarfe bangs a heavy hand on her desk to block her from leaving. He repeats, 'You have two suspects in custody – what are you doing about them?'

'We're letting them go,' she glares back at him, annoyed at his interruptions. 'They haven't done anything.'

Grace has made Sunday roast, bless her soul. She was cooking for six, but now there are only four of them, sitting over a table laden with deep-brown glazed potatoes, a huge fat turkey with a grotesquely swollen breast and thighs, and two dishes brimming with vegetables.

'Sean, pet, you'd better get on with carving the turkey,' Grace directs Sean and passes him the carving knife. The knife slides smoothly through the skin and the white fibres of the turkey, the perfectly measured slices falling like roof tiles over each other. Sean takes Mildred's plate first.

'Not too much for me, Sean – half a slice will do,' she tells him, but she knows he'll give her more than she asks for. He always does. It's his way to make her better: overfeed her, spoil her rotten. He puts three slices on her plate.

'So, tell me again, how it came to Stella and David being arrested?' Grace is a curious old gossip, there's no two ways about it.

'They weren't arrested exactly,' Sean corrects her. 'Your plate, Colleen?'

'Assisting the police with their inquiries,' Esme quotes.

'Isn't that the same thing? As being arrested?'

'No.'

Mildred has been wondering about that, too. Isn't that what they call it these days: *assisting the police with their inquiries* while, in fact, it is the same thing as arresting people because the police can prove they've done something – committed a crime. Mildred shudders. It is an involuntary reaction.

'You cold, Mildred?' Grace brings a blanket from the sitting room and places it over Mildred's lap. 'The heating's on, you'll warm up soon. I say, it's been a bit of a cold snap of late. It's the wind that does it.'

Grace is blabbering on. She forgot all about David and Stella. Sean is putting turkey on Esme's plate and slides the plate across the table to her, but she doesn't look up at him. Esme is staring into the table. She is probably fearing the same as Mildred does, and it is *her* mother who was arrested – or taken to assist the police with their inquiries.

'Go on, Mildred, don't make me wait on you, dish out the veg!' Grace's voice breaks through her musings. 'You eat while it's hot – that'll warm you up no end!'

'They're wrong,' Mildred says out loud, meaning it for Esme. She doesn't want Esme to feel bad for her mother; she wants her to know that Mildred doesn't blame her. She doesn't blame either of them. 'The police are wrong. I didn't bring David up to be a... murderer. And your mum – she couldn't kill a fly.'

Esme lets out a sob.

'Now, now... they're wrong. I should know.'

'They *are* wrong,' Sean puts his hand on Esme's shoulder. 'Hear me?'

Colleen is sitting, her plate full, her mouth gaping – she is gaping at Sean and at Esme, and she's blinking as if she wants to hold back tears. Not Colleen, too! She mustn't start now!

'Well, I say, they'll clear their names... if... they be innocent.' Grace dishes out one of her Solomon's

244

wisdoms.

They hear what sounds like a car door being shut and footsteps soon follow on the steps outside. Corky hasn't barked – not a squeak from him. He knows the visitors.

'That'll be them now!' Grace pronounces.

It isn't them. It isn't David or Stella – it's that policewoman again; and another one by her side. All the trouble started when that woman, DI Marsh – Mildred has her name burned into her memory – first entered their lives. It was Liam who brought her here, making daft complaints about Sean. Sean, of all people! He is such a good man, looking after Mildred, unfailing in his devotion. He is like a son to her, even more so now that her own son is gone. It all started with that damned policewoman. Mildred scowls at her. She isn't welcome here.

'I'm sorry to interrupt, again.' The cheek of her!

'Then don't come bothering us all the time,' Mildred growls at her.

'It is the last time that I'm doing it -' She walks over to Sean, who is standing stiff as a poker, a carving knife pointed in his hand.

'This really isn't a good time,' Grace is the only one able to speak.

She is ignored by DI Marsh, who addresses Sean. 'Sean Corrigan, I'm arresting you on suspicion of the murder of Liam Cox and the manslaughter of Dimitri Papariakas. You don't have to say anything, but anything you do say may be taken down in writing and used in evidence against you. DC Macfadyen, handcuff Mr Corrigan.'

That damned policewoman – she is not human! Not a twitch of emotion comes into her voice. It should. She and Sean, Mildred knew from the first, are close. Sean is fond of her. Sean is a good, caring man! What is she doing to him?

'What are you doing to him?' Mildred says it out loud. 'You ought to be ashamed of yourself!'

'I'm sorry I have to do this – in front of you – but we have witnesses who -'

'No! No, you're wrong! You stirring trouble, you are! You can't do this to people – good, God-fearing people, you can't! Leave my house! Get out of my house!' Mildred feels her chest is swelling with all that anger, and there is no stopping it: it will boil over!

'Macfadyen,' DI Marsh nods to her sidekick and she leads Sean out, holding him by his cuffed wrists like some sort of a criminal.

'She can't do that, Sean! Tell her!' Mildred urges him.

'Sean?' Esme is only asking. She should be standing up for him. She's young and strong.

'I'm sorry, Mildred. I wanted to protect you. He was going to have you locked up in a home, away from… this… everything you love. I couldn't let him do that to you.'

'You bastard!' Esme speaks so loudly it makes Mildred flinch.

'It isn't true… it isn't true… God knows it's all lies…' Mildred mutters defiantly. That is all she can do – mutter to herself like a woman possessed, because everything else has failed her: her legs, her strength, her mind. Sean is a good man – that's what her heart tells her, that's what she knows for a fact.

Gillian came straight home after Liam Cox's funeral. She didn't attend the wake – didn't want to intrude on their lives more than she already had. Colleen invited her to come and that, apparently, was done with Esme's blessing. Esme owns the farm now and she is in charge of everything: both Mildred's wellbeing and the dairy farming. Colleen went back to what she does best – teaching little people how to read and write, no surprises there - but Esme surprised everyone. She has a good business head on her shoulders and, like her father, she's a ruthless negotiator. She will have to be if she is to make a success of the farm.

Mildred has given up the ghost. She prays all the time, which seems like such a mindless activity, especially when you look at her fingers dancing manically with the rosary beads and at Mildred's lips moving in a repetitive chant of Hail Marys. Little else comes out of her mouth. Stella and David are staying in Britain. They're thinking of buying a house in the Lakes, away from all this bad blood, as soon as the dust settles and Stella receives the insurance payout on the house.

Gillian is sitting on her soft, doughy settee, with her feet up on the coffee table, contemplating all that information. Colleen hasn't mentioned Sean. No one mentions Sean. Gillian, too, has blotted him out of her memory – the side of him that doesn't stand accused of murder and manslaughter, that side of him that made her believe – briefly and foolishly – that she had found her man, her soulmate. In a few months' time she will be testifying at his trial – so much for soulmates!

All he had to say to her, when they were alone in the corridor between the interview room and the cells, was, 'She was like a mother to me, and I as good as killed her too. It's my curse, Gillian. Remember Dermot McAuley and his mother?'

'I can't talk to you off the record, Mr Corrigan,' she said stiffly and walked away without a second glance.

Fritz has rolled himself up into a fluffy ginger ball next to her on the settee. She ruffles his silky fur; he raises his head, disturbed and disoriented. He produces an admonishing yodel and goes back to sleep. His ear has healed, but the evidence is there for all to see – it is only half-an-ear, the other half is gone, just like a chunk of Gillian's battered heart. She must stop feeling sorry for herself – it's a sign of a feeble mind.

The ringing telephone brings distraction.

'Tara! How are things with your dad?'

'Really good, Mum!' Her daughter's voice is a soothing dressing on Gillian's emotional wounds. 'So good in fact that we all agree that he may be able to travel!'

'Well, that's great! That means that you can travel, too! Coming home could be an option.' It doesn't hurt to try. Tara has only missed two months – she could catch up with her uni work if she came now and put her mind to it. 'Are you coming, then?'

'Yes!'

Gillian can't believe her luck. Someone up there is watching over her. 'Well, excellent! When?'

'On Sunday. Arriving at Heathrow at six forty-five in

the morning. I was wondering if you could collect us – would be so much easier than to take a train.'

'Did you say *us*?'

'Yeah, me and Dad. Didn't you hear me – Dad is fit to travel. I thought it'd be a good idea to bring him home to convalesce while I catch up on things. Don't you want me to keep up with my uni courses?'

'Yes, I do, but -'

'I thought so. That's settled then. Dad wants to see Jack so he'll be gone for a couple of days. Jack's in boarding school in Shropshire. Of course, we could invite Jack to our place…'

'Who the hell is Jack?'

'Jack, Mum! My half-brother – Jack! He's eleven this month. We could throw an impromptu birthday party for him, invite him into the lap of the family, what do you say?'

'I don't know what to say?'

'Just say yes!' Tara is too bubbly, too excited to say no to, so Gillian says nothing. 'Oh, and I hope Sean won't mind. He has nothing to fear from Dad, reassure him or something, OK? Dad is sooo over you, trust me, so he won't try to compete with Sean. Tell Sean, all right?'

'I don't have to. Don't worry about Sean, he's gone.'

'Aw,' Tara puts on a concerned voice, which she clearly doesn't mean. 'Sorry to hear that. I thought you were good for each other. Why did you split up?'

'It's a long story. He's just gone, all right? Let's not go into details.'

'Must've hurt you, I can tell by your voice. Bastard! I'll have a word with him when I get there.'

249

'No!' Gillian says the first thing that springs to her mind to cover up her embarrassment. She doesn't know why she is embarrassed and why she has to lie to Tara, but that's what she does. 'It's nothing like that. We parted ways amicably...'

'I don't believe you!'

'We did! I'm even looking after Corky for him.'

'The dog? That huge, scary German Shepherd?! How does Fritz feel about that?'

'They had words to start with, but now they're quite fond of each other.' Gillian nudges Corky with her foot. He lifts his head, alert and keen, though she can still detect melancholy in his deep brown canine eyes. He misses his master, but at least he has abandoned his hunger strike and this morning even helped himself to Fritz's food.

THE END

MORE IN THE GILLIAN MARSH SERIES

Just when things seem to be going right for Nicola Eagles, she disappears without a trace. Was it a voluntary disappearance, or was she abducted – or murdered? When her absence is noted back in the UK, DI Gillian Marsh is sent to investigate.

Gillian is a good detective but as she delves deeper into the case, she realises that she may be out of her depth, because Nicola's disappearance is just the beginning…

After a head-on collision resulting in four deaths and a fifth person fighting for his life, DI Gillian Marsh is sent to investigate.

Nothing seems to add up. How did four capable drivers end up dead on a quiet, peaceful country road?

As Gillian unpicks the victims' stories, she edges closer to the truth. But will she be able to face her own truth and help her daughter before it's too late?

Á

Proudly published by Accent Press

www.accentpress.co.uk